Praise for the Ghost Finders novels

GHOST OF A DREAM

"Green once again mixes and matches genres with gleeful abandon . . . Readers who enjoy a roller-coaster ride through a haunted house (well, theater, but I'm mixing metaphors here) will love this novel . . . A terrific continuation of the Ghost Finders' adventures, with loads of horrors, thrills, and shocks."
—*SFRevu*

GHOST OF A SMILE

"*Ghost of a Smile* is a lovely blend of popcorn adventure and atmospheric thriller, and good fo[illegible] traction and entertainm[illegible] Green's books always l[illegible] list."

GHOST [illegible]

"If future novels in Green's new Ghost Finders series are as engaging as this one, they will hold up admirably against his previous work . . . Readers will appreciate the camaraderie and snappy dialogue."
—*Publishers Weekly*

Ghost Finders Novels

GHOST OF A CHANCE
GHOST OF A SMILE
GHOST OF A DREAM
SPIRITS FROM BEYOND

Novels of the Nightside

SOMETHING FROM THE NIGHTSIDE
AGENTS OF LIGHT AND DARKNESS
NIGHTINGALE'S LAMENT
HEX AND THE CITY
PATHS NOT TAKEN
SHARPER THAN A SERPENT'S TOOTH
HELL TO PAY
THE UNNATURAL INQUIRER
JUST ANOTHER JUDGEMENT DAY
THE GOOD, THE BAD, AND THE UNCANNY
A HARD DAY'S KNIGHT
THE BRIDE WORE BLACK LEATHER

Secret Histories Novels

THE MAN WITH THE GOLDEN TORC
DAEMONS ARE FOREVER
THE SPY WHO HAUNTED ME
FROM HELL WITH LOVE
FOR HEAVEN'S EYES ONLY
LIVE AND LET DROOD
CASINO INFERNALE

Deathstalker Novels

DEATHSTALKER
DEATHSTALKER REBELLION
DEATHSTALKER WAR
DEATHSTALKER HONOR
DEATHSTALKER DESTINY
DEATHSTALKER LEGACY
DEATHSTALKER RETURN
DEATHSTALKER CODA

Hawk and Fisher Novels

SWORDS OF HAVEN
GUARDS OF HAVEN

Also by Simon R. Green

BLUE MOON RISING
BEYOND THE BLUE MOON
DRINKING MIDNIGHT WINE

Omnibus

A WALK ON THE NIGHTSIDE

SPIRITS FROM BEYOND

SIMON R. GREEN

ACE BOOKS, NEW YORK

THE BERKLEY PUBLISHING GROUP
Published by the Penguin Group
Penguin Group (USA) Inc.
375 Hudson Street, New York, New York 10014, USA

USA | Canada | UK | Ireland | Australia | New Zealand | India | South Africa | China

Penguin Books Ltd., Registered Offices: 80 Strand, London WC2R 0RL, England
For more information about the Penguin Group, visit penguin.com.

SPIRITS FROM BEYOND

An Ace Book / published by arrangement with the author

For information, address: The Berkley Publishing Group,
a division of Penguin Group (USA) Inc.,
375 Hudson Street, New York, New York 10014.

ISBN: 978-0-425-25993-1

PUBLISHING HISTORY
Ace mass-market edition / September 2013

PRINTED IN THE UNITED STATES OF AMERICA

10 9 8 7 6 5 4 3 2 1

Cover art by Don Sipley.
Cover design by Judith Lagerman.
Interior text design by Laura K. Corless.

Life is complicated.
Why should death be any different?

Ghosts are real, whether we want them to be or not. People have reported seeing ghosts throughout the whole history of human civilisation. We may argue over how to interpret the phenomenon, but the phenomenon remains a real thing.

How the living cope with the dead defines who we are.

PREVIOUSLY, IN THE GHOST FINDERS

The secret organisation known as the Carnacki Institute exists to Do Something about ghosts. Hunt them down, sort out their problems, and if need be, send them packing with existential prejudice. The Institute's most experienced and successful team of field agents currently consists of JC Chance, team leader and positive thinker; Melody Chambers, girl science geek; and Happy Jack Palmer, team telepath and heavily medicated depressive.

On a mission to solve a mass haunting in Oxford Circus Tube Station, JC met and fell in love with the ghost of a murdered young woman, Kim Sterling. He almost died fighting to save her from a demonic presence on a tube train, when Something from Outside reached into our world and gave him new strength. His eyes glow golden now.

The living and the dead aren't supposed to fall in love, for any number of really good reasons.

On their next assignment, the team went up against Robert Patterson, a trusted high-up executive in the Carnacki Institute who turned out to be a traitor and the servant of an Outside force called The Flesh Undying . . . a powerful Being that fell into our world from another dimension, exiled by its own kind. The Flesh Undying sees our world as a trap and is ready to blow it apart if that is what it takes to escape.

JC and his team killed Robert Patterson, only to see him rise again, possessed by another traitor within the Institute. Ghost girl Kim drove that mind out by possessing the body herself, but when the time came for her to emerge again, she was gone.

JC nearly lost his mind.

They saw Kim again, briefly, during the Case of the Phantom of the Theatre. She told them they couldn't trust anyone in the Carnacki Institute. And then she silently vanished away again.

It's been six months since then. But everyone knows time means nothing to the dead.

ONE

THERE IS A WORLD BELOW

Sometimes he slept right through. Sometimes he got into bed and fell asleep and didn't wake up again until the alarm bell rang. But mostly JC couldn't sleep. He did all the right things, went to bed at the right time, but no matter how hard he tried, something wouldn't let him sleep.

There are few things worse than lying in bed, in the dark, waiting for the endless hours of the night to pass. Dozing off and waking up repeatedly, convinced that after so many wakings, it must be four, five o'clock in the morning . . . and then looking at the bedside clock and seeing it's barely 2:00 A.M. The night barely begun, and all those long hours still stretching away . . . JC Chance hadn't slept properly since his ghostly girl-friend, Kim, disappeared. In all the months she'd been missing, JC couldn't remember a single good night's sleep.

He still got tired at the end of the day, still went through all his usual routines before retiring . . . but mostly he lay flat on his back in his bed, in his marvellous new apartment in London's West End, dog-tired and bone-deep weary . . . and prayed for sleep that never came. Too tired to sit up and read, or even watch television, too tired to do anything but stare into the dark and wait for the night to end.

Sometimes he would get up and sit on the edge of the bed, head hanging down . . . and sometimes he would get up and walk around the room in the dark, trying to convince his body how tired it was, and how late it was . . . hoping against hope that just this once his body would give up and let him sleep. But mostly he lay there, legs crossed and hands folded neatly across his chest, as though wanting to be ready for the undertaker if he should happen to die in the night. Opening and closing his eyes though it didn't really make much difference. Because in the end, it was another night without Kim.

Until one night a scattered aetherial glow appeared at the foot of his bed, slowly concentrating into the form of the ghost girl, Kim. She hovered at the foot of his bed, looking just as she had the first time he had seen her in the London Underground. A beautiful pre-Raphaelite dream of a woman, forever in her twenties, the age she was when she was murdered. A great mane of glorious red hair tumbled down past her shoulders, framing a high-boned, sharply defined face, with vivid green eyes and a wide, smiling mouth. She wore a long white dress that clung tightly here and there to show off her magnificent figure; and she shone and shimmered in the gloom of the bedroom like a star fallen to Earth.

How nice, thought JC. *I'm finally asleep and dreaming of Kim.*

"You're not dreaming, darling," said Kim. "I'm here. I'm back."

JC sat bolt upright in bed. A fierce golden glow blazed from his wide-open eyes, the only outward sign of how deeply he'd been touched by forces from Outside. JC froze where he was, afraid to do anything that might disturb the vision or frighten her away.

"Hello, JC," said Kim. "Have you missed me?"

"More than life itself," JC said hoarsely. "Because it isn't living if you're not with me. Are you really back now? Tell me this isn't only another brief encounter because I don't think I could bear to lose you again."

"I'm back," said Kim. "But if you want to keep me, you're going to have to fight for me. You have to come and get me, right now."

"Where are you?" said JC.

"Where you lost me," said Kim. "Outside Chimera House. I'm there now, waiting for you."

Then she was gone; and the only light in the darkened room came from JC's eyes as he glared desperately around him.

He grabbed up his phone from the table beside his bed and called his team-mates, Happy and Melody. He had their number on speed dial, right next to a twenty-four-hour exorcist and dentist. He was shuddering all over, clinging to every detail of what he'd just seen, fighting to convince himself it had been real and not a dream. He'd only got through to Melody and Happy's apartment and heard Melody's voice at the other end, when the phone went dead in his hand and the television set at the other end of his bedroom suddenly turned itself on, blasting light into the darkened room. And there on the screen were Happy and Melody, staring out at him from their bedroom all the way across the city, in North London. They were sitting together on the end of their bed, shoulder to shoulder, wearing matching towelling dressing gowns and matching furry Sasquatch slippers. JC slowly put his phone down.

"I can see you!" he said to the faces on his television. "And you can see me, can't you . . . ?"

JC became suddenly self-conscious and pulled his bedclothes securely about him. Because he slept in the raw.

"Yes, we can see you," said Melody. "And will you please put on your sunglasses, because you're blinding us with the glare."

JC picked up the very dark sunglasses from his bedside table and slipped them on. The golden glare cut off immediately though a little light still spilled around the edges. JC gathered his dignity about him and glared at his television set.

"All right," he said steadily. "How are you doing this?"

Melody smiled briefly. "You're not the only one who liberates useful items from the Carnacki Institute warehouse. Now and again. When no-one's looking. After everything that's happened to us, I thought it important we have a method of communication that no-one else could intercept and listen in on."

"And you didn't tell me about this before because . . . ?" said JC.

"Didn't want to worry you," said Happy.

"And we weren't entirely sure it would work," said Melody.

"So we thought we'd better save it for a real emergency," said Happy.

"Hold everything," said JC. "All our phones have industrial-strength security scramblers already built in! The Institute installed them personally, once we were officially designated an A team. So they could discuss important mission details in confidence."

Happy looked at him pityingly. "Don't be naïve, JC. The people who installed the scramblers for the Institute are the very people who make sure to leave a back door open so they can eavesdrop if they want to. Given our current circumstances, with The Flesh Undying on our backs and at our throats, and God knows how many traitors inside the Institute, raging paranoia is a survival instinct. Of course, with me that comes naturally."

"Look!" said JC. "This is important! Kim was just here—in the room, with me."

"We know!" said Melody. "She was right here in the room with us, too."

"She was speaking to both of us at the same time?" said JC.

"And giving us the same message," said Happy. "The dead aren't as limited as the living. They love to multitask. Show-offs." He stopped, to snigger briefly. "Good timing, too. If she'd turned up ten minutes earlier . . . someone would have blushed, and it wouldn't have been me or Melody."

"She said we have to fight for her, back at Chimera House," said Melody, giving Happy a fierce dig in the ribs with her elbow. "And I have to wonder. How was she able to manifest in our apartments? Given that both our places are positively lousy with aetheric defences, specially designed to keep out spooky apparitions? One of the few real perks you get working for the Carnacki Institute is that major-league protections come as standard, in case something from the Other Side should take a fancy to one of us and follow us home."

"Right!" said Happy. "But I still check under the bed every night. How was Kim able to appear to us?"

"Because Kim isn't any old ghost," said JC. "Something from the Outside touched her, down in the London Underground, just as it touched me. It changed us both."

"I can confirm," said Happy, a bit diffidently, "that what we all saw wasn't any kind of trick, or illusion. It really was her. Though of course *really* might not be the best choice of word, given that we're dealing with a ghost here . . ."

"Shut up, dear," said Melody.

"Yes, dear, shutting up right now," said Happy.

"Should we contact our revered Boss, at the Institute?" Melody said carefully. "Tell her what's going on?"

"Best not bother her," JC said immediately. "Given that we don't know what's going on, as yet. Catherine Latimer has always been big on questions. Besides, she might order us not to go, and I'd have to defy her to her face. Instead of behind her back, which is quite definitely safer for all concerned."

"I thought the Boss was supposed to be on our side?" said Melody. "Are you saying we can't even trust the person who runs the whole damned Institute?"

"No-one is on our side but us," said JC.

"Now you're taking!" said Happy. "I know; shut up, Happy."

"Get yourselves ready," said JC. "I'll fire up the company car and come get you."

"We're really going back to Chimera House?" said Melody. "On the word of a ghost, and a pretty vague word, at that?"

"It's Kim," said JC.

There must have been something in his voice because Happy and Melody both looked away for a moment. Happy sighed loudly.

"Have I got time to update my will?"

"You're always updating your will," said Melody.

"I find it calming," said Happy.

The television set turned itself off. JC waited a moment to make sure the screen stayed blank, then he threw back his bedclothes and swung out of bed. The early-morning air was pleasantly cool against his bare skin. He stretched easily. He didn't feel tired at all.

He dressed quickly, then prowled through his apartment, snatching up things he thought might prove useful. Finally, he stopped before the full-length mirror in his hall and looked himself over. He wanted to be sure he was looking his best, for Kim.

His reflection smiled cheerfully back at him: a tall, lean, and only slightly sinister-looking fellow, perhaps a little too handsome for his own good. JC had just hit thirty and was putting a brave face on it. He had pale, striking features, dominated by the very dark sunglasses he had to wear in public and a huge mane of dark rock-star hair. He wore a rich, ice-cream white three-piece suit of quite staggering style and elegance, along with an Old School tie he wasn't in any way entitled to but which he wore anyway because it opened doors.

JC Chance—Ghost Finder Extraordinaire.

"I'm on my way, Kim," he said. "And God help anyone who gets in my way."

He left his apartment block, quietly and surreptitiously, and strode down the street to where he'd parked his car. He'd commandeered it from the Carnacki Institute car pool sometime back because it was the brightest shade of red he could find. He certainly intended to return it someday. He was entitled to a company car now he'd been officially upgraded to A-team status, and he really didn't see why he should go through all the hassle of filling out paper-work every time he wanted a car, like ordinary mortals. So he took one, and kept it. No doubt someone had noticed by now, but they couldn't come and reclaim it until they'd filled out all the necessary paper-work. By which time he would probably have crashed it or lost it in some other dimension.

JC always left his car parked outside in the street because the rents the local garages charged were nothing short of extortionate. He never worried about anything happening to the car because it was, after all, a Carnacki Institute official vehicle and could look after itself.

It wasn't particularly flashy or interesting because the Institute didn't want its field agents driving anything that might get them noticed, but it got the job done. JC drove his car swiftly through the deserted streets of early-morning London, by the straightest if not necessarily most legal route to Happy and Melody's apartment. There was hardly any other traffic on the roads anyway at this hour of the morning, and JC found that what there was usually got out of his way quickly enough if he hit the horn and drove straight at them. He kept his foot hard down on the accelerator, confident the traffic police wouldn't bother him because all Carnacki Institute cars carried Corps Diplomatique plates. It saved time and helped avoid awkward conversations that weren't going to go anywhere useful.

JC had a definite feeling there was something odd about the streets he was driving through. Not only the quiet and the lack of other traffic, which meant he could drive on whichever side of the road he felt like . . . It took him a while to realise it was all the empty parking spaces. During the day, you didn't see a parking space unoccupied anywhere in London. Unless it was a trap.

JC turned on his music, and the gently rasping melancholia of The Smiths filled the car. JC always played The Smiths when he was feeling reflective and in the mood to kick the crap out of someone deserving. Someone had been keeping his Kim from him, all this time, and JC was quietly determined that when he found out who, he was going to make that Someone very unhappy.

* * *

He finally slammed his car to a halt in front of Melody and Happy's place, shut off his music with a flourish, and threw open the car doors. Happy and Melody were already standing outside on the street, waiting for him;

but it couldn't be said that either of them looked particularly enthusiastic. JC decided to be charitable and put it down to their being disturbed so early in the morning.

Melody looked exactly as she always did. Pretty enough in a conventional way, short and gamine thin, and burning with enough nervous energy to scare off anyone with working survival instincts. In her thirties now, and quite openly resentful about it, Melody wore her auburn hair scraped back in a tight bun, never bothered with makeup, and wore severe glasses with old-fashioned granny frames. Along with clothes so anonymous they wouldn't have recognised style or fashion if they'd tripped over it in the gutter. Melody was all business, all the time.

Happy Jack Palmer lurked slouching beside her, wearing his usual put-upon look. Well past thirty but resigned to that as the least of his troubles, Happy was short and stocky, prematurely balding, and might have been handsome if he ever stopped scowling. He wore grubby old jeans and knock-off sneakers, along with a T-shirt bearing the message ASK ME ABOUT MY DAY. GO ON. I DARE YOU. under a battered old black leather jacket whose occasional rip and tear had been repaired with black duct tape. Happy made a point of telling everyone that he Saw the world more clearly than anyone else and was therefore entitled to feel clinically depressed.

On their own, they both made a strong impression. Together, they looked like they could kick arse for the Olympics. And take a bronze in fighting dirty.

Happy was first off the mark and into the car, grabbing shotgun. Melody threw a bulging knapsack into the back seat, and dropped heavily in after it.

"Just a few things," she said loudly. "Useful items. Because you never know."

"Girls and their toys," Happy said vaguely.

The car doors slammed shut, JC stomped hard on the accelerator, and the car jumped forward like a goosed dowager aunt. Off through the empty streets of London, on their way to rescue a ghost.

''''''''''''''''''''''''

It didn't take them long to get to Chimera House, not with Happy on board. His marvellous telepathic mind could detect short cuts, avoid obstacles, and when necessary make other people get the hell out of the way without even knowing why they were doing it. And it did help that JC drove like a demon, ignoring the occasional wails of distress from his passengers. As they entered the home-stretch, JC shot Happy a thoughtful gaze.

"I know the streets look empty. But could anyone be following us? Are we being observed, perhaps, from a distance?"

"No, and no," said Happy, clinging to his seat belt determinedly with both hands. "Accompanied by a large side order of Not A Chance In Hell. I'd know."

"I could check," Melody said immediately, determined not to be left out of things. "I've got a down-and-dirty sensor package somewhere in my back-pack."

"By the time you've got it out and adjusted the settings, we'll be there," Happy said witheringly.

"Someone's looking for a short sharp visit from the Slap Fairy," said Melody.

Chimera House was right in the middle of London's business centre; but when JC finally brought the car screeching to a halt in front of the massive office building, the entire area was completely deserted. Not a living soul in sight. Which was a bit suspicious because there's always someone about in every part of London, whatever the hour. Everyone from the police to the homeless, party-goers, and minor celebrities—all of them out and about doing something they shouldn't because there was no-one around to see . . .

Melody was immediately out of the back of the car, her hand-held scanner at the ready. She waved it around, adjusting the dials and hitting the thing with the flat of her hand when it didn't do what she wanted it to do quickly enough. Happy took his time getting out of the car, so he could get his slouch exactly right, and show everyone how unhappy he was at being more or less awake at such an uncivilised time of the morning. JC got out of the car, locked it carefully, then sat on the bonnet and looked thoughtfully about him.

"No life signs anywhere," Melody said briskly. "No dead signs, either. We are strictly on our own here. Sorry, JC."

"Bad vibes," Happy said wisely. "People can sense this is a bad place, and go out of their way to avoid it, even if they couldn't tell you why. I wouldn't be here if I didn't have to be. Of all the places Kim could have chosen to show up again. I don't like it here. I've got the shudders. Have you got the shudders? Even the homeless wouldn't sleep in these doorways. This entire area is spiritually polluted, right down to the stone and concrete."

The three Ghost Finders stuck close together, looking the area over with professionally discerning eyes. None of them had been back here since the distressing Affair of the New People. Which . . . could have gone better. Chimera House still dominated the area, a massive steel-and-glass business edifice towering over the open square before it. The square itself felt cold and empty, laid out under an open night sky full of stars, and a pale full moon. The main illumination was the unwavering flat amber light from the street-lamps.

Everything had been carefully cleared up since the great battle of Chimera House. No sign anywhere of the great cracks in the ground or the shattered windows in the surrounding buildings. All the blood and bodies gathered up and spirited away . . . Someone had gone to a great deal of trouble to make it all seem as if *nothing happened*.

Chimera House itself stood silent and empty. No lights on anywhere, and heavy steel chains hung from the closed front doors. No-one allowed in or out, by order; and if you were wise, you didn't ask on whose order. JC looked the building over carefully. He couldn't avoid an uncomfortable feeling that the building was looking back at him. And not in a good way.

"Shouldn't there be guards outside that building?" said Happy. "I mean, armed guards, heavily armed, to make sure no-one messes with whatever's left inside?"

"Chimera House was supposed to be pulled down," JC said steadily. "Completely destroyed, reduced to rubble, and built over because of all the really bad things that happened inside it. More than enough to make the entire building a strange attractor, drawing in nasty people, and things, from all around. So I have to ask: why is it still here?"

"You should keep up on your interdepartmental

memos," said Melody. "Somebody very high up on the food chain over-ruled the Carnacki Institute. And I mean someone with really impressive clout. They insisted on preserving the building until a full investigative study could be performed on its contents. The Boss was mad as hell. Took her argument all the way to the top. And got nowhere."

"Are we talking political or business clout?" said Happy.

"Yes," said Melody.

"Ah," said Happy.

"Pretty much the same thing, at that level," said JC. "What was the name of the big company in charge of the medical experiments that went wrong, in Chimera House?"

"Mutable Solutions Incorporated," said Melody. "One of the biggest drug companies in the world. Where does the eight-hundred-pound drug company sit? Anywhere it wants . . ."

"But what good does it do them, keeping Chimera House intact?" said Happy. "No-one will be able to work in it for ages. It'll take years, more likely decades, to get the psychic stains out. You've heard of Sick Building Syndrome; well, Chimera House is the psychic equivalent of the Ebola virus. That whole building is crazy on a stick, waiting to happen."

JC couldn't help noticing that Happy didn't even want to look at Chimera House as he spoke. They could all hear the open strain in the telepath's voice.

"Maybe what happened inside the building is what makes it valuable," said JC. "Valuable to The Flesh Undying, or its agents . . . Maybe it wants to maintain bad places, to make weak points in the walls of the world, so it can break out and get back where it came from."

"Don't you start," Melody said firmly. "It's bad enough having to live with a paranoid depressive, without having two of them on the team."

"I don't like it here!" Happy said loudly. "I feel . . . vulnerable. Like a target. Like I'm standing at ground zero, right in the middle of a bloody big bull's-eye. With a target painted on my forehead."

"Will you please calm the hell down!" said Melody, waving her hand scanner around. "There's no-one else here!"

"There's always something here," said Happy. "We're never alone, wherever we are. The world is packed full . . . I can See things, feel things . . . I want to get out of here!"

"We're not going anywhere until Kim turns up!" JC said firmly. "However long that takes. Get a grip on yourself, Happy. This isn't your first time at the rodeo."

Happy sniffed miserably and stared determinedly down at his shoes. "Still want to know why there aren't any guards."

"He may be paranoid, but he has a point," said Melody. "I'm pretty sure that was a condition on the building being allowed to stand. So where are they?"

"Someone must have called them off," said JC. "Which implies . . . someone knew we were coming here before we did."

The three of them stood close together. It was still the early hours of morning, cold and quiet and empty. No sign of the living, or the dead. But not exactly peaceful. JC and Happy and Melody hugged themselves against the chill and stamped their feet hard on the ground to keep warm.

"This is just like last time," said Melody.

"Bloody better not be," said Happy. "We were lucky to come out of that mission with all our important parts still attached. Dead men walking, insane doctors with cutty things, rogue transplant organs on the loose, Gog and Magog and the New People . . . We should get danger money. We should get unionised!" He scowled about him, still carefully avoiding looking at Chimera House. "I never thought it would be like this when the time came to get Kim back. I thought we'd have to storm some kind of castle, fight some monsters, to win back our lost princess."

JC smiled at him. "You would, too, wouldn't you?"

"Of course!" said Happy, surprised and even a little outraged that JC could think otherwise. "She might be your girl-friend, but she's our team-mate, too."

"Damn right," said Melody. She draped an affectionate arm across Happy's shoulders. "He's very sentimental, on the quiet."

"Of course," said Happy. "There are limits. I'm giving Kim ten more minutes, then I'm going back to wait in the car. With the heater full on."

"Sentimental, but practical," said Melody. And then she stopped, grabbed Happy by the chin, and jerked his head around, so she could look him straight in the eye. "Happy, what is wrong with you? You're shaking all over, and it isn't from the cold. Are the psychic impressions here really that bad?"

"This whole area is saturated with weird energies," said Happy, jerking his chin free. "And I mean, really strange stuff. It's all information, you see, soaked into the surface of the world, radiating back and forth like emergency broadcasts from Heaven and Hell . . . And it's getting more difficult all the time to keep it outside my head."

Melody checked the readings on her scanner again. "I'm not picking up anything I'd consider . . . out of the ordinary."

"Science is limited," said Happy. "Science deals with the surface of the world, not what's Below or Above."

"Compared to your marvellous mutant mind, I suppose," said Melody, testily.

"Yes," said Happy.

"Oh come on," said JC. "It can't be that bad. I See stuff too, sometimes, but . . ."

He broke off. Happy was glaring at him.

"You never get it, do you? What it's like to See the world as it really is, all the time, to know what's really going on, all around us. All right! See the world through my eyes, for once!"

He grabbed JC and Melody by the arms; and immediately, all three of their minds were linked tightly together by the sheer force and power of Happy's telepathy. He couldn't have done it with anyone else; but the three of them had linked before. They weren't just everyday Ghost Finders, after all.

The everyday view of London in the morning disappeared, replaced, or rather overwritten, by a larger view. The world around them was suddenly packed full of life and death, Heaven and Hell, and everything in between. Overlapping layers of spiritual and spatial dimensions, interspersed with spiralling moments of Time.

Past, Present, and any number of Futures, all happening at once. Ghosts coming and going, following paths that didn't exist any longer in the physical world. Stone tapes everywhere, ghostly images imprinted on their surroundings, playing back loops of repeating Time, over and over again.

JC almost cried out, as he saw old images of the A team who died inside Chimera House. Jeremy Diego, Monica Odini, Ivar ap Owen. Legends in their field; caught by surprise and killed in a moment. Still there, held forever in a repeating moment, like insects trapped in amber. Forever going to their deaths, and not knowing it. And there was nothing JC could do to help them or even warn them.

He'd never liked them much. Somehow, that made it worse.

More images now, layer upon layer, with people from every period of history, all shouting at once. An endless din of dead voices. Unfinished bodies walking in and out of buildings as though they weren't even there. Because they weren't, once. Dead men and women walking in and out of each other, teeming like the unseen microscopic images that swarm in a drop of water. How many ghosts can dance on the head of a pin? Depends on the tune . . .

More voices, more sounds, human and inhuman. Great booming Voices, shouting at the world from Outside. Sounds that might have been screams or laughter, or human interpretations of Voices beyond our comprehension. The dead, reaching out for answers, or comfort, or simple human contact. Crying out against the dying of the light or the rising of the dark.

Flashing images of this world and that and countless others, coming and going, superimposing themselves, turning and twisting and combining to make new things, the way two colours can mix to make a third. And always . . . creatures, strange things, moving through our world from one unknowable place to another. The apparently empty open square before Chimera House was like the Grand Central Station of the supernatural. And this, JC and Melody slowly realised, was what it always looked and sounded like in Happy's world.

The telepath jerked his hands free from JC and Melody, breaking contact, and the world was quiet and empty and sane again.

JC swayed on his feet, his heart hammering, struggling to win back his mental equilibrium. His face was wet with sweat. He looked at Melody; and she looked the same. They both looked at Happy, who stared back defiantly.

"You see?" he said. "That's what I see and hear all the time. All the things that never go away, never shut up, never leave me alone. I have to fight with everything I've got to keep them out of my head. So the only thoughts in my mind are my own. So I only see and hear what everyone else does. The pressure never stops, never lets up for a moment; and I get so tired, so tired . . ."

"Oh, sweetie," said Melody. She took him in her arms and held him close; and Happy let her.

"There's nothing we can do to help, is there?" said JC.

"No," said Happy. "Though I am working on something." He pushed Melody gently away from him. "We're not here for me. We're here for Kim. Where is she?"

"Back at the Haybarn Theatre, she said she wasn't

abducted—just missing," said JC. "That she was busy, following leads of her own. She said she saw, or experienced, something important here while she was possessing Robert Patterson; and that she had to pursue it. So where has she been all this time? And what has she been doing?"

"Out in the world," said the ghost girl Kim. "And walking up and down in it."

They all looked around sharply; and there she was, standing before them. Glowing very faintly in the gloom, her bare feet hovering an inch or two above the ground, smiling happily on them all. JC rushed forward, reaching out to take her in his arms, only to remember at the last moment. He stumbled to a halt before her, and they stood face-to-face, smiling into each other's eyes. Lost in each other but unable to touch. After a respectful moment, Happy and Melody came forward, and Kim turned away from JC to smile on them. Happy put up a hand for a high five; and Kim put up a hand that almost touched his. Melody threw the ghost girl a quick salute, and Kim nodded in return.

"Where have you been, Kim?" said JC.

"I've been tracking down the individual who was inside Patterson's head, before me," said Kim. "The servant of The Flesh Undying; the secret traitor at the heart of the Carnacki Institute."

"Who?" said JC. "Who is it? Who are we talking about here?"

"I can't tell you," said Kim. "Not yet."

"Why the hell not?" said JC.

"Don't you raise your voice to me, Josiah Charles

Chance," said Kim. "I can't tell you because I'm protecting you. I know the name; but they can't read my mind."

"They?" said Happy, his ears pricking up immediately.

"Exactly," said Kim.

"Why didn't you come back to us before this?" said Melody.

"Because the traitor saw me," said Kim. "Saw and knew me. And so The Flesh Undying sent its agents after me, physical and spiritual, chasing me all across the world, and Above and Under it. The living and the dead, in hot and cold pursuit. It's taken me a long time, travelling through the sacred and profane places of the world, to shake them all off . . . and to search out what I was looking for."

"All that matters is that you're back," said JC.

"Not quite," said Kim. "I'm sorry, JC, but we're not alone here. Something unfriendly is here in this place with us."

"What?" said Happy. *"What?"*

He spun quickly around in circles, as though hoping to catch something by surprise. Melody slapped her scanner with the flat of her hand again.

"Still not picking up anything!" she said angrily. She shook the thing fiercely. "You are seriously underperforming! You can be replaced!"

"I'm not Seeing anything!" said Happy. "I Spy with my third little eye . . . nothing out of the ordinary! So to speak."

"The Flesh Undying knew I would reappear here," Kim said calmly. "I had to return to this place because this is where I'd left from. Closing the circle was the only way I could come back, to the material world I left. There are rules, you see, for the dead as well as the living. Perhaps especially for the dead. And The Flesh Undying took advantage of that. It's set a trap here, for me, and for you. It's not too late for you to leave if that's what you want."

"Never," said JC.

"Well, I don't know about never," said Happy. "But I'm here now."

"He's so brave," said Melody. "Isn't he wonderful? Of course we're not leaving, Kim! You're part of the team."

"Then brace yourselves," said Kim.

JC and Melody and Happy moved quickly to stand back-to-back-to-back; so they could watch and cover all the open space around them. So nothing could sneak up on them or catch them by surprise. Melody put her scanner away and produced a machine-pistol. She swept it smoothly back and forth with professional ease, looking for a target. JC had to smile.

"All right," he said, "I give up. Where do you keep that gun, Melody?"

"Trust me," said Happy. "You don't want to know."

Kim stood very still, looking at whatever ghosts looked at.

"I can See layers of protection, still in place," said Happy. "Laid down around Chimera House. But it's standard off-the-shelf stuff. The kind of defences that would collapse in a moment if anything seriously demonical even leaned on them."

"The threat to us isn't inside the building," said Kim. "It's out here, with us."

"Okay," said Happy. "I am now running for the car. Try to keep up."

"Too late," said Kim, sadly.

The ground before them split violently apart—soundlessly, jaggedly. Solid stone and concrete tore like paper. The ground shook and juddered, and the three living Ghost Finders staggered back and forth, clinging to each other for support. A deep chasm opened up, stretching across the open square, full of darkness. Kim turned a stern gaze on the wide gap, and like that the ground was still again. Everything was quiet. Melody took a cautious step forward, peering down into the great dark crevasse. Happy moved in behind her, staring over her shoulder. JC looked at Kim, who looked calmly back at him.

"More major structural damage, right in the heart of London's business centre," said Melody. "Someone's insurance premiums are about to go right through the roof. What do you want to bet that the powers that be will find some way to blame all of this on us?"

"No wonder the security guards were called off," said JC. "Someone didn't want any witnesses . . ."

"This isn't like the last time," Happy said slowly. "It feels different . . ."

They all eased forward, right up to the edge of the chasm, and looked down. A long range of old stone steps headed down into the darkness. Scuffed and much-used stone steps, without any banister or railing, falling away, apparently forever.

"Impressive," said JC.

"They're not real," said Kim.

"What?" said Happy.

"The steps aren't really there," said Kim, apparently entirely unimpressed. "This is merely a transition, from one place to another. Your mind interprets what's there as steps to make life easier for you."

"How come you can See that when I can't?" said Happy, frowning hard at the steps, which still insisted on looking like steps.

Kim smiled. "Because I'm dead. It's very revealing, being dead. You should try it sometime."

"Not right now," said JC. "We've got work to do."

Melody took out her hand-held scanner again and aimed it down into the dark chasm. Smoke immediately poured out of the machine, from every side at once, and the whole thing overheated so quickly, Melody had no choice but to throw it away before it burned her hand. It dropped away into the darkness and quickly disappeared. Happy looked at Melody but had the good sense not to say anything. JC peered dubiously into the chasm.

"All right," he said. "Where do these steps that aren't actually steps go, Kim? And why do we want to go there?"

"Hold everything," said Melody, blowing gently on her scorched fingers. "Before we go into that, I want to know; who actually broke open the ground? Who provided this extremely dramatic transition; and who wants us to go down there, into London Undertowen?"

"Into what?" said Happy.

"Is this you, Kim?" said Melody. "Did you crack open the world?"

"No," said Kim.

"Is this the trap?" JC said carefully. "The trap The Flesh Undying has set for you, and us?"

"Yes," said Kim. "But for once, I think The Flesh Undying has outsmarted itself. It's so used to thinking of itself as the most intelligent and superior creature on this planet that it has never stopped to consider that wasn't always the case. There's something else, waiting for us down there, that we can use against our enemy."

"Will somebody please tell me," Happy said doggedly. "What the hell is London Undertowen?"

Melody sighed loudly. "Am I really the only one on this team who takes the time to read the regular reports the Carnacki Institute circulates among its field agents every month?"

"Yes," said Happy. "You sweet little girl swot, you."

"We get regular reports?" said JC. "Really?"

"Information is ammunition in our line of work," Melody said primly.

"That would look good on a T-shirt," said Happy.

"Never wear them," JC said firmly.

"We noticed," said Happy, crushingly. "Maybe we could stencil it on the back of your jacket."

Kim looked at Melody. "They haven't improved while I was gone, have they?"

"No," said Melody. "Men . . . Evolution; I'm looking forward to it. Hey! Both of you shut the hell up and listen! Thank you . . . London Undertowen is the city beneath the city. Or perhaps even the world beneath the world. Catacombs, set deep in the earth, that the Romans and everyone else built London over."

Happy glared down the long series of stone steps, concentrating hard, as though he thought he could make them look like something else if he tried hard enough.

"Don't," said Kim. "Steps are good. Learn to love the steps. Because all the alternatives are worse."

"So . . . what's down there, exactly, in this Undertowen?" said Happy.

"I've been trying to get a straight answer on that for months," said Melody. "I'm pretty sure someone somewhere in the Institute knows, but I've never been able to hack the security around those files. You'd have to turn up at the Carnacki Institute's Secret Libraries, in person, and read what they've got there. Except mere field agents like us don't have a high enough security clearance to get in there."

"Ooh! Ooh!" said Happy, bouncing cheerfully up and down on the spot. "I've always wanted to get inside the Secret Libraries!"

"The Boss did promise us access," JC said slowly. "But she never got around to updating our security rating . . . Which may or may not have been an oversight on her part . . . Kim; do you know what's down there, in the Undertowen?"

"Something very old," said Kim. "Something The Flesh Undying thinks it can use against us. That's one of the reasons why I stayed away so long, guys. Because I didn't want to put you in even more danger. But I finally saw a chance to come home again, and I took it. I have a plan; so let's hope I'm as smart as I think I am. If you want to keep me, JC, you're going to have to go down there into the dark and fight for me."

JC grinned. "Isn't that how we first met?"

They smiled at each other.

"I can't help noticing," Happy said loudly, "that I still haven't had an answer to my question. *What the hell is down there?*"

"Tell me," said Kim. "What do you guys know about Druids?"

"Oh hell," said Happy. "The answer hasn't even started yet, and already I hate it. You mean the real Druids, the original Druids? Scary, and I mean seriously scary. Not like the current bunch, the Stonehenge botherers. Big, hairy, refried-hippie, tree-hugger types. The original pre-Roman bunch were seriously nasty, bad-arse, mystic warriors. Heavily into murder magic, human sacrifice, burning their enemies en masse in giant Wicker Men . . ."

"Good film, that," said JC.

"Bloody good film," said Happy. "Which only goes to show we shouldn't mess around with anything that involves real Druids. We're only supposed to deal with ghosts. I think we should back away, very carefully and at speed, and turn this whole thing over to someone with more experience in this field. Like the Droods."

"You've got to be kidding," said Melody. "They're scarier than the Druids ever were."

"True," said Happy.

"You deal with the dead," said Kim. "And what's waiting for us down there very definitely qualifies."

"Only back ten minutes, and already I'm getting into situations that give me twitches in the backstairs department," muttered Happy.

"Tell me more about Druids," said JC. "I never was very big on ancient history."

"The old-time Druids dealt with wood and water, fire and earth," said Melody, patiently. "And like the Nature they worshipped, the Druids were red in tooth and claw.

So seriously hard-core they actually shocked the hardened Roman Legionnaires. Three times the Roman armies tried to invade Britain, and twice the Druids drove them back into the sea, till the waters ran red with blood up and down the coast. The Romans only won the third time, in 55 B.C., because they were able to sneak in agents and get the various British tribes fighting each other. The Romans practically invented Divide and Conquer. But, you have to remember that the Druids had an entirely oral tradition of knowledge, with information passed only from mouth to mouth. Nothing was ever written down, to preserve their ancient mysteries. So the only written records we have of the Druids at that time are Roman writings. People with no interest in presenting the Druids in a good light."

"So they were actually good guys?" said Happy.

"No," said Kim. "Not by any definition we could be comfortable with."

"Druids worshipped the triple goddess," said Melody. "Macha, Badb, Neman. More gorecrows than gods, they thrived on slaughter and butchery. And then, there was Lud . . ."

"And then there was Lud," said Kim. "A very ancient Being, he predated the Druids who worshipped him. Long dead now, of course."

"Good," said Happy. "Anyone the Druids worshipped is not someone you'd want to meet in a dark catacomb. You are sure he's dead?"

"Oh quite definitely," said Kim. "I've seen the body. That's why we're going down into the Undertowen—to talk with him."

They all looked at her.

"Are you saying," Happy said carefully, "that somewhere down there, is the ghost of an old god?"

"Ghost of an old monster, anyway," Kim said cheerfully. "Surrounded, of course, by all kinds of other dead things of an equally upsetting and dangerous nature."

"Including a whole army of dead Druids, perchance?" said Melody.

"Exactly!" said Kim.

"I'm going home," said Happy. "Right now. Really. Watch me."

"I thought you wanted to fight for me?" said Kim.

"Well, yes, but," said Happy.

"And there you have his entire character, in a nutshell," said Melody.

"Come along, children," said JC. "Lovely night for a stroll in the Undertowen. We are going down!"

"Of course we are," said Melody.

And then she broke off, as Happy produced a pill bottle from one of his jacket pockets. He studied the handwritten label carefully, put the bottle away again, and fished out another. He nodded over the label, undid the screw cap, and knocked back two of the pills quickly, swallowing hard. Melody stared at him, openly shocked.

"Happy!" she said finally. "You swore you didn't need those any more . . . You promised me you'd thrown them all away!"

"I lied," said Happy, meeting her angry gaze unflinchingly. "I do that sometimes. When necessary. To keep the peace."

"You don't need pills any more!" Melody said fiercely. "You've got me!"

"You make me feel safe," said Happy. "But you can't

make me feel brave. To go down into a place like this takes more of me than I've got."

Melody turned to JC. "Do Something! Say something!"

"He's a grown man," said JC. "He can make his own decisions. He knows what he needs better than you or I."

"Sorry, Melody," said Happy. "But love can only take me so far. After that, it takes chemical courage to push me over the edge."

His eyes were already glassy, and his smile was a lot wider than they were used to seeing of late. Melody glared at him coldly.

"We will talk about this later."

"If there is a later," said Happy. He went right up to the edge of the great chasm and looked down the long steps into the dark. "Ooh . . . You're right, Kim. They really aren't steps at all, are they?"

"What are you Seeing down there, Happy, that the rest of us aren't?" said JC. And if he was as surprised and shocked as Melody at Happy's return to a chemical crutch, he kept it out of his voice. He had a job to do.

"Let's just say . . . When I say *It's quiet, too quiet*, that means something," said Happy. "In this case . . . it means Something's down there waiting for us. And not in a good way. Let's go say hello!"

He went clattering quickly down the stone steps, taking them two at a time, and the others had no choice but to hurry down after him.

''''''''''''''''''''''''

The stone steps felt real enough, solid enough, under JC's feet as he took over the lead from Happy. On the grounds that if you were heading into danger, the one leading the way should have at least some of his survival instincts still working. The small group moved steadily down into the depths, surrounded by a small pool of moon-pale light with no obvious source. JC couldn't help noticing that none of their feet made any noise at all on the apparently solid stone steps. Without any landmarks, it was hard to get any real sense of descent, or time passing, until the stairway suddenly stopped without warning, and they were Somewhere Else.

The catacombs stretched away before them: ancient stone galleries, with corridors and passageways, endlessly turning and branching. Rough stone arches, all of them full of shadows and darkness. Dusty openings and endless grey avenues led off in every direction. Old stone, without markings or character, constructed to serve a purpose and a function, not decoration. The silence was complete, hanging heavily over everything. JC looked at Melody, who was hanging on to her machine-pistol like a security blanket. She actually jumped slightly when he turned to her.

"Yes! What? I don't see anything!"

"I was wondering. How big is London Undertowen supposed to be?"

"How big is London?" said Melody. "They say you can find everything that London's lost down in the Undertowen. Lost people, lost secrets, lost civilisations."

"Albino alligators!" Happy said brightly, smiling about him beatifically. "Grown from small pets flushed down toilets when they got too big."

"First, that's an urban myth," said Melody. "And second, it's an entirely American urban myth. Alligators as pets never caught on over here because we are a sane people."

But Happy had already stopped listening to her. He'd spotted thick mats of blue moss growing over most of a nearby wall. In fact, there were heavy splashes of the stuff all over the place. It looked moist, and springy; and JC thought the moss might even be breathing, rising and falling very slowly. Happy darted forward to study the nearest patch of blue moss, pushing his face right into it.

"I know what this is!" he said loudly. "I've read about it, in the kinds of magazines you never find in supermarkets . . . Supposedly, whoever eats or smokes this stuff is supposed to receive visions of Heaven and Hell. And a chance to have actual conversations with the inhabitants of both places."

"Are you intending to try it out?" said Melody, pointedly.

"No," said Happy, backing away reluctantly. "I have enough problems as it is. Besides, you should never talk to the dead. You can't trust anything they say. They always have their own agenda." He stopped and looked back at Kim. "No offence."

"Dear Happy," said Kim. "You haven't changed at all."

"Is that a good or a bad thing?" Happy said earnestly. And then his head came up suddenly, and he turned his back on the blue moss to stare out into the surrounding gloom. "Heads up, people! Company's coming!"

JC looked quickly about him. The pale moonlight that fell from nowhere stretched away in all directions but didn't reveal much.

"What's coming?" he said. "And from which direction?"

"From everywhere," said Kim. She was glowing more brightly now, her face eager and intent. "Hold your ground, guys. And don't do anything to draw their attention."

Melody pulled Happy over to stand at her side and held her machine-pistol at the ready. JC stood beside Kim, who didn't even look at him. Someone was coming, or Something; JC could feel it, like a pressure on his skin. Something unnatural, from out of the dark.

They came from every direction at once, emerging from the tall arches or appearing suddenly out of narrow stone corridors, glowing faintly like poisoned candles. Walking in silence, drifting along as though blown by an unfelt wind, staring straight ahead and saying nothing. Walking the low road, the paths of the dead, driven by needs and purposes that only the unliving could understand. Ghosts of dead soldiers, in uniforms from armies across the ages; deserters from every force that ever marched through the streets of London. Ghosts of plague victims, dumped in mass graves and unmarked burial pits. Still huddled together for comfort, even in death. The marks of the plagues that killed them still vivid on their faces, like deadly kisses. Ghosts of small children, worked to death in sweat-shop businesses, or abandoned to die cold and alone, in the streets and back alley-ways where civilised people never went.

All the ghosts London doesn't want to remember.

And all the Ghost Finders could do was stand very still and watch the dead file past, disappearing back into the dark. The ghosts didn't even look at them. When the last of them was finally gone, JC turned almost angrily to Kim.

"There must be something we can do to help."

"You can't," said Kim.

"But there were children!" said JC. "There shouldn't be children in a place like this. I won't stand for it!"

"London is a city built on the dead," said Kim. "You know that, JC. You'd need an army of exorcists, working in shifts for years, to wipe London clean of its past. And even then, a lot of those ghosts would almost certainly come back again. Because they've nowhere else to go, or because they're not ready to let go. Ghosts are all about unfinished business, and this many ghosts, together . . . They have a spiritual weight, a spectral impact on their surroundings, that is way beyond our understanding. And a purpose beyond our comprehension."

"But . . . there were children," said JC. "That's not right. We can't just leave them down here, in the dark."

"I love it that you care," said Kim. "And it's sweet that you feel the need to Do Something . . . but you can't help those who don't want to be helped." She looked briefly at Happy, then stared out into the dark again. "We have to keep moving, JC. There are far more dangerous things in the catacombs than ghosts."

"Could any of them help us?" said Happy. "With whatever it is we're here to fight? I need information, and clarification, and possibly a very big stick with nails sticking out of it."

"This isn't like you, Happy," said JC. "It's an improvement, but it isn't like you."

"There is thunder and lightning in my veins," said

Happy. "And a lion growling in my heart. Point me at something, before it wears off."

* * *

Kim led the way, into the dark heart of the catacombs. The stone passageways radiated out before them, with doors and rounded openings and high stone arches leading off in every direction. They all seemed extremely real and solid, but JC wasn't entirely convinced. He trailed his fingertips through the thick dust covering the walls, and rubbed the stuff between his fingertips. More dust rose with every footstep they took though it took its own sweet time about falling back down again. Couldn't get much more real than dust . . . JC peered over his sunglasses, now and again, to check out his surroundings with his altered eyes, but it all looked exactly the same. The catacombs were certainly real enough to contain and guide him and his team.

At least he could hear his footsteps now, even if they didn't seem to echo, along with Happy's and Melody's. Kim made no sound at all as she moved, even when her bare feet did seem to make contact with the floor. And she didn't leave trails in the dust, like the others. JC kept a careful eye on the trail they left in case they needed to get the hell out in a hurry.

"The air down here smells bad," said Melody, after a while. "Dry, and sour . . ."

"We're a long way from the surface," said Kim. "And I hate to think what else here has been breathing this air before us."

"Oh, gross," said Happy.

"Wish I still had my scanner," Melody grumbled. "I'll bet the carbon-monoxide levels are appalling."

"Is it only me?" said Happy. "Or can anyone else smell blood?"

"We're entering the oldest part of the catacombs now," said Kim. "Built centuries before the Romans even thought of invading Britain."

"Who by?" said JC.

"Good question!" said Kim. "I'm not sure there's anyone still alive, or dead, or in between, that could tell you. We're passing out of history and into legend. Into the place of myths and madness. I can say these are Druid things. Their subterranean galleries. Miles and miles of them . . ."

"The Druids were supposed to be all about the Nature," said Happy. "Why would they bury themselves away down here?"

"To do the things their triple goddess wouldn't approve of," said Kim. "And given some of the things they got up to in the open, in the forests . . ."

"This isn't just a catacomb," JC said slowly. "This is a maze . . . Built, perhaps, to keep Something in . . ."

"Or to keep Something out," said Kim.

JC looked at her thoughtfully. "What is this place a home for, now?"

"The dead, mostly," said Kim. "Those not departed enough."

"Depends on whom you talk to," Melody said sternly. "There are sites on the Net . . ."

"And you've argued with most of them," said Happy.

"I don't necessarily believe everything I hear," said Melody, ignoring Happy. "But there are some fascinating stories out there, concerning what lives or perhaps more properly speaking exists, down here in the Undertowen."

"I know I'm going to regret saying this," said JC. "But such as . . . ?"

"Some say . . . the results of scientific experiments, run wild, having broken out of very secret laboratories," said Melody. "Or, the abandoned offspring of Snake Deities and Alien Greys. Refugees from the Nightside, hiding out until the pursuit goes cold. The last surviving remnants of ancient races and species long thought extinct in the world above. The lost and the strayed, the forgotten and the damned."

"Happy's right," said JC. "You will believe absolutely anything."

Melody brandished her machine-pistol angrily. "At least I'm prepared!"

"You really think a gun is going to help you down here, in the place of the dead?" said Kim, not unkindly.

"Couldn't hurt," said Melody.

JC looked at Kim. "What, exactly, are we going to be facing?"

"The ghost of a dead god and what remains of his court," said Kim. "But don't press me for details. The Flesh Undying has been meddling here. There are rumours, in certain places, that these days the corridors are full of his creatures. The weaponised dead . . ."

Happy leaned in close beside JC. "Remind me again why we wanted her back?"

* * *

The Ghost Finders walked on through the stone galleries, which slowly and subtly changed their shape and nature until the group realised they were walking through a dead grey forest, made up of twisted and distorted trees, looming above them, made of stone. Branches protruded stiffly, with no leaves anywhere. Mottled tree-trunks thrust directly up out of the grey stone floor, with no sign of roots. The stone trees were packed close together, with only a narrow, twisting trail to lead the Ghost Finders on. Happy leaned in close for a good look at one of the grey trees; and then never did that again.

"Fossilised trees?" said Melody, after a while. "How is that even possible? I mean, how old would trees have to be, before . . ."

"Maybe there's a Gorgon down here," Happy said brightly.

"The trees continue because the Druids continue," Kim said quietly. "Because this is the world they remember. From when they were alive. There are old sleeping powers here, and people. The Flesh Undying has promised to aid them if they will serve him. They know we're here. They know we're coming."

"All right," said JC. "How do we fight them?"

"We can't," said Kim. "But the ghost of the old god Lud, he can. If we can persuade him that such actions are in his best interests."

"Marvellous," said Melody. "What can we promise him that The Flesh Undying can't? What does a dead god want, anyway?"

"Broad band?" said Happy.

"Come on," said JC, "We can do this! Slapping down ghosts is our business."

"You can be so cocky sometimes," said Melody.

"I know!" said JC. "it's one of my most endearing qualities."

''''''''''''''''''''''''''

Kim insisted on taking the lead as they pressed on between towering stone trees, following a trail or direction only she could see. The moonlight that fell from no moon took on a blue-white, shimmering aspect, while the surrounding shadows seemed to grow deeper and darker all the time. The air smelled close and bad, as though something had breathed all the goodness out of it long ago. JC strode along beside Kim, quietly trying to get her to open up and answer some questions; but she had nothing further to say. Melody clung firmly on to her machine-pistol with one hand and hauled Happy along with the other. He kept wanting to go off and chase butterflies. But in the end, he was the first one to realise they were not alone in the stone forest. That something, or rather some large number of somethings, was following along with them. Sticking to the more extreme shadows, staying well out of sight; a presence more felt than properly observed.

JC pulled everyone in close and kept them moving. He trusted Kim's sense of direction, but he still had to wonder if they were being herded . . . Whatever was moving silently along with them between the grey trees felt bad. A threat to the spirit as well as the body. Something that served the kind of forces that could only be found in the dark. JC could hear them, after a while, moving in closer, behind and around them. Surrounding them, forever on the edge of vision, barely glimpsed out of the corner of the eye. Melody waved her machine-pistol around until JC made her lower it again. He didn't want to start something he wasn't sure he could win. Until finally the trees fell suddenly back to either side, revealing a huge open space before them—a vast natural amphitheatre. A carefully arranged setting for what was waiting for them.

The Ghost Finders came to a halt. JC looked up, half-expecting to see an open night sky above, complete with full moon. But there was only stone and gloom above. So JC had no choice but to look at the terrible thing sitting on its throne, before them.

Lud was huge. A massive, towering, mostly human figure, sitting unmoving on a throne so old . . . that both Lud and his throne seemed impossibly ancient. And equally fossilised. Like the trees in his forest. JC had never seen anything, living or dead, as big as Lud. In his time, in his prime, Lud could have intimidated dinosaurs. His shape and proportions were subtly wrong, even disturbing to any normal human sense of aesthetics; but in the end the thing on the throne looked more like a man than anything else. Its skin was grey and dusty, like the trees. It almost looked like a statue, a nightmare carved in old stone; but it was clearly, unsettlingly, so much more than that. It had a huge, horned, almost skeletal head, with an elongated muzzle packed full of blocky teeth, and two deep, dark, empty eye-sockets. The horns looked more like branches than bone, and even more like branching antlers.

JC hated to think how big Lud would be if he ever rose from his throne again.

"He's been dead for centuries," Kim said softly. "And

he hasn't moved from that throne since the Romans left Britain."

"But, he's still . . . here," said Happy. "A physical presence; not just a spirit. Like you."

"That is the ghost of a god," said Kim. "The rules are different."

"Rules?" said Melody. "There are rules? Who sets them?"

"Such things are decided where all the things that matter are decided," said Kim. "On the shimmering plains, in the Courts of the Holy."

"If anything, I think I feel even less confident than before you started explaining things," said Happy.

"We're currently standing under that part of London known as Ludgate," said Kim. "Where St. Paul's Cathedral is now. A Christian holy site, put in place over an old pagan site. They did that a lot, to hold the old things down. Lud's Gate, where the first Wicker Men were ignited; whose awful burning light illuminated Druid Britain from coast to coast. And here before us, on his throne, all that remains of the old god Lud. People have attributed all kinds of stories and powers to him; sun god, warrior god, protector of his people during the long winter . . . but Lud was here long before there were humans around to worship him. He chose to become a humanlike form, so humans could more easily worship him. He wanted to scare them, not scare them off. Lud isn't even his real name. I don't think anyone knows what Lud was, originally. Faith is fuel, to his kind. They feed on emotions, and death, and souls. You don't think The Flesh Undying had the shape it does now, the one we saw in the vision, before it was kicked out of the greater world it came from? No; it was forced into its present shape, contained by the physical limitations of this world, to punish it. Its shape and conditions are the true bars of its cage."

She drifted silently forward, to stand directly before the throne, tilting her head all the way back to look up into Lud's awful face, half-lost in shadows.

"Lud, forgotten now, no longer worshipped by anyone or anything, outside of London Undertowen. Oh yes, JC, there are those here who still look up to him. The Flesh Undying has given them new shape and power, so they can raise Lud from his long sleep. So The Flesh Undying can bargain with him. Appeal to him, as one outcast to another."

"Hold it," said JC. "Are you saying Lud came here, to this world, from some other place? Like The Flesh Undying?"

"They weren't the first, and they won't be the last," said Kim. "Other-dimensional remittance men, slumming it in the lower dimensions. But it's all conjecture. If Lud was forced through a crack in the sky, there was no-one human here to see it. This all happened long ago, before human history, let alone human civilisation."

"We are not the original owners of this world," said Melody, unexpectedly. "We merely inherited it."

"She reads a lot of H. P. Lovecraft," said Happy, a bit apologetically. "I never read horror fiction. Gives me nightmares."

"She could be right, this time," said Kim.

"Oh thanks a bunch," said Happy. "I may never sleep again."

"Good," said Melody, unfeelingly. "So I won't have to put up with your snoring."

"I do not snore!"

"Cut it the hell out, right now, both of you; or I will slap you both, and it will hurt!" said JC. "We are standing before the ghost of an old and very dangerous god. Keep the noise down."

"Lud is the trap," said Kim. "But he is also the way out of the trap. The Flesh Undying promised Lud that if he would destroy me, and all of you, then it would make Lud powerful again. Worshipped again. A force to be reckoned with in the world of men. Question is—is Lud desperate enough to actually believe that?"

"Kim," JC said carefully, "I have to ask. How do you know all this? I mean, you're talking about things that even the highest levels of the Carnacki Institute almost certainly don't know about."

"I have travelled in many places," said Kim. "And I have witnessed many things. I will tell you everything, JC, eventually. When it's safe. But right now, down here, I need you to trust me. So we can concentrate on what's before us."

"I trust you," said JC. "If only because the thought of not being able to trust you scares me more than anything else."

Kim laughed softly. "Dear JC, always so wonderfully practical."

Happy put his hand in the air and waved it around. JC looked at him.

"What is it, Happy? Do you need to be excused? I don't think there are any facilities around here. Use a tree.

Take your pick. It won't care. We won't look. Though I can't promise anything for what's out there."

"I have a question!" said Happy, with great dignity. "Why does the appallingly powerful Flesh Undying need help to destroy us? We're only human. Apart from Kim, obviously. No offence. Have I said that before? Oooh . . . flashbacks . . ."

"He may be out of his skull, but he has a point," said Melody.

"The Flesh Undying is stuck at the bottom of the ocean," Kim said patiently. "To try anything directly would use up a great deal of power. So instead, it prefers to act in this world through agents. Like the Faust, or the Phantom of the Haybarn. Or the traitor who possessed Robert Patterson. Lud would make a far more powerful local agent. Even if he is much diminished from what he once was. Only a ghost of his former self . . . As to why The Flesh Undying is so determined to wipe us out. I think it's scared of us."

"Us?" said Happy. "Really? Gosh; I do feel proud . . ."

"But why us?" said Melody. "Out of all the Ghost Finders in the Carnacki Institute? I mean, remember poor Jeremy Diego and his team, back at Chimera House? Wiped out in a moment, without a second thought!"

"I think . . . it's because of what happened to me, down in the Underground," said JC. "When Something reached down from Outside and touched me. And Kim."

Happy looked at Melody. "I don't feel touched. Do you feel touched? I don't remember being touched even though we were both right there, alongside these two cocky drawers . . ."

"On the other hand," Melody said slowly, "did you

notice . . . when the four of us linked together, that time, our eyes glowed golden, too. That has to mean something."

"I don't feel different," Happy said stubbornly. "I don't want to be different . . ."

"Even if it makes you stronger?" said Melody.

"Being stronger means they expect more from you," Happy said wisely. "Like right here! We're supposed to fight the ghost of a god? Come on! There aren't enough chemical combinations in the world to make me that brave. Or that stupid."

Melody sniffed and turned to JC. "He may be chicken, but he has a point."

"I am not chicken! I am just survivally orientated!"

"The ghost of a god is so far above our pay grade we can't even see that far from here," said Melody. "This is not what we do! I am keeping my machine-pistol handy in case I need to shoot myself repeatedly in the head."

JC looked steadily at Kim. "She may be a girl science geek with a weapons fetish, but she has a point. This is so way outside my experience, I don't even know where to start."

"Good thing you've got me, then," said Kim, smiling widely. "I know where to start. We start with Lud."

"Heads up, people!" said Happy. "Enemy forces on the move!"

"Where?" said JC, glaring quickly about him, into the gloom between the stone trees.

"Everywhere!" said Happy. "Whoever or whatever was following us is now closing in from all sides. I don't see a possible exit route anywhere, and I am looking really hard!"

They came forward, out of the dark, from every side at once. The last Druids, emerging from the shadows of London Undertowen. Thousands of them, stalking forward, as grey and dusty as the trees through which they moved. Some of them were splashed with blue woad. For old time's sake. Human in size and shape, they no longer moved like anything human. They had spent far too long down in the Undertowen, in the dark. In the dead forest. Their flesh glowed unnaturally pale, like mushrooms. Their puffy faces held no human emotions. And their eyes were deep, dark, empty sockets, like their god. They carried weapons carved from human bones—ugly, brutal, deadly things.

"All that remains of the original Druids, driven underground by the invading Roman forces, two thousand years ago and more," said Kim. "The Romans built London over the catacombs, at least partly to keep the Druids down here."

"So the catacombs were built to contain the Druids?" said JC.

"No," said Kim. "The catacombs came first. They were expanded and strengthened to keep the Romans out."

"I'm getting seriously confused here," said Melody, sweeping her machine-pistol steadily back and forth, to cover the nearest approaching figures. "What exactly are we dealing with here? Two-thousand-year-old Druids? Are they dead, or liches, or ghosts? They can't still be alive after all this time, can they?"

"They don't feel human," said Happy. "As such. And I can't get inside their heads . . . It's as though they're all wrapped inside something. Something that reminds me very much of The Flesh Undying, and I do wish it didn't."

"The Druids died out down here long ago," Kim said steadily. "Nothing to eat and drink but each other. Must have been a bad way to go . . . They've been nothing but old bones for centuries, haunted by an undying hatred for those who lived on, in the world above. Now these old bones have been given new life, wrapped in new flesh provided by The Flesh Undying. So they can have their revenge at last."

"Revenge on whom?" said Happy. "The Romans are gone!"

"But we are their inheritors," said Kim.

"So, essentially, these are the ghosts of old Druids," said JC. "We can handle ghosts." He stepped forward and challenged the approaching figures in a loud and carrying voice. "What is it you want? Speak up! I'm listening!"

And all the grey dusty figures stopped moving, standing very still, right at the edge of the open amphitheatre. And when the answer came, it seemed to come from all of them at once. A single dry and dusty voice, still packed full of hatred after all the centuries.

"We will have our vengeance for what was taken from us. We will make a Wicker Man here and burn you alive in it, as a sacrifice, to make Lud strong again. We will have power and life again, and leave this place for the sun and light of the forests. We shall rule all the peoples of this land, as we did before, and we shall burn out everything that does not follow Druid ways. We shall serve Lud, and he will serve us, and it will be a glorious time of blood and slaughter. We shall take your precious civilisation and nail its guts to the old oak tree."

"Long-winded buggers, aren't they?" said Happy. "I'll bet they've been rehearsing that for ages."

"Your time is over," JC said steadily, to the dusty figures. "You must know that; or what are you still doing down here? You wouldn't even recognise the world above, now."

"With Lud awakened and empowered, we shall leave the Undertowen and rise up," said the mass whispering voice. "We shall set bale-fires from one end of this island to the other, and delight in the screams of our enemies as they burn. We remember what it is to be Druid; and we will make the world remember."

Happy moved in beside Kim. "You brought us down here. You must have a plan. How are we supposed to stop this?"

"You can't," said Kim.

"What?" said Happy.

"Our only chance is to make a deal with the ghost god Lud."

"Everyone stand back," said Happy. "I'm going to dig a way out."

"Stand still," said JC.

"I need another pill," said Happy.

"I don't think the whole of the Carnacki Institute working together has enough power to deal with the thing sitting on that throne," said JC. "We can't fight a god, and even if we did . . . Hold it. Hold everything. Fighting . . . is what The Flesh Undying wants. It wants us to fight because it knows we can't win. That's why he enfleshed the Druids—to distract us!"

"Trust me, it's working," said Happy. "I am feeling very definitely distracted."

"So let's try talking," said JC. "Not with the dead Druids. All they have are old grievances, old hatreds, that they'd rather die than give up . . . Happy, can you make mental contact with Lud?"

"Not on the best day I ever had!" said Happy, loudly. "That may be only the ghost of a god, but they key word there is still *god*! My brains would boil in my head and leak out my ears. Unless . . ." His voice trailed off as he looked around at the others, his brows falling into a serious scowl. He took out a silver pill box. "I suppose . . ."

"No!" Melody said immediately.

"Yes," said JC. "Sorry, Melody; but we need our team telepath firing on all cylinders."

Happy had taken a single pill out of the box, a long yellow-and-green-striped one. He rolled it back and forth between his fingertips, studying the pill thoughtfully. "Now this . . . is the good stuff. I distilled it from some weird esoteric chemical traces I found in Chimera House, left behind by the passing of the New People." He looked at Melody. "You never did appreciate my talents as a chemist."

"Happy," said Melody. "Please, don't . . ."

"It won't put me in the same league as Lud," said Happy. "Not even close. But it should hold me together long enough to get his attention."

Melody glared at JC, her voice cold and fierce. "You don't care whether he lives or dies, as long as he gets the job done!"

"I care," said JC. "But the job has to be done."

"This isn't about the job!" said Melody. "This is

all about your getting Kim back! Your unnatural girlfriend!"

"Right now," said JC, "Kim, and what she knows, is the job. Because what she knows about The Flesh Undying might be enough to save the whole Earth, and everyone on it."

"Can't argue with that," Happy said cheerfully. He dropped an arm across Melody's shoulders, ignoring the stiff rejection he felt there. "We have to do this. We can't get out of here, we can't win the fight, and we don't have any kind of future . . . as long as The Flesh Undying is still out there. We have to work together to do this, all four of us. Like we did before, remember? And I have to be able to control the contact we're about to make with the ghost of a dead god. And that's a sentence I didn't expect to be saying when I got up this morning. You mustn't worry, Melody. Really. The pill will keep me sane. Or at least sane enough that you'll still be able to shout at me afterwards."

"If you want to help Happy," said JC, "you need to work with us, Melody. Be his anchor; root him in the real world. Give him something to come back to."

"There will be harsh words later," said Melody, nodding reluctantly.

"No change there, then," said JC. "Do it, Happy."

Happy hesitated, then took out several more pill boxes. He spilled the contents onto his palm, rolling the multi-coloured pills back and forth, as though judging the best possible combinations, and the most bearable side effects. JC leaned in close beside Melody.

"Did you know he had that many pills on his person?"

"Of course not!" said Melody. "And he didn't stop to

load up before we left the apartment. Which means he must have been carrying them around for some time. Must have been planning to use them, for some time. Why didn't I notice?"

"Because he didn't want you to," said JC. "He didn't want you to worry. And I think he's been waiting for the right moment, or the right excuse, to start using them again. Being a junkie comes as much from the soul as the body."

He moved over to stand before Happy, who was bouncing lightly up and down on his toes, in a thoughtful sort of way. He put away all the pills but one, the original striped pill. And then he smiled easily at JC.

"This can only go well," he said, and swallowed the pill. All the colour dropped out of his face at once, and beads of sweat popped out on his forehead.

"Damn . . ." he said. "The dosage in that one is so strong it starts working almost before you take it."

"How do you feel?" said JC.

"Good, good, good . . ."

"What's in that pill?"

"A bit of this, a lot of that, all of it entirely illegal, unethical, and unnatural," Happy said rapidly. "Does you good on a spiritual level, with only the slightest chance that my liver will dissolve."

"Are you sure you can link us all, to make contact with Lud?"

"Of course! Piece of cake. Don't worry, JC. Overconfidence is all part of the ride. I couldn't Do Something this dangerous and this scary if I were in my right mind; and neither would you. I'm not enough, you see, on my own. Never was. I need something to lean on. For a while that was Melody; but I always knew that wouldn't last."

"She didn't know that," said JC.

"Yes, she did," said Happy. "I'm a telepath, remember?"

He reached out and pulled them all together. Four minds, not merged, but working in tandem. All their eyes burned golden in the gloom, then their whole bodies blazed with light. The Druids fell back, slowly and reluctantly, retreating into the protecting shadows of the stone forest. The four Ghost Finders, the living and the dead, turned to face the throne; and the dead god slowly lowered his head to look down on them. The Druids cried out, to see their old god move, for the first time in centuries. When Lud spoke, his voice reverberated in the heads and in the souls of all who heard him.

"At last," said Lud. "A voice calls out to me. A human voice . . . I remember the way things used to be, when all of Britain bowed down to me and burned for me. Life and death at my command, and at my whim. Worship to sustain me and purpose to give me a reason to go on. But all that passed, and I fell away, to become so much less than I was. Now . . . I see the world above, and I see a world with no room in it for such as me. And there is nothing down here that I would wish to be a part of. So let me go. Break the chains that hold me to this city, this London, that I no longer recognise nor understand. Let me go wherever gods go when they die."

"Fair enough," said JC. He gathered up all the strength generated by the binding of the four Ghost Finders, locked in harness with him, and reached out in a direction he could sense, if not understand. A great Door appeared in the amphitheatre, beside the great throne. A

Door into the Hereafter. And Lud stood up. He reached out a huge grey hand and ripped all the flesh off the Druids watching from the stone forest. The given flesh flew away from the old bones, burned in mid air, and was consumed long before it ever reached Lud. The new flesh that The Flesh Undying had provided . . . gone in a moment, leaving nothing behind but old bones, lying scattered on the forest floor. Lud had taken the flesh of his worshippers and burned it in sacrifice to himself, to raise the power he needed, to do the thing he needed to do.

He opened the Door. It swung smoothly open before him, and a great light spilled out, forcing back the darkness. Lud shrunk suddenly, falling in on himself in fits and starts, until he was of a proper size to walk through the Door. The light was so bright that JC and Kim, Happy and Melody, had to turn their heads aside, unable to face it. The old god paused, on the very threshold of the Door, and looked back at them.

"I see the touch of Outside upon you all. Something reached into your world, from my homelands, and altered you according to its purposes. Something like me. That is what has made this moment possible. Like calls to like . . . and pays its debts. I owe you a debt; so call on me, one last time, when you have need . . . But beware gods bearing gifts; none of you were ever meant to burn this brightly. Be careful of what such a light attracts . . ."

Lud strode through the Door, and it closed behind him, and was gone. The Ghost Finders fell apart and fell back into their own heads.

When they finally got their thoughts straight again, and looked, Lud was still sitting on his throne. Or at least his body was. The shape he'd made, so he could be worshipped and adored by the little human creatures. It looked a lot more like a statue now: grey and dusty, with cracks all over it.

"That's it?" said Happy, rubbing at his aching forehead in a bemused kind of way. "No more trap? We're all safe now?"

"Yes," said Kim. "For now."

* * *

They retraced their steps, back through the stone trees, kicking bones aside as they went. Back through the stone catacombs, heading for the surface. Back through London Undertowen to the world above. JC and Kim stuck close together, or as close as they could get without touching. They talked happily together, half-intoxicated with each other's presence. Melody made a point of walking alone, swinging her machine-pistol moodily at her side, staring straight ahead. Happy didn't even notice, tripping lightly along, sorting through the contents of his head.

"If you love me, JC," said Kim. "If you really love me, don't ask me where I've been, or what I've done. What I had to do, to get back to you. I will tell you, someday. When I'm ready. When you're ready."

"You can tell me anything, Kim," said JC. "You know that."

"Yes," said the ghost girl. "But not yet."

TWO

THE UNOFFICIAL RECORD

Everyone else wanted to go home and get some rest. But JC was the man behind the wheel, and he insisted on driving them all the way across London, to the Carnacki Institute's Secret Libraries. So Happy and Melody slumped down in the back seat and sulked, while Kim hovered serenely an inch or so above the seat next to JC. She had to concentrate, to keep her spirit self moving along at the same speed as the car because the physical world no longer had any hold over her. She could have teleported straight to the Secret Libraries and waited for the rest of them to catch up; but being only recently reunited with JC, she was loath to leave him even for a moment. JC stared straight ahead, lost in his own roiling thoughts. It was one thing to feel under threat from so many directions at once when it was just him, or his team; they'd always been able to look after themselves. But now that Kim was back, he felt an added responsibility.

He needed information on how best to defend himself and on exactly who or what he was defending himself against. And for that, he needed the Secret Libraries.

Often called the Unofficial Record, because the books in the Secret Libraries covered everything in the world that didn't officially exist, or shouldn't exist but unfortunately did.

JC's Boss, the redoubtable Catherine Latimer herself, had given him password access to the Libraries sometime back; and he wasn't prepared to wait for an official security upgrade any longer. He was fed up guessing and theorising; he wanted to know. So he aimed his car like a bullet through the empty streets of early-morning London, heading for the south-east of the city and the Woolwich Arsenal. The Secret Libraries were located directly below the Arsenal itself, presumably so that if they ever came under direct attack, the Army would already be there to defend them.

The streets didn't stay empty for long. In fact, JC barely had Chimera House in his rear-view mirror before vehicles came pouring in from every side street at once, and the road filled up with regular early-hours traffic. Buses and taxis, newspaper deliveries and food trucks, and people coming and going as shifts ended and started. Almost immediately, JC was forced down to a merely legal speed and method of driving. There wasn't enough room on the roads for anything else. JC scowled fiercely. Clearly someone had gone to great lengths to keep the traffic away from Chimera House and its environs, to make sure that what happened there would remain private, unobserved, and uninterrupted. But who had enough power, or influence, to shut down a whole section of London? Presumably someone inside the Carnacki Institute itself . . . JC made the mistake of musing on that one aloud and was immediately hit with loud reactions from the rest of his team.

"I don't care!" Happy said flatly. "I don't know, and I don't want to know. Don't want to go to the Secret Libraries, either. Want to go home. My system's crashing, I feel awful, and I am currently sweating chemicals so corrosive they will almost certainly eat holes in your leather upholstery. And I'm getting car-sick. Please can we go home? Pretty please? Can't the Libraries wait?"

"You used to say you would sacrifice a whole bus load of blind orphans for one peek inside the Institute's Secret Libraries," JC said calmly. "All those years of rabid paranoia, and saying the truth is out there . . . Well, the truth is out there, out in Woolwich Arsenal, and I'm taking you right to it. You always said They were out to get you; here's your chance to get Their home address and personal-contact details. So you can sneak up on them and do appalling things in revenge."

"Let Them finish me off," said Happy. "The way I feel now, it would be a mercy killing."

JC glanced at Melody in his rear-view mirror, expecting support; but she sat stiffly upright with her arms tightly folded, staring straight ahead and saying nothing. She was in a mood. She wasn't talking to Happy, making that very clear by giving him as much space as possible on the back seat; and from the look on her face, she didn't feel at all inclined to join in the conversation. JC sighed, quietly, and looked at Kim, who smiled sweetly back at him. She was currently manifesting as a Flapper girl, a bright young thing from the 1920s, complete with canary yellow dress, a long string of beads, and cute little cloche hat. Since Kim's appearance was composed entirely of ectoplasm, she could change the details of her look on a whim and frequently did.

"Nothing wrong with a visit to the Library!" she said brightly. "I'm sure it will be very educational!"

"These are the Carnacki Institute's Secret Libraries we're talking about!" snapped Melody, unable to maintain her silence in the face of such open provocation. Melody lived for the opportunity to shove someone's ignorance back in their face. "Nothing good or instructive is to be found there, only forbidden knowledge, all the nastier parts of the hidden history of the world, and things you're better off not knowing. People can't order you killed for things you don't know about."

"Unfortunately, that turns out not to be the case," JC said mildly. "The Flesh Undying wants us dead just for knowing it exists even though we don't know what it really is or who works for it. I say ignorance is not bliss and is actually dangerous to our continued good health and existence. We need to know things, and we need to know them now. Information is ammunition. Remember?"

"But, given that the Secret Libraries are in fact protected by large numbers of the British armed forces," said Happy, "how are we going to get in?"

"Oh, they're much better defended than that!" JC said cheerfully. "Layers upon layers of psychic protections, backed up by wholly unnatural forces of a downright malevolent nature. Plus a whole lot of guns and booby-traps and bad shit. But not to worry, team, because I have a plan!"

"This can only go well," said Happy.

He slumped back in his seat and gave all his attention

to feeling miserable. JC studied him in the rear mirror. Happy really didn't look well. He was going through hot and cold sweats, shaking and shuddering, and his face was the colour of a fish's belly. Every now and again, he would glance out the car window and jump briefly as his mental control slipped, and he Saw something he didn't want to. It was obvious the pills he'd taken were wearing off and kicking the crap out of his immune system on the way out of his body. He used to be able to cope with sudden changes in his brain chemistry; but that was before JC and Melody persuaded him to stop taking the pills. The road to someone's hell is always paved with someone else's good intentions.

Melody deliberately didn't look at Happy. "You did this to yourself," she said loudly. "After you promised me you wouldn't. So don't look to me for sympathy."

"I thought you weren't talking to me," said Happy, managing a small smile.

"I'm not! I'm merely . . . thinking aloud!" She glared at the back of JC's head. "Why are we going to the Secret Libraries? All right, any other time I might have been . . . interested, but why do we have to go there now?"

"Lud got me thinking," said JC, bullying a black London taxi out of his way and openly intimidating a London bus. "The Druids knew a lot of things now lost to the world, but maybe some of them are retained on file in the Unofficial Record. Lud said he recognised something on me, from where I was altered by some force from Outside. Maybe the Druids had a name for it . . .

"If not, the Faust said I actually died down there in the Underground, before the Outside brought me back. I want to know if that's true. And if it is, I want to know a lot more about it. I want to know Who or What did it, and I very definitely want to know Why. Because there's always a price to be paid . . .

"While I'm busy doing all that, the rest of you can search the stacks for anything they might have on The Flesh Undying and its servants' infiltration of the Carnacki Institute. And any of the other secret subterranean organisations. Bound to be something there even if they don't know they've got it . . ."

"You don't want much, do you?" said Happy. "Pardon me if I admit noxious gasses."

JC made a point of lowering all the windows. Bracingly fresh air rushed into the car from all sides.

"I thought Catherine Latimer was supposed to be carrying out her own investigation into potential traitors and double agents?" said Melody, drawn into the conversation in spite of herself. "Wouldn't she have told us if her people had turned up anything? I mean, she is our Boss. In her own scary and very efficient way. She's supposed to have our back on this."

"Good point, well made," said JC. "But I haven't heard a single word from our revered Boss on this subject; and I don't feel like putting up with that one moment longer. Not while The Flesh Undying and its rotten agents are taking open pot-shots at us."

"How are we supposed to find something useful in the Libraries if all the Boss's people couldn't?" said Melody.

"You are supposing someone has actually looked," murmured Kim; and everyone in the car sat quietly for a moment, considering that.

"A fresh pair of eyes is always useful," JC said vaguely,

swerving his car in and out of the packed traffic perhaps a little more casually than was safe or desirable. "Perhaps a pair of unprejudiced eyes will turn up something new . . . Preferably something we can use as a defence. Or a weapon. Either way, I want answers. I demand answers! I need to know things for sure. Whether the Boss wants me to know them or not."

"You're starting to sound a bit like me," said Happy. "Which is not necessarily a good thing. "

"How are we going to get in?" demanded Melody. "You said it yourself: the Secret Libraries are surrounded by some of the most powerful, appalling, and openly distressing defences anywhere in the land. I've tried to hack their on-line presence any number of times, for the challenge, of course; and I never got anywhere."

"The Boss provided me with password access after the events at Chimera House," said JC. "What happened to Robert Patterson shook her."

"You've had access all this time?" said Melody, her voice rising dangerously. "And you never said anything?"

"So the Boss isn't the only one who's been keeping things from us!" said Happy accusingly.

"Do I detect the sound of mutiny in the air?" said JC. "I'll have any one keelhauled who dares dispute my authority! I was content to let the Boss do the hard work, digging up proof of hidden informants; but when someone aims the ghost of a dead god and his enfleshed followers at me, my patience evaporates. It is clearly time to take matters into our own hands."

"You're not wriggling out of it that easily," said Melody. "Why did the Boss give you a password, and not us?"

"Because I'm team leader," said JC.

"Only because we all voted, and you lost," said Happy.

"Exactly," said Melody. "Somebody had to take responsibility for our actions; and it sure as hell wasn't going to be us."

"I've missed all this jolly banter," said Kim.

At the Woolwich Arsenal, JC parked his car in someone else's private parking space. The car's CD plates should ensure that no-one bothered it; and if someone was foolish enough to do so, the car was quite capable of looking after itself. In a thoroughly mean-spirited and unpleasant way. No-one messes with the Carnacki Institute. Dealing with the restless dead, the monstrous, and the demonic on a daily basis gives you a rather short temper when faced with more everyday annoyances.

The team disembarked from the car in their own various ways. Happy got out slowly and painfully, with many loud, creaking noises from his joints, and peered dubiously around him into the harsh electric light of the car park. He gave the appearance of something that had crawled out from under a rock and was seriously considering going straight back again. Melody kicked her door open, hauled herself out in one lithe movement, and glared about her in the hope that someone would come along and give her some grief. So she could cheer herself up by punching them repeatedly in the head. Kim floated through her door without opening it and drifted over to hover beside JC as he stood in front of the car and looked thoughtfully about him.

The Woolwich Arsenal was basically a collection of barracks and assorted anonymous military buildings, some more interesting to look at than others. JC gestured grandly at one particular structure, set a little away from everything else. Old brickwork, a slanting roof, and a single door with the word STORES set out in peeling paint.

"And there we are, children. The gateway to a place of wonders. Or so I'm told. I've never been inside the Secret Libraries, and I don't know anyone who knows anyone who has. There's always the chance that this is all one big con, a distraction from the real secret repository of hoarded knowledge. And all we'll find down below is a collection of old *Reader's Digest*s and a bunch of Dan Browns. Still, on the chance that this is the Real Deal, act confidently, like we have every right to be there, and no-one will challenge us. Kim, I hate to say this . . . but I think you'd better wait in the car. You do draw people's attention . . ."

"No-one will see me," said Kim.

"This is a Carnacki Institute site," JC said patiently. "They maintain all kinds of surveillance here, to keep out uninvited spirits."

"But I am not any old ghost, darling," said Kim. "No-one can see me now unless I want them to. Disappearing from the world's eyes was one of the first things I had to learn when I went on the run. In fact, I learned many strange and unusual secrets on my travels. I am wise and wonderful and know many things, and don't you forget it. You are my sweetie and my love, JC; but you are not the boss of me."

JC shot a quick glance at Happy and Melody, but they were carefully looking somewhere else.

"Very well," said JC. "On your own ectoplasm be it. But, we will talk about this later . . ."

"Yes, dear," said Kim, demurely.

"You're not fooling anyone," said JC.

"Hold everything, hit the brakes, go previous," said Happy. "What did you mean when you said, 'Act like we have every right to be here'? If the Boss gave you the password, then we do have every right to be here. Don't we?"

"Oh, she gave me the word," said JC. "Right there in her office. Made a big presentation out of it. I had to sign a whole bunch of very official papers first. She very definitely gave me the password. But whether she ever intended me to use it, that's a whole different matter. For all I know, she changed the password the moment I left her office."

"Terrific," said Melody. "What do we do if the password doesn't work?"

"I shall be sprinting for the car," said Happy. "Try to keep out of my way, or I will run right over you."

"You faced down the ghost of an old god," said JC. "Are you really worried about getting past the one uniformed soldier they've got guarding the door?"

"If you could See the kind of defences and protections surrounding that building, you would wet yourself," Happy said firmly. "There are booby-traps set in place that could turn you inside out and play you like a concertina. There are others that could blow your soul right out of your body. This place is more private than a very private place with extraordinarily private tendencies."

"Do I need to give you a paper bag to breathe into?" said JC.

"Couldn't hurt," said Happy.

JC led the way across the half-empty car park, heading straight for the nondescript building ahead of them. He had a strong feeling of being watched by cold unfriendly eyes. But then, he often did. He squared his shoulders and put a bit of a swagger into his walk. Never give them an inch, or they'll walk all over you. He strode straight up to the single uniformed soldier standing in front of the only door and nodded to him briskly. He could hear the rest of his team shambling to a halt behind him but didn't look back. The soldier gave every appearance of being as ordinary as the door and building he guarded: average height and weight, with a face you wouldn't look at twice . . . but his smile and his eyes were very cold.

JC gave the solider his best charming smile, to no obvious effect. JC carefully avoided looking at the soldier's rifle, which happened to be pointed right at him, and glanced back at his team-mates. Melody was scowling, Happy was sweating, and Kim was smiling sweetly.

"Step forward, children, and make a good showing. Allow me to present to you . . . the official guardian of the Carnacki Institute Secret Libraries. Not just any British soldier; this is Tommy Atkins. He's not real, as such, but don't hold that against him. Mr. Atkins here is the ghost of every British soldier who ever fell in battle, defending his country; with some stain still on his character. This is his last chance to do penance and make amends for his sins, before he moves on."

The team took it in turns to blink at Tommy Atkins, who looked calmly back.

"And you know all this how, JC?" murmured Melody.

"The Boss told me," said JC. "I think we can all guess why."

"So," Happy said carefully to Tommy Atkins, "you're not only you; you're a whole bunch of you. Are you all volunteers?"

"That's the idea, sir," Tommy Atkins said easily. "Each of us stepped forward, grateful for one last chance to put our papers in order. You've heard of the Unknown Soldier? Well, we're the Known Soldier. Guilty as charged, every one of us, for sins small and large."

"How many of you are there?" said Melody.

"As many as needed, to do the job, miss," said Tommy Atkins. "We take it in turns to stand guard, do our duty, protect the contents of the Secret Libraries. Until we've done enough to put things right and move on; and then the next man steps up. We will guard this door till Judgement-Day, if need be. Never any shortage of Tommy Atkinses."

"The very best kind of guard," JC said cheerfully. "Never gets tired, never sleeps, never loses concentration. Because he's dead and therefore beyond such weaknesses."

"Professional soldier, that's me, sir," said Tommy Atkins. "Now and forever; or at least until my time's up. Now, sir, I'm all for a nice chat now and then, but either you present to me the proper password, or I'm afraid I will have to blow several large holes through you."

"Of course," said JC, still carefully not looking at the soldier's rifle. He presented his left hand to Tommy Atkins, palm down, and carefully pronounced a certain Word. A glowing eye appeared on the back of JC's hand. It swivelled around to look at Tommy Atkins, blinked once, then disappeared. The soldier nodded briefly and lowered his rifle. He looked thoughtfully at the rest of the team.

"They're with me," JC said firmly.

Tommy Atkins nodded again, turned around, and pushed open the door to the building. Nothing showed beyond it but a dim, unwavering light. JC glanced at the back of his hand, but the eye had already disappeared.

"Hell of a library stamp," muttered Happy.

"Shut up," muttered Melody.

JC led the way in, and they all took turns to shuffle sideways past Tommy Atkins. He seemed solid enough, but up close he still made the hair rise on the back of their necks. Apart from Kim, of course. Tommy Atkins looked at her thoughtfully.

"Pardon me, miss; but you are a ghost, aren't you? Yes, thought so. Not the first I've let go past, and won't be the last, probably. They say there are books down there that only the dead can read. Probably just as well. But you watch yourself down there, miss; there are much worse things than dangerous books in the Secret Libraries."

"Thank you, Tommy Atkins," said Kim. "Always nice to meet a ghost with manners."

The door closed firmly behind them, and the Ghost Finders huddled together, looking around a small room not much bigger than the average washroom. A single bare light bulb hung down, providing the only illumination. No furniture; no window; no other door. Happy looked at JC.

"So who was that, outside? Really?"

"He's Tommy Atkins," said JC. "Or at least I have been given no reason to believe otherwise. And no-one has ever got past him that shouldn't have. Until now."

"What do you mean?" said Melody. "We're the good guys!"

"That's not the point," said Happy. "We are not officially supposed to be here, password or no, because the Boss didn't specifically approve it. So who else might have got in here, on equally spurious grounds?"

"Still not talking to you," said Melody.

Happy turned to JC. "Where do we go from here? I can't See anything, with all these protections in place."

"Probably because you're looking in the wrong direction," said JC.

He pointed down at the floor, where there was a large trap-door. JC leaned over, grabbed the heavy ring set into the trap-door, and hauled it open. He let it fall back onto the floor with a loud, echoing bang; and they all looked down into the dark opening. A heavy iron staircase went winding and spiralling down into the gloom.

"Down we go!" JC said cheerfully.

"You are definitely getting on my nerves," said Melody. "I don't care if Kim is back; it's not natural to be that cheerful all the time."

"I have defeated a living god, I am close to answers that have been kept from me, and my girl-friend has returned!" JC said grandly. "If I were any happier, I'd have to be more people."

"You say the nicest things, JC," said Kim.

Happy shuffled uneasily beside the dark opening. "That staircase does not look safe to me, JC. And God and the Boss alone knows how far down it goes. No; I am not going down that stairway without a parachute."

"Go!" JC said firmly. "Be a brave little Ghost Finder, and there shall be Jaffa Cakes for tea. And tea!"

"After you," said Happy, just as firmly.

JC stepped down onto the stairway with exaggerated calm and started down the spiralling iron steps. His feet clattered loudly on the bare metal, but the stairway didn't shake in the least under his weight. Melody went down next, and Kim drifted down after her, leaving Happy standing alone in the room. He took out a pill box, looked at it for a long moment, then put it away again. He sighed loudly and went down after the others.

A pleasant glow with no obvious source surrounded the team as they descended. The light didn't spread far, moving along with them as they went down and down, into darkness after darkness. JC peered over the top of his sunglasses from time to time, but even his altered eyes couldn't pierce the dark beyond the stairs. JC carefully pushed his sunglasses back into place and glanced back up at Happy.

"Can you See anything out there, Happy?"

"Yes . . ." said Happy. "Enough to make me not want to See any more, so I'm going to stop looking. Trust me on this, JC; you don't want to know. Some transitions are more distressing than others. Let's just say . . . the Secret Libraries aren't where we thought they were. You take me to the weirdest places."

They carried on down the spiralling staircase, all of them being very careful to stay well away from the edges, which lacked any kind of railing. Kim got bored pretending to walk down and dropped quietly down through the open space in the middle, sticking close to JC. He'd already lost all track of how far down they'd come. His leg muscles had begun to seriously ache when a light suddenly flared up, and he stepped off the bottom of the staircase and onto solid floor. He stumbled away from the stairs to give the others room to get off, and looked around him.

He was standing in a huge underground cavern, packed with row upon row of tall, sturdy bookcases. A stone floor, and a stone ceiling high above. And book-shelves, book-shelves everywhere, stretching away further than the human eye could follow, in every direction JC could think of, plus a few more.

Melody and Happy stared about them with wide, hungry eyes, making *Oooh!* and *Aaah!* noises, both of them forgetting the sour moods they were supposed to be in. Kim laughed softly, clapping her hands silently together.

"So many secret places turn out to be something of a disappointment when you finally get to see them," said JC. "But not this! It's like they have every book in the world here, including all the ones that no-one's supposed to have."

Melody took hold of herself and sniffed loudly, striking a conspicuously unimpressed pose. "Who needs all these books? Why not put them all on e-files? Then there'd be no need for so much storage space."

"Because you can't hack books, of course," Happy said witheringly. "If you want to know what's in a particular volume of forbidden lore, you have to come down here in person, check out the book, and read it. Except you can't because that isn't allowed. Mostly."

"What about remote viewing?" said Melody, to be stubborn.

"With the shields they've got in place here? Any wandering spirit that tried to sneak in here would get its ectoplasm kicked so thoroughly it would end up in another dimension, with its arse on fire. And besides, most of the books down here are so dangerous in their own right that they would deep-fry your brains inside your skull if you tried to read them without taking the proper precautions." Happy paused. "Or so I've heard. There are an awful lot of stories about the Carnacki Institute's Secret Libraries, and every single one of them contradicts all the others. Does your password give us access to everything, JC? Or should we lurk quietly to one side and not touch anything?"

"We can look at anything we want to, now we're in," said JC. "Or so I was given to understand."

"And if you're wrong?" said Melody.

"Listen for the bang," said JC. "Ah, here comes the Librarian."

They all turned to look as the current Librarian came strolling forward to meet them. Everyone in the team took their time looking him over because this particular individual was in fact an empty suit of rather old-fashioned clothes, inhabited by nothing obvious or indeed visible. There was clearly something inside the clothes from the way they bulged and moved and wrinkled. But nothing protruded from the starched collar or the stiff cuffs or the bottom of the trouser legs. There were also subtle and somewhat worrying indications that whatever was inside the clothes wasn't necessarily, entirely, human. The clothes came to a halt in front of the team and struck a sort of respectful pose.

"Well, hello there!" said a dry, dusty voice from somewhere in the vicinity of the starched white collar. "Visitors! How very unexpected and unannounced! Don't get many visitors these days since I put down the enchanted man-traps. And the head-eating things. Never can remember what they're called . . . Anyway, nice to see you all! I'm in charge here, inasmuch as anyone is, or can be. I prefer to be called the Keeper of Secrets; but unfortunately that never caught on. Mostly, I'm called the Empty Librarian. Guess why? Never mind, never mind, moving on . . . How can I be of service to you good ladies and gentlemen?"

JC looked at the others, and the others looked right back at him, making it very clear they had no idea of what to say either and were therefore leaving it to the team leader. JC gave them all a cold glare that promised exacting retribution in the near future and turned back to the Empty Librarian.

"Pardon me, sir," he said very politely, accompanied by his most winning smile. "But are you dead or alive?"

"Almost certainly, sir," said the Empty Librarian.

"All right," said JC. "Absolutely definitely moving on . . . I am here to inquire about whatever material you might have concerning the original Druids."

"Hardly any, I'm afraid, sir," said the Empty Librarian. "Given that the Druids possessed no written tradition of their own. Modern Druidry is a whole different thing, being mostly made up by a bunch of woolly-minded second-guessers."

"Doesn't anyone know anything about the original Druids?" said JC.

"You could always ask the Droods, sir . . ."

"I'd rather not," said JC.

"Very wise, sir," said the Empty Librarian. "Simply thinking about that horrible family is enough to make me mess my underwear. If I wore any."

"Far too much information," muttered Melody.

"We had an encounter with the ghost of the old god Lud," said JC, talking quickly over Melody. "Down in London Undertowen."

"Consider me officially impressed, sir," said the Empty Librarian. "Did he have anything to say? I could always add another page to his official biography."

"He said he wasn't of this world, originally," said JC. "That he came from another place, Outside our reality. And that there were others like him. One of whom recently reached down and made . . . alterations in me."

"Wouldn't surprise me at all, sir," said the Empty Librarian. "You're not the first visitor I've seen down here with eyes like those."

JC knew a distraction when he heard one and shouldered it firmly to one side. "Have you any books on the subject of people being touched and changed by forces from Outside?"

"Stacks and stacks of the things, sir. Everything from the original *Siggsand Manuscript* to *Jane's Field Guide to Abominations from the Outer Rings*. We used to have an illustrated edition of that last one, but it kept freaking people out, and I got fed up cleaning up after them. So now I only show it to people I don't like. There are any number of very useful books on the subject, sir. However . . ."

"I just knew there was going to be an however," said Happy. "Didn't you just know there was going to be an however?"

"Shut up, Happy," said JC.

"However," said the Empty Librarian, firmly, "these are the kind of books where you have to study for years to be able to read them. Never mind understand them. Some scholars have been visiting here for years, working their way through a particular volume one page at a time. While making copious notes. And occasionally having to stand up face-to-face shouting arguments with other scholars over what it all really means. Fist-fights, head-butting matches, and rolling-around-on-the-floor biting contests were not uncommon until I got bored and started fining them body parts for each infraction. Nothing like losing the odd ear to calm someone down. In my experience, sir, you can't get two of these so-called experts to agree on anything, where forces from Outside are involved. That's Academe for you. Is there anything else I can help you with, sir?"

"Yeah," muttered Happy. "Because you've already been so helpful . . ."

"Shut up, Happy," said JC. He gave the Empty Librarian his best determined smile. "How about . . . books on suddenly not being dead any longer?"

"Oh, there's no shortage of those, sir," said the Empty Librarian. "Most of them entirely contradictory, of course."

"Of course," said JC. "How about, more specifically, books on people dying, then being brought back again by forces from Outside?"

"Quite a lot of those, too, sir. Some days it seems like forces from Beyond can't keep their hands off us. Hanging around our reality like ambulance-chasing lawyers. Or winos outside a bar, looking for a hand-out."

"Is that what happened to you?" said Melody.

"Nothing happened to me, miss," said the Empty Librarian.

Melody gave him a hard look, then decided to rise above it. "Do you have any computers here? Anything on-line I can look at?"

"Nothing like that in here, miss," said the Empty Librarian. "The very idea . . . We are a Library; not a video arcade. We do have an Index you might find useful. Connected to every volume here, and voice-activated for easy use. If you'd like to follow me this way, miss . . ."

He shambled off, and the team hurried after him. Seen from the back, the empty suit of clothes appeared even more disturbing, if anything. The Empty Librarian led them through several sets of book-shelves, took a sharp left, and stopped abruptly. He waved an empty sleeve at an oversized volume set out on a gleaming brass reading stand. The book reminded JC of an old-fashioned family Bible. Someone had left it open, and the huge pages overflowed the sides of the reading stand. The Empty Librarian gestured for Melody to come forward and stand before the book.

"This is the Index for the entire Secret Libraries, miss. Like many useful things, it is bigger on the inside than it is on the outside. Thinking about that makes my head hurt, and I don't even have a head. Blame the Travelling Doctor; he founded the Libraries, after all. Speak your wishes aloud, miss, and the Index will give you the name and location of the volume most likely to be of help. Do try to speak clearly. If you mumble, the Index gets confused, then people shout at it, and I have to put up with its sulking, afterwards."

"Got it," said Melody. "Now go away and help the others. I don't like people peering over my shoulder."

"Of course, miss. I feel the same way. And I don't even know who's down here to peer over my shoulder . . ."

The Empty Librarian led the rest of the team away. Melody glared at the Index.

"What have you got on strange occurrences down in the London Underground railway system? Ancient and modern? I want book titles, and a précis, if possible."

The heavy pages fluttered quickly back and forth before her, so fast the print became a blur, then stopped abruptly to show her a double-page spread of book titles, complete with every detail, and a précis. Melody sniffed loudly, to make it clear she wasn't going to be impressed that easily, and leaned eagerly forward to work her way through the various entries. It soon became apparent to Melody that there was no shortage of books on the subject: private and personal and professional. Strange sightings, encounters with ghosts and demons, weird happenings, and alien encounters. Reports of strange things went all the way back to when the first railway tunnels were dug out of the earth under London. Interestingly, though, there were no reports of any encounters with the old catacombs of London Undertowen. Which confirmed what Melody had already suspected—that the

Undertowen wasn't necessarily, literally, underneath London itself any longer. Melody turned her search to those volumes dealing with intrusions into the Tube system from Outside and was genuinely shocked at how many books there were on the subject. The Empty Librarian had been right; whatever happened to JC was neither a new nor a rare thing . . .

Melody asked the Index on where these books could be found and received her second shock. According to the notes that appeared on the pages before her, each and every one of these books had been recently removed from the Secret Libraries. On the orders of Catherine Latimer.

Melody called the Empty Librarian back to her, in a loud and carrying voice. He came striding through the stacks, his empty suit of clothes positively radiating outrage at being summoned in such a peremptory manner; but when Melody showed him how many books were missing, he was genuinely shocked and appalled.

"But this . . . this is simply not allowed! Books are never taken out of the Secret Libraries, under any circumstances! And I can tell you for a fact, miss, Catherine Latimer has not paid a visit down here in over a year. Whoever removed these books may have done so in her name, but she did not do it herself. More importantly . . . I have no record, and no memory, of these books' leaving the Libraries. And I am always here! I do not sleep, I do not rest, and I never turn aside from my duties. Though I am forced to admit . . . this is not the first time such a thing has happened." He leaned in close for a conspiratorial murmur, his empty collar close to her ear. "More and more, I get the feeling . . . that I am not alone down here."

"Okay," said Melody. "Let's concentrate on the missing books, shall we? Look at the details set out in the Index; do you by any chance remember the contents of these books? What they were about?"

"Of course, miss!" said the Empty Librarian. "I have read every book in the Secret Libraries! Not much else to do down here, you understand . . . That title, there, was a detailed account by a young Institute field agent, on how she was attacked on a mission in the Underground, and how Something from Outside intervened to save her. I had the honour of speaking with this remarkable young lady on several occasions. Her eyes glowed like Mr. Chance's until she learned to control it."

"Who was this?" said Melody. "Do you remember her name?"

"Of course," said the Empty Librarian. "It was Catherine Latimer."

Sometime later, the Empty Librarian escorted Happy deep into the stacks, to the Acquisitions Suite. Not books, but rather Items of Special Interest that had been gifted to the Carnacki Institute, down the years. Basically, the Suite was an open space set aside to hold several rows of display cases, of varying size, with solid steel and silver surrounds and heavily reinforced glass. Containing things, objects, and general weird shit that had proved important or significant in the past. Happy looked them over dubiously.

"So these are all the important bits and pieces the Institute has gathered to itself, apart from those the Boss keeps in her office?"

"Exactly, sir," said the Empty Librarian. "All Heads of the Institute like to hang on to reminders of their own time out in the field. Until they retire, and it all ends up down here. In the end, everything turns up down here, one way or another. There was a move, some years back, to have all dead field agents buried down here, as a security measure. But that was considered disrespectful. To the books. Some of them are very sensitive, sir."

Happy nodded in a way he hoped indicated he neither believed nor disbelieved what he was hearing. He waited until the Empty Librarian had moved off before moving slowly up and down between the rows of display cases, studying their contents thoughtfully, while being very careful to touch nothing. Most of the items on display were simply . . . objects, presumably of some importance at some time but now without even a name or case history attached. Only an Index number. A single marble finger, a brass mezzotint, a bottle of comet wine, and a stuffed cat's head with three eyes and drooping whiskers. A few still had names, or titles: *The Merovingian Crown*, *Cardinal Woolsey's Scrapbook*, *The Doom That Came To Liverpool*, *The Sword Sacnoth*.

And then . . . Happy looked at the thing in the case before him and felt his strength drop away. He tried to examine it with his Sight, to make sure it was what it claimed to be, but the layers of protection laid down around the display case defeated him. So he stepped back and raised his voice, calling the others to him in an increasingly loud and hysterical tone. The Empty Librarian arrived first, running into the Acquisitions Suite, waving its empty sleeves.

"Please, sir, remember where you are!"

"Go to Hell!" said Happy. "How long have you had this? You had *this* here; and you didn't think to tell us?"

Kim appeared out of nowhere to stand next to Happy, calming him with her proximity. JC and Melody came running through the stacks to join them. The Empty Librarian fell back, as Happy gestured wildly at the thing in the display case.

"That, right there, is supposed to be an actual part of The Flesh Undying!" he said loudly.

They all gathered together before the display case, maintaining a safe and respectful distance. Beyond the reinforced glass was a small, pulsating blob of . . . something. Something that didn't belong in this world. It was no colour they could name, no consistency that made any sense, and it never stayed one shape for long. It rose and fell, turning itself inside out, throwing itself back and forth against the sides of the steel-and-glass case that contained it. Like a caged animal, desperate to be free.

"Someone put a bit of The Flesh Undying inside a box?" said JC.

"That is not a box, sir," said the Empty Librarian. "That is a display case. Though I am forced to admit, it is one of our more secure display cases."

"How was it brought here?" said Melody, staring fascinated at the writhing, pulsating thing.

"I'm not exactly sure, miss. It appeared here, a few weeks ago, already contained within its case. Along with an account of its acquisition."

With the end of an empty sleeve, he indicated a heavy note-book set beneath the display case. JC and the rest of his team looked at the note-book, each of them quietly wondering why they hadn't noticed it before. JC finally picked up the note-book, very carefully and very gingerly, and opened it, holding it out so they could all see. The handwritten pages contained a brief account of how this particular piece of The Flesh Undying had come into the possession of the Carnacki Institute.

They all recognised the handwriting. It was Catherine Latimer's.

Apparently, a large communications company had been laying a new section of transatlantic cable. The machinery hit something, on the very bottom of the ocean, and the ship laying the cable was mysteriously lost, with all hands. Other ships went to investigate; and as a result the cable was redirected to another section of the ocean, many miles away. And to hell with the extra expense. Somewhere along the way, a small piece of what the original cable-laying ship had encountered had been acquired, then gifted to the Institute. No names, no details. And there the record ended.

JC put the note-book back under the display case and looked at the others. And then they all looked at the raging thing in its case.

"I've been trying to examine it through my Sight," said Happy. "But forcing my mind through the defensive shields takes so much out of me . . . What I can See makes no sense at all. There's so much of it, I can't get a grip on it. As though it's denser, realer, than everything else."

"I wish I had my equipment with me," said Melody. "I'd make this thing talk. Hell, I'd make it sing and dance and give up all its secrets."

"It's been tried," said the Empty Librarian.

Melody bristled and glared at him. "You don't even know what I have in mind!"

"I don't need to, miss," said the Empty Librarian. "It's been tried. It's all been tried. Long before it got here. It's all in the back of the note-book."

Kim drifted forward and stuck her face right up against the glass side, so she could look directly at the blob. It became increasingly agitated under her steady gaze, throwing itself back and forth and flailing at the glass sides. It suddenly expanded, growing greatly in size, pushing outwards until it filled the entire display case, pressed flat against each of the glass walls. And the heavily reinforced glass began to crack. Jagged lines shot across the sides of the case, splintering the glass. Everyone fell back sharply, including the Empty Librarian.

"It's a trap!" shouted Happy. "It's another bloody trap! The Flesh Undying gave up part of itself so it could be brought here! I can hear it now; its thoughts are as loud as a thunderstorm, powerful as an earthquake . . . That blobby thing may be separated from the main body, but it's still connected, still part of The Flesh Undying!"

"But what does it want?" said JC. He grabbed Happy by the shoulders and held him in place. "Concentrate, Happy. Why did it want to be brought here?"

"Because it knew we'd come to look at it!" said Happy. "It wants us dead, JC. The whole team! It wants us destroyed because . . . we're dangerous to it! Damn. I didn't know that. Kind of heartening, really . . . JC, you've got to Do Something! It's getting out! The glass is cracking and the shields are failing and once that thing has escaped from its cage, there's nothing here that can stop its growing big enough to . . . Oh. Oh no . . .

You really don't want to know what it wants to do to us . . ."

The blob had filled every square inch of its container now, not a gap or bubble anywhere, seething and straining against the glass sides of the display case. Strange lights sparked and flared inside it, multi-coloured threads of energy snapping back and forth like illuminated blood-vessels. Melody pointed her machine-pistol at the case, then lowered it again, uncertainly. Happy stepped forward and put himself bodily between her and the thing in the case. Melody smiled briefly and stepped forward to stand beside him. She put an arm across his shoulders, and he put an arm around her waist.

JC took off his sunglasses and turned the full force of his golden eyes on the thing in the case. The blob shook and shuddered but didn't withdraw an inch.

"Rather hoped for more than that," said JC. "Kim, this might be a good time for you to teleport out of here."

"I won't leave you," said Kim. "I only just got you back. There must be something you can do."

"I don't have my equipment," said Melody.

"We could still run," said Happy. "Running's always good. But I don't think we'd get very far . . ."

"And we can't leave the Libraries undefended," said JC. "We stand and fight; that's the job. Except, we have no tech, no weapons, no magics or special Institute techniques that would do any good. I suppose we could eat it . . ."

"After you," said Happy.

"The Acquisitions!" JC said sharply. "That's the answer! Objects of Power, right? Smash the cases, everyone, and grab anything that looks useful!"

"That really won't be necessary," said the Empty Librarian. Everyone stopped and looked at him. The empty suit of clothes didn't seem at all worried.

"What?" said JC.

"Refreshing though your zeal to protect the Libraries is, before you go wild and start smashing all the exhibits, I feel I should point out that we here at the Libraries are perfectly capable of dealing with a rogue exhibit. Tommy Atkins! Your presence is required!"

The uniformed soldier appeared out of nowhere, standing before the display case. And then there was another soldier, standing on the opposite side. And then more, and more, dozens of Tommy Atkinses, surrounding the case in row after row. They didn't raise their rifles; they simply glared at the blob in its case, concentrating their full attention on it. The blob faltered and fell back, falling in upon itself, until there was nothing left of it in the display case but a small ball of suppurating organic matter, barely moving at all.

"Of course," said JC. "That . . . thing, is just flesh. While Tommy Atkins, all of him, are pure spirit. It has no effect on them and no defences against them. They outnumbered it, and overwhelmed it, through sheer spiritual presence."

"Yeah, more or less," said Tommy Atkins. "I was hoping I'd get a chance to bayonet it . . ."

He was the one they recognised, from outside the door. All the others had disappeared, gone in a moment. He leaned over the display case, wrinkling his nose at what remained of the blob. "You, behave yourself! Don't make me have to come down here again. Or there will be trouble."

He straightened up, nodded easily to the Empty Librarian; and disappeared.

Melody and Happy realised they were still holding each other. They quickly let go, stepped back; and then looked at each other. JC went for a little walk, to calm himself down. He was used to being the one who saved the day at the last moment; and he didn't like being upstaged. And he was pretty certain his plan to use the Objects of Power would have worked, in a generally destructive kind of way . . .

The Empty Librarian looked thoughtfully at the ghost girl Kim.

"You're not the first restless spirit we've had down here, my dear; not by a long shot. Some field agents have difficulty letting go . . . The filters keep most of them out, but you're something different, aren't you? I can see the mark of Strangeness on you, like your Mr. Chance. And your two other friends, of course."

"Don't tell them," said Kim. "They don't know. They don't need to know, yet. It would only upset them."

"As you wish, miss," said the Empty Librarian. "Now, is there any way in which I can be of service to you?"

"Is there anything here especially suited to my . . . special nature?"

"There are the Ghostly Reads, miss. The last aetheric remains, of books that no long exist on the material plane. Ghosts of lost books; perfect reading material for the not yet departed."

"Show me," said Kim.

But when the Empty Librarian led her to a collection of glowing, semi-transparent books on a dusty shelf, flickering like dying light bulbs, Kim found that although she could take the books off the shelf, and even open them and read them, they were all of them written in dead languages she couldn't understand.

She went back to join the others and found JC glowering at the Empty Librarian.

"These are the Carnacki Institute Secret Libraries! One of the biggest repositories of hidden knowledge in the world! There must be something here that can help us!"

"JC . . ." said Kim.

"No! I need to know this. I need to know why Outer forces brought me back from the dead!"

"Ah, sir," said the Empty Librarian, not unkindly. "You don't need books for that. You don't need anything we have here. We deal only in the Past; and you are concerned with the Future. You need to get back out in the field, sir, take names, and kick bottoms, and get your answers direct from the horse's mouth, as it were. You need to go to the source, sir."

JC and his team sat quietly in the car, in someone else's private parking place. Thinking, considering, what to do next. The sun was finally up, shedding a cold grey light across the Woolwich Arsenal. A few birds had started singing, in a half-hearted sort of way. People in uniforms came and went, but went nowhere near the car. Word had got around.

JC turned suddenly, to look at Melody in the back seat. "Did you bring your lap-top with you?"

"Of course," she said. "It's in my back-pack."

"Get it up and running," said JC. "Can you get a signal here?"

"This lap-top could get a signal anywhere," said Melody. "It's very well trained." She soon had it open on her lap. "All right, I'm signed in. What am I looking for?"

"Catherine Latimer," said JC. "Dear old Boss of Bosses. Her fingerprints were all over what just happened. See if there's anything new about her in the Carnacki files. See what people are saying about her."

"No problem," said Melody, her fingers flying across the keyboard.

"What's going on?" said Happy.

"Damned if I know," said JC. "But I'm starting to get a really bad feeling . . ."

"Welcome to my world," said Happy. "We have T-shirts and decoder rings and everything. And you don't even want to know what the and everything involves."

"Mouth is open, should be shut," said JC.

"Yes, boss."

It took a while, with Melody frowning more and more severely as she jumped from site to site, looking at things she definitely wasn't cleared to know, but finally she let out a long breath and looked at JC.

"If the Carnacki Institute was a business," said Melody, "I would say I was looking at a hostile takeover. Someone is trying to remove Catherine Latimer from her position as Head of the Institute, and replace her with someone else. Loyal to . . . someone else."

"Is that necessarily a bad thing?" said Happy. "Would be nice to have a Boss who didn't make me want to wet myself every time she looks at me."

"She may be an ogre," said JC, "but she's our ogre. And better the ogre you know . . . Who's plotting against her, Melody?"

"I can't tell," said Melody, scowling. "Whoever it is is hiding their tracks with great thoroughness, behind walls and walls of secrecy. There are lots of people involved in this, with a hell of a lot of the left hand not knowing what the right foot's doing . . . but this is all very definitely being organised by someone already deep within the Carnacki Institute. And, fairly high up . . . Someone is quite definitely informing against Catherine Latimer, easing the path for whoever's trying to oust her."

And that was when Catherine Latimer's grim face suddenly appeared on the lap-top screen, glaring out at them all. Melody made a loud squeak of surprise, then tried very hard to look as though she hadn't.

"What the hell are you people doing, looking at things that are none of your business?" the Boss said loudly. "And what were you doing back at Chimera House? I didn't authorise any return visit! Come and see me in my private office. And yes, that does include the ghost. Welcome back, Kim. It's about time. Be in my office at 9:00 A.M. sharp! All of you! Or there will be trouble."

Her face disappeared from the lap-top screen, and Melody quickly slammed the lid shut.

"Well," said JC. "This should be interesting."

"Have I got time to change my trousers?" said Happy.

THREE

INTERVIEW WITH A SCARY PERSON

Some days, it's all hurry up and wait, JC decided. He and Happy and Melody sat together in the Boss's outer office, on the uncomfortable visitors' chairs provided. Deliberately designed that way, to keep visitors from feeling too important, or even welcome. It was twenty past nine in the morning, and the Boss still wasn't ready to meet them. The three of them had of course arrived at 9:00 A.M. on the dot because it was more than their lives were worth to keep Catherine Latimer waiting one moment if she wanted to see them . . . But the Boss did like to keep people waiting, to remind them she was the Boss.

The Waiting Room was small, stuffy, and entirely windowless, tucked away in the back of Buckingham Palace. In a part of the building that didn't officially exist. Dozens of portraits covered all four walls, without even the smallest space left for a clock or a calendar. All head-and-shoulder shots, of Carnacki Institute agents who had fallen in the field and never got up again—the Honoured Dead. The faces all looked worryingly young because few field agents ever survived long enough to reach retirement. Or even middle age. It wasn't a job you did for the honour or the glory, and definitely not for the money; you did it because you believed it was a job worth doing. The job was its own reward because you certainly weren't going to get any other kind.

The oldest portraits were oil paintings, moving steadily on through daguerreotypes to sepia prints, and all the way up to the latest digital photos. You posed for your official portrait the day you were accepted into the fold because you might not get another chance. The only thing all the portraits had in common was that none of the faces were smiling. They were all the same size, the same frame, with no names and no histories. Not even a *Lest We Forget*. The Carnacki Institute didn't encourage sentimentality. Perhaps because everyone involved knew that tragedy came as standard.

JC looked around the room, from wall to wall. As far as he could make out, there was no obvious progression, from past to present. No obvious pattern or design to the layout. Except that they were always in different places every time he visited. JC was convinced the portraits changed their positions all the time, when no-one was looking. Possibly fighting out savage alpha-dominance clashes, like antlered stags butting heads, for superior position or prominence. JC decided that coming up with ideas like that was a sign he'd been sitting there far too long.

JC and Melody and Happy sat side by side, hiding their impatience as best they could because it didn't do to show weakness in the face of the enemy. Melody was playing a game of Angry Chavs on her phone. Happy was scribbling frantically in his private note-book, trying to get down everything he'd seen and heard and read in the Secret Libraries before he forgot it. So he could go on all his favourite conspiracy sites, boast of his new knowledge, and win all the arguments. Or at the very least, start a few new ones.

JC looked thoughtfully at the heavily reinforced steel door at the back of the Waiting Room. The only entrance to Catherine Latimer's personal and very private office. The door was tall and broad and looked solid enough to stop a tank moving at speed. Happy had studied the door once, with his Sight cranked all the way open, and had to be carried out of the Waiting Room crying, with a headache that lasted for days. The Boss's office was protected on levels that didn't even bear thinking about.

The most obvious line of defence was Catherine Latimer's private secretary, Heather. Who sat happily at her desk, day in and day out, typing away and running interference for the Boss, so the rest of the world didn't bother her unnecessarily.

Heather was already there on duty when the three field agents arrived and gave every indication of having been there for some time, despite the early hour of the morning. She was always just Heather; if she had a surname, no-one knew, for security reasons. Or possibly because she liked messing with people's heads. JC sometimes wondered if she ever went home.

Heather was a calm, easy-going, professional type, pleasantly pretty in a blonde, curly-haired, round-faced way. She dressed neatly rather than fashionably and looked like she would have trouble bench-pressing a bench. But you could only get to the Boss if you could get past Heather; and that didn't happen. Heather was rumoured to be the most heavily armed person in the entire building, which took some doing, and more than ready to use excessive force on anyone who gave her any lip. Or tried to get past her without an appointment. As far as JC could see, she only ever stopped typing to ceremonially move a piece of paper from the in-tray to the out-tray. JC had never seen either of the trays empty.

Melody looked up from her game abruptly to glare at JC. "Correct me if I'm wrong, which I'm not, but we are an A team these days, aren't we? One of the most successful field teams in the entire Carnacki Institute? Then why are we being kept waiting out here like errant schoolchildren summoned to see the Headmistress?"

"We are here because the Boss wants us here," said JC. "And we are sitting patiently and very definitely not complaining because the Boss is Catherine Latimer. Voted most scary person in the entire world seventeen years running by anyone who knows anything about anything." He looked across at Heather. "You work with the Boss every day, Heather. Do you find her scary?"

"Hell yes," said Heather, not looking up from her typing.

Melody sniffed loudly and gave JC her best meaningful stare. JC sighed, inwardly. He knew it wasn't going to do any good, but sometimes you had to do things anyway, to keep your team quiet. He gave Heather his best ingratiating smile.

"You're looking very yourself today, Heather. Is that a new hairstyle? And wonderfully efficient, as always."

"Don't waste your famous charm on me, JC," said Heather, still not looking up from what she was doing. "It's no use asking me about anything because I don't know anything."

"Not even a hint as to what's going on?" said JC. "For old times' sake?"

"What old times?" said Heather.

"How soon they forget," said JC.

Happy looked up from his scribbling. "You must know something, Heather. You run the Boss's appointments book. Can't you at least tell us what kind of mood she's in? Are we in trouble? Answer the second question first."

"She'll tell you herself," said Heather. "When she's ready."

And then she stopped typing and turned around in her chair to look at them thoughtfully, catching them all by surprise.

"I did hear," she said, "that Kim is back."

"Yes," said JC. "She is."

Heather waited a moment, until it became clear JC wasn't going to say anything else. "Then why isn't she here with you?"

"Sorry," said JC. "That's strictly need-to-know."

Heather gave him a long, hard look and turned her attention to Happy. "I did also hear that you are back on the mother's little helpers again."

"You leave him alone!" Melody said immediately.

"It's all right, Melody," said Happy. "I can look after myself." He smiled easily at Heather. "You do realise, I could slip absolutely anything into your coffee mug. And you'd never know until it was far too late."

Heather looked at him coldly and moved her coffee mug to the other side of her desk.

They all looked round as the outer door flew open, and a thoroughly annoyed middle-aged man in a very expensive three-piece suit burst in. He stomped over to Heather's desk and scowled at her, conspicuously ignoring the three waiting field agents. He had the look of a man who had lunched not wisely but too well, on many occasions, and for some reason had stretched his remaining thinning hair across his bald pate in a tragically unconvincing comb-over. His face was flushed, his eyes were blazing, and he had a mean, pinched little mouth. He planted both hands on Heather's desk, so he could lean forward and glare right into her face.

"I am the newly appointed Minister for Supernatural Affairs!" he said loudly. "As in appointed first thing this morning! I didn't even know we had a Ministry for Supernatural Affairs! I was promised Education, or Health, one of the big sexy top jobs, come the next reshuffle of the Cabinet. And this is what I get! Well, if the Prime Minister thinks he can shut me up by pushing me out into the backwaters, he's got another think coming! I know how to get noticed . . . If I have to run this half-baked Ministry, whatever it is, I will put my personal stamp on things! Oh yes . . . I'll reorganise this place till people's heads spin and get everyone doing things my way! Till they're afraid to do anything without checking with me first! I demand to see Catherine Latimer, right now, so she can brief me. And so I can brief her on all the changes that will be taking place around here!"

Heather smiled at him, politely, not budging an inch. "Do you have an appointment?"

"I don't need an appointment! I am the newly appointed Minister, and I am in charge of this . . . Department, or whatever it is."

"No, Minister," said Heather. "You answer to Catherine Latimer, not the other way round. It's a common misconception, among the newly appointed. The Boss will call you in when she needs to speak to you. Go back to your office and wait."

"Now you listen to me, young lady, this is precisely the sort of attitude I intend to put a stop to!" The Minister's voice was rising sharply now. "All Departments in this Government answer to the Ministers of the elected Government, not to some jumped-up civil servant!"

"Not here," said Heather. "The Carnacki Institute was founded on the orders of Her Most Royal Majesty, Queen Elizabeth I, in 1587. So we are therefore a Royal Prerogative, and not a Government Department. Which is why we're situated here, in Buck House. Strictly speaking, we answer to the sitting Monarch, not the Prime Minister. Because all successive Governments have preferred it that way. Don't ask; don't want to know. Your Prime Minister really doesn't like you any longer, does he? Or he would have warned you . . ."

"This is worse than I thought," said the Minister. "I know all about career civil servants and their own private fiefdoms . . . Well, if this is a fiefdom, it's going to be my fiefdom! Following my orders! This kind of sloppy thinking and wilful independence has no place in modern Government! Now you do as you're told, young lady, if you like having a job! I demand to speak to Catherine Latimer, immediately!"

"I'm afraid that these waiting field agents have the only appointment today," said Heather.

The Minister looked at JC, Happy, and Melody properly for the first time, and gave no indication of being in any way impressed. He sniffed loudly and turned his scowl back to Heather.

"They can wait. They're nothing more than little people."

JC smiled at Happy. "There you are. It's official. We are little people. Doesn't that make you feel all safe and protected, knowing we're too small to be any real danger to anyone?"

"I've always wanted to be little people," said Happy. "Too small to be noticed by the powers that be."

"Size isn't everything," said Melody. "Except for when it is."

The Minister glared at them. "I have never found humour funny. You can be sure I'll be looking into your files very thoroughly."

"Good look finding them," said JC.

"Right," said Happy. "I've been trying to hack into them for years; and I know my name. Which you haven't asked."

"Tell me your names!" snapped the Minister.

"Jeremy Diego," said JC.

"Monica Odini," said Melody.

"Ivar ap Owen III," said Happy.

The Minister looked at them suspiciously. He could sense they'd slipped something past him, but he couldn't tell what. So he went back to frowning at Heather, regarding her as an easier target for bullying and intimidation. "You tell Latimer I'm coming in. And open up that damned door right now, or I'll send for some security men to come in here and break it down!"

Heather sighed and pushed her chair back from her desk. JC felt an immediate need to hide behind or possibly under something. Heather came out from behind her desk, and the Minister smiled, thinking he'd won the argument—the fool. Heather strode right up to the Minister, grabbed his nose between the middle fingers of her closed left hand, and twisted the Minister's nose savagely. He let out a howl of such pain and misery it must have been heard three corridors away. Heather twisted the Minister's nose back and forth unmercifully while he cried like a baby; and then she let go and stepped back. The Minister raised both hands to his bleeding nose and looked at Heather with wide-eyed horror. And then he turned and ran from the Waiting Room. Heather closed the door behind him, went back to her desk, and resumed typing. Not appearing in the least disturbed or even out of breath.

JC looked at Happy and Melody. "You have to know how to talk to these people."

There was a long pause. Melody went back to her game of Angry Chavs, Happy went back to scribbling exaggerations in his note-book, and JC went back to staring thoughtfully at the portraits on the walls, trying to catch one of them not looking at him. Time passed.

"Come on, Heather," JC said finally. "Help us out. What sort of mood is the Boss in? Should we have brought flowers or updated our wills?"

"You'd know better than me," said Heather. "She summoned the three of you here directly instead of going through me and this office." She didn't actually stop typing, but JC couldn't help noticing that she did look a bit put-out. "And that's not like her! The Boss is normally a stickler for following protocol. I think something's worrying her. She's hiding things from me. She's hiding things from everyone."

"Situation entirely normal, then," said JC.

And that was when the door slammed open, again, and the newly appointed Minister for Supernatural Affairs stormed back in. There was dried blood all down the front of his nice suit, and two thick tufts of cotton wool protruded from his nostrils. He was accompanied this time by half a dozen large and heavily armed security types. The Minister struck an aggrieved pose before Heather's desk and pointed a quivering finger at her.

"That's her! That's the bitch! I want her arrested, and dragged out of here, and thrown in a cell! In handcuffs!"

Heather was already up on her feet, behind her desk. Two really big guns had appeared in her hands, out of nowhere. The Minister's jaw dropped, and he stood very still. The six security guards lowered their weapons immediately. The man in charge nodded respectfully to Heather, then looked witheringly at the Minister.

"You idiot. This is who you wanted us to arrest? Catherine Latimer's personal secretary? Are you insane? Sorry, Heather. We didn't know. Please don't kill us all and dump our bodies in a mass grave."

"It's all right, Dave," said Heather. "He didn't know. He's new."

"Well, he's not going to get old, acting like that," said the security guard. "Come on, lads, let's get going while the going's still good."

They left in a rush, pushing and shoving each other in

their hurry to get through the open door. The Minister stood alone, staring in an almost hypnotised way at the really big guns Heather was now pointing exclusively at him.

"So," he said finally. "If I'm not in charge . . . what, exactly, is my job here? What do I do?"

"You get to talk to the media and convince them that we don't exist," said Heather. "And that's it."

"Ah," said the Minister. "Yes. I think I'll go now if that's all right."

"I would," said Heather.

The Minister left, closing the door quietly and very politely behind him. The really big guns disappeared from Heather's hands, and she sat down again and resumed her typing.

"Potentially bright sort, I thought," said JC. "He learned quickly."

Catherine Latimer's voice sounded suddenly in the office, from no obvious source. "Chance, get in here with your team. Heather; we are not to be interrupted. Unless it's that thing we talked about."

"What?" Happy said immediately. "What thing?"

"That thing the Boss and I talked about that the likes of you don't need to know about," said Heather.

"Unless it's that thing we already know about," said JC.

"The thing with the thing?" said Melody.

"No; the thing with the other thing," said Happy.

"You all think you're so funny," said Heather, crushingly.

"Get in here, Chance!" said Catherine Latimer's voice.

The extremely solid steel door at the back of the Waiting Room swung slowly open, as though daring the three field agents to enter. JC made a point of swaggering in, while Melody stuck her nose in the air, and Happy slouched along in the rear. The door closed very firmly behind them.

The Boss's private office hadn't changed much since the last time JC and his team had been called before her. Large and comfortable, but in no way cosy or inviting, with only the most luxurious and expensive fittings and furnishings. Catherine Latimer sat upright behind her Hepplewhite desk and gestured for the three of them to arrange themselves on the even more uncomfortable visitors' chairs set out before her. She then looked them over with her usual cold gaze. JC made a point of not looking at her, pretending an interest in the contents of her office. Which was actually quite interesting in its own right. The Boss's antique desk might be covered with all the most up-to-date electronic equipment, but there was no doubt Catherine Latimer had placed her own personal mark on her surroundings. Strange objects leapt to the eye everywhere, demanding the visitor's attention.

There was a large goldfish bowl, half-full of murky ectoplasm, in which the ghost of a goldfish swam calmly backwards; flickering on and off like a faulty light bulb. A glass display case, remarkably similar to the ones JC had encountered down in the Secret Libraries, here containing the Haunted Glove of Haversham, known to have strangled seventeen young debutantes in 1953. The long white evening glove had been very firmly nailed to its wooden stand. It looked ordinary enough until you realised the fingertips were still twitching. Another display case contained an exceedingly large tooth labelled, simply but worryingly, *Loch Ness 1933*. A portrait of Queen Elizabeth II took pride of place on the wall behind the Boss's desk. It was said to have been painted directly after her Coronation, but that it had aged along with the Queen, in real time. It was also said that the Boss talked to the portrait concerning important matters of the day. It was not known whether she ever received a reply; but there was a great deal of discussion on the subject.

JC reluctantly returned his attention to Catherine Latimer to find she was still looking the field agents over, taking her time, saying nothing. So JC looked her over, taking his time.

The Boss had to be almost eighty now, but she still projected an air of unnatural strength and vitality. She was medium height, unapologetically stocky, her grey hair cropped in a bowl cut. Her face was all hard edges and cold grey eyes. She wore a smartly tailored grey suit and smoked black Turkish cigarettes in a long, ivory holder; supposedly an affectation that had survived from her old student days in Cambridge. There was a longstanding rumour that a long time ago, Catherine Latimer had made a deal with Someone, but no-one had ever been able to prove anything.

"You've all come a long way," she said abruptly. "From C-team agents with disreputable backgrounds and quite appalling business interests to full-time A-team agents. With an impressive record of cases solved and a series of impressive victories against the Institute's enemies. I'd put you all down for a commendation if we did that sort of thing. I am pleased to see you're all giving the Institute your full attention these days." She looked at JC. "Mr. Chance, you used to run an antiquarian bookshop, in the Charing Cross Road, specialising in the kind of esoteric forbidden lore that would give any reputable scholar nightmares. The literary occult equivalent of the back-pack nuke."

"Guilty as charged," JC said easily. "It's all in storage now. Just don't have the time, any more. And A-team pay is so much better than C-team. As long as the money continues, I see no reason why I should have to go back to my bad old ways."

Catherine Latimer turned to Happy, who sat up straight in his chair, trying hard not to look guilty. Or at least, no guiltier than usual.

"Mr. Palmer," said the Boss. "You used to be an accountant. A very creative accountant, by all accounts."

"I find numbers comforting," said Happy, hardly meeting her gaze. "They are what they are. But like JC said, the money's good enough now that I have no need for outside income. No need at all. Honest."

"And you, Miss Chambers," said the Boss, switching her cold gaze to Melody. "You used to publish . . . Well, let's be polite and call it specialised erotica."

"Filth," said Melody. "For the discerning connoisseur. But like JC said, I don't need the money now. Though I do still have a lock-up full of really quite interesting stuff. In case times get hard . . . Banks may come and banks may go, but filth goes on forever."

"We all give the Carnacki Institute our full attention,

these days," said JC, quickly cutting in. "If only in self-defence. So why don't we forget the pleasant conversation and get down to business?"

"By all means," said Catherine Latimer. "What the hell were you doing, back at Chimera House? Is it connected with what happened to Robert Patterson?"

"Kim is back," said JC. "We had to go back to Chimera House to pick her up."

The Boss nodded briefly. "Why isn't she here with you? I said I wanted to see all of you."

"Apparently she doesn't trust you, or the Institute," JC said flatly. "And she really didn't feel like being interrogated."

"She's been gone some time," said the Boss, avoiding the pointed comment. "What did your ghost girl have to say for herself? Where has she been? What's she been doing? What did she learn?"

"She can't remember," said JC, calmly.

"What?" said Catherine Latimer. She actually leaned forward in her chair, glaring right into JC's sunglasses. He met her gaze unflinchingly.

"Some form of traumatic amnesia, apparently," said JC. "I'm sure her memory will return, in time. As long as she's not . . . pressed. But for now, she can't tell us anything. Such a pity."

Catherine Latimer switched her gaze to Melody, then to Happy. They both presented the Boss with their best poker faces though everyone present knew they weren't fooling anyone. The Boss looked back at JC.

"Did anything happen at Chimera House?"

"Like what?" said JC, not giving an inch.

"Don't play games with me, Chance."

"I wouldn't dare," said JC. "I did happen to notice that Chimera House hasn't been pulled down and bulldozed, even though everyone was promised it would be. And it wasn't in any way whatsoever under armed guard."

"I know," said the Boss. "I took the guards away. Chimera House is being left intact, as a trap. To see who or what tries to move back in."

"You didn't tell us that," said Melody.

"I don't have to tell you everything."

"And you don't," said JC. "What can you tell us about what's really going on, Boss? How far have your investigations progressed, into the infiltration of the Carnacki Institute? Any names, or facts? Anything you'd care to share with us?"

"I have learned nothing useful, as yet," said Catherine Latimer. "I have to be careful with what I ask and who I talk to, and even more careful not to reveal how much I know and, more importantly, how little I know, for certain . . ."

"Would you tell us?" said Happy. "If you did know something?"

"He's being very brave, all of a sudden," said the Boss, still looking at JC. "Back on the pills again, is he?"

"It's no thanks to you if he is!" said Melody, bristling immediately.

"Happy goes his own way," said JC. "He always has."

"Why is everyone talking about me as if I weren't here?" said Happy, loudly. "Oh hell; I haven't gone invisible again, have I? I hate it when that happens . . ."

"You are entirely visible, every appalling inch of you," JC reassured him. "Now hush, while the grown-ups talk." He gave Catherine Latimer his best hard look. "You have been working us very hard, Boss. Working us into the ground, in fact. It's no wonder some of us are feeling the pressure. It's been one case after another, often without the mandatory downtime between cases that the rules call for, to help us get our heads back together again."

"That's what being an A team means," said the Boss, sitting back in her chair, entirely unmoved. "You get the most important, and the most dangerous, missions, as and when they arise. Whether you're rested or not. Now stop changing the subject. I haven't finished haranguing you yet. I want to know what you were all doing down in the Secret Libraries?"

"You gave me the password," said JC.

"Yes!" said the Boss. "I gave it to you! I thought with the understanding that you had enough sense to keep it to yourself. At the very least, I expected you to avoid exposing your team members to toxic spiritual material. I'm surprised those two came back out with their souls still attached . . . Well, what's done is done. Hopefully. Did you at least turn up something useful?"

"Not . . . useful," said JC. "Not as such . . . But we did uncover a few interesting things. For example, I was looking for information about past strange happenings down in the London Underground; and imagine my surprise when I discovered that all relevant materials had been removed from the Secret Libraries. On your orders."

Catherine Latimer removed the dark cigarette from her ivory holder and stubbed it out in an ash-tray shaped like a lung. She made no move to light another. She sat in her chair, thinking. She didn't look particularly surprised or even shocked; but she was quite definitely thinking.

"I gave no such order," she said finally. "The fact that someone was able to use my name and falsify my authority, in such a way that no-one even questioned it . . . is interesting. I shall have to look into that. Makes me wonder what else might have been done in my name that I don't know about . . ."

"Did you know about the piece of The Flesh Undying that had been gifted to the Acquisitions Section?" said JC.

"Of course I know!" said the Boss. "I arranged for it to be put there, in a safe location, as far as possible from the Institute itself. Tell me you haven't damaged it!"

"More like . . . muzzled it," said Happy, smiling unpleasantly.

Catherine Latimer shook her head slowly. "He worries me; he really does . . ."

"You're doing it again!"

"This is what I'm talking about!" said Catherine Latimer. "Disobeying orders, blundering around, interfering in things you don't understand!"

"Only because you won't explain them to us!" said JC.

"You've all been making too much noise," said the Boss. "Drawing too much attention to yourselves. And that . . . is getting in the way of my investigations. So I'm sending you away for a while. To deal with a haunted inn, down in the south-west."

JC, Melody, and Happy all sat up straight in their chairs. They looked at each other, then back at Catherine Latimer.

"What?" said Happy.

"You're . . . sending us away?" said JC. "With everything that's going on here, after all we've uncovered . . ."

"That's why you're going," Latimer said firmly.

"What if we don't want to go?" said Melody. "We're getting close to some real answers! I can feel it!"

"You're making waves," said Latimer. "And that's not what I need right now. So off to the West Country with you. It's standard stuff, practically a text-book haunting, nothing too difficult. Not really worthy of an A team, but it'll do to keep you occupied, and out of the spotlight, until the interest in you dies down."

"Interest?" said Happy. "What interest? Who's interested in us?"

"You don't need to know," said Catherine Latimer.

"Story of my life," muttered Happy.

"Treated like mushrooms," Melody said harshly. "Kept in the dark and fed shit."

"Go sort out the haunted inn," Latimer said flatly. "Do a good job. Don't talk to strangers. Don't get killed. And take your time coming back."

Happy was up and out of his chair and heading for the slowly opening door the moment it was clear to him the meeting was over. Melody took her own sweet time getting up, to make a point, and still managed to catch up with Happy before he was out the door. JC stood up, checked that his incredible white suit was hanging properly, and only then looked at the Boss.

"So what did happen to the Empty Librarian?"

"Nothing, as far as I know," said Catherine Latimer.

FOUR

GHOST STORIES

Later that evening, following a series of railway journeys that went on that little bit longer than body and soul could easily bear, JC and Happy and Melody arrived at that old country inn, the King's Arms, outside the small country town of Bishop's Fording. An old farming community, of old houses in an old setting.

The three Ghost Finders disembarked at a very small station, only to find they were still some way short of their destination. They had to take a taxi ride through the town and out the other side to reach the King's Arms. And it was raining hard. Really hard. The kind of storm that makes you want to head for the high ground and build an ark. Chucking it down, with malice aforethought, adding an extra layer of misery to an already cold and desolate evening.

JC and Happy and Melody crammed themselves into the battered back seat of the only taxi-cab on duty because the driver didn't allow anyone to sit next to him. Apparently he found this . . . distracting. He didn't even want to take them to the King's Arms and went all sulky and silent when JC insisted. He drove his taxi through the pouring rain with great concentration, staring straight ahead, ignoring his passengers. There wasn't really room for three people in the back seat, especially when two of them were ostentatiously not talking to each other. Happy and Melody sat jammed shoulder to shoulder and still managed to find two completely different directions to look in. They'd had a loud and emotionally messy argument on the train coming down, about any number of things, but always coming back to Happy's return to supportive chemical maintenance. So now there was a frosty silence in the back of the taxi to match the sullen silence up front.

JC stared straight ahead, peering past the driver to look through the windscreen because it was better than getting involved. He studied the town as they passed quickly through it: squat dark buildings with brightly lit windows and absolutely no-one out and about in the streets. Hardly surprising, he supposed, on a night like this. And it was late, heading out of evening and into night. The town fell suddenly behind them, and the taxi shot down a long, narrow road into the countryside beyond. Tall trees with heavy foliage lined both sides of the road, their heavy tops leaning out and forward, to form a dark canopy overhead; so it seemed they were travelling through a long, dark green tunnel. There were no streetlights outside the town, and with the moonlight cut off, all JC could see was the road directly ahead. Water splashed up around the taxi, thrown up by the taxi's progress through the flooded road, the waters pouring in from the saturated fields beyond the trees. And still the rain came down, shining in the headlights.

The great green tunnel suddenly disappeared, the trees falling away behind them. The taxi slowed down even though there was clearly still some way to go. At first, JC thought it was because the flooding had grown worse, but then he saw the driver's face in the rear-view mirror and knew it was nothing to do with the flooding. The man's face was pale and sweaty, the eyes wide and staring. And JC realised the driver was genuinely scared.

"Is everything all right?" he said carefully.

"You wanted the King's Arms," said the driver. "Don't distract me. I need to keep my eyes on the road."

Everything was not all right. JC could hear it in the driver's voice. And they hadn't even reached the inn yet.

''''''''''''''''''''''''''''

The taxi finally slammed to a halt right at the edge of the King's Arms car park. The driver couldn't get any closer because the wide-open area was packed with parked vehicles, crammed together from one low stone boundary wall to the other, with hardly a space left in between. Everything from family runabouts to Land Rovers to expensive muscle cars. As though the whole community were waiting at the inn to welcome them. The taxi-driver sniffed loudly and peered out through the windscreen. He addressed his passengers without looking around, without taking his eyes off the view before him. As though to do so might be dangerous . . .

"This is it. King's Arms. Close as I can get. That'll be eight pounds. Please."

He said the last word as though it were part of some foreign language he didn't normally use.

"Get the baggage out of the boot," JC said firmly. "And don't bang it about if you expect any kind of tip."

He pushed his door open and got out, hunching his shoulders against the pouring rain. Happy and Melody got out different sides of the cab, then came forward to join him; and the three of them stood close together, scrunching up their eyes as water trickled down their faces. None of them had thought to bring an umbrella because the weather reports for the area hadn't even mentioned the likelihood of even a gentle shower. JC glared about him. Shimmering blue-white moonlight reflected back from the rain-soaked open fields, filling the car park with an eerie, uncertain light.

"I hate rain," Happy said miserably. "It's cold and wet and it sinks into your clothes and gives you chills. Hate it."

"Weather forecasts," Melody said bitterly. "A very basic contradiction in terms."

"Let's get inside," JC said diplomatically. "I'm sure we'll all feel a lot better when we're all warm and cosy in the main bar."

"I don't like it here," said Happy. "I can feel the pressure building. There's a storm coming; and it's going to be a monster . . ."

They all looked across at the inn, on the far side of the crowded car park, and the inn looked back at them. The taxi-driver hauled their suitcases out of the trunk, muttering under his breath all the time. It sounded like he was making hard work of it, but none of them offered to help. The King's Arms was a large, blocky building, with bright lights burning cheerfully in all the downstairs windows. Up above, everything was dark. The inn looked solid, well established, as though it had endured time and weather and other things, and was still here in spite of all of them. The sign swinging noisily above the main entrance looked surprisingly modern, a stylised crowned head. Happy regarded it suspiciously.

"So which King was the pub originally named after? George V, maybe? Though the building looks to be a lot older, maybe even sixteenth-century . . ."

"Some people can't help showing off their ignorance," Melody said loudly to JC. "The King's Arms is much older than that. This particular building goes back so many centuries, under so many names, that there's no way of telling which monarch it was named after. I do wish at least one of you would read the briefing files . . ."

"But then you wouldn't have the fun of lecturing us," said JC. "You're annoyed because the truck bringing your main equipment is delayed by the weather." He did his best to sound patient and understanding but couldn't quite bring it off. It's hard to feel civilised with rain trickling down the back of your neck. "I'm sure it'll be here tomorrow, and you can shout at the drivers. Won't that be nice?"

Melody sniffed loudly and moistly. "I swear they do this deliberately, just to mess with me. Good thing I packed some basic tech in my suitcase. Enough to make a start . . ."

"Would that be the really heavy case that the driver is struggling with?" said JC innocently.

"Don't you dare bash it about like that!" said Melody.

She went hurrying back to rescue her bag from the

driver. JC and Happy exchanged an understanding glance. And then they both looked at the inn again.

"Are you picking up anything, Happy?"

"Yes . . . It feels like we're being watched."

"From inside the pub?" said JC, frowning.

"No," said Happy. "From all around . . . Something knows we're here. And it's not pleased."

"What kind of something?" said JC.

"Old," said Happy. "Very old."

Melody came back, dragging a large suitcase behind her on protesting casters. The taxi-driver followed after, bringing JC and Happy's much smaller suitcases. He dumped them both at JC's feet and glowered at him meaningfully. He didn't actually stick out his hand for payment, but he was clearly thinking about it.

"What's your hurry?" said JC. "You weren't in any rush to get here."

"I need to get back to town before the flood-waters cut off the only road," said the driver.

Which was reasonable enough; but there was something in the man's voice, and in his manner, which suggested there was a lot more to it than that. When JC didn't respond immediately, the driver glanced about him in a jumpy sort of way. He was definitely scared of something. He wouldn't even look at the inn itself. JC took pity on the man and gave him ten pounds. The driver stuffed the note in his pocket without even looking at it and hurried back to his taxi. He opened the door, then stopped and looked back, as though prodded by some last vestige of conscience.

"You're not actually thinking of staying the night here, at the King's Arms; are you?" he said roughly.

"Yes," said JC. "Any reason why we shouldn't?"

The taxi-driver shuddered briefly. "Then may God have mercy on your souls."

He clambered quickly back behind the wheel, slammed the door shut, turned the taxi around, and set off down the waterlogged road, driving a lot faster than was safe. His lights soon disappeared into the dark green corridor and were gone. The three Ghost Finders looked at each other, then at the inn. Seen through the driving rain, the bright lights shining through the old-fashioned leaded windows seemed especially cheerful and inviting.

"Looks cosy enough to me," JC said determinedly. "We can check out the pub's history tonight, do whatever needs doing tomorrow, after Melody's equipment has arrived, then maybe take a few days off, for a nice little holiday. I think we've earned one. Good food, good drink, good company, and all of it at the Institute's expense. Doesn't that sound splendid, my children?"

"Your optimism never ceases to amaze me," said Happy. "You should know better than that by now. I told you; this is a bad place! I mean, look at it! That pub's thirty feet away if it's an inch, and already I'm getting bad vibes. Given the sheer age and accumulated history of that place, it's probably crawling with ghosts and ghoulies and long-leggity beasties. And I hate long-legged things. Including supermodels. It's not natural to be that bony."

"We only deal in ghosts," said JC. "For anything else, they can call RentaKill."

"Can we please get in out of the rain?" Melody said forcefully. "Before we all drown?"

And she headed determinedly for the main entrance,

hauling her large suitcase along behind her like a reluctant dog. Happy picked up his suitcase and went after her, splashing deliberately through every puddle along the way to demonstrate what a rotten day he was having. JC grabbed his case and started after them, then stopped and looked about him.

"Kim?" he said. "Is that you? Are you here with us?"

There was no reply. JC went after the others.

He had to turn this way and that, squeezing his way through the narrow gaps between the closely packed vehicles. *Big and small, rich and poor—must be a hell of a turnout at the pub,* thought JC. *Maybe it's quiz night . . .* And then he stopped, as he realised Happy and Melody had stopped, barely half-way through the car park. JC moved forward to stand beside Happy, who was clutching his lightweight suitcase to his chest.

"Tell me that case isn't just full of pills," said JC.

"It isn't just full of pills," said Happy, not even looking round. "Travel light, travel fast, that's what I always say. Because you can't make a hurried exit from a scene of imminent peril if you're dragging heavy luggage along behind you. I know; I've tried. Amazing what you can bring yourself to abandon if Something is catching up with you. These days my suitcase contains a thermos full of hot chicken-and-sage soup, an assortment of useful items, and my pyjamas. I don't normally bother with such things, but I always wear pyjamas when I'm away. In case there's a fire. Or a burglar. Everyone knows burglars are frightened of pyjamas. Or is it a chair and a whip? I can never remember . . ."

"You took something in the toilet on the last train, didn't you?" said JC.

"Possibly," said Happy. "Who can say? I might be naturally cheerful. It does happen. On occasion."

"Junkie," said Melody.

"Kill-joy," said Happy.

"Children, children," said JC. "Why have we stopped?"

"Because we're not alone," said Happy. "There's someone else here, in the car park with us. Or, more likely, Something."

JC looked carefully around him. Moonlight and light from the pub's windows washed across the great hulking shapes that filled the car park. Everything seemed still and peaceful. And then something moved, between the parked cars, a dark, shadowy shape, moving quickly in and out of sight. JC pressed forward, threading his way through the parked vehicles to where he saw the shape; but when he got there, there was no-one. JC and Happy and Melody moved quickly back and forth between the cars, splashing through the puddles. Again and again, they all saw the dark shape, flitting soundlessly, disappearing in a moment, but they couldn't even get close to it. In the end, JC got fed up with being led around by the nose and turned his back on the cars. He walked determinedly towards the pub, and the others went after him. And if they caught a swift movement out of the corner of their eye, they ignored it.

"Probably someone playing games," JC said loudly.

"Or Something," Happy said helpfully.

"Look, are you picking up on anyone? Or anything? No? Then we are going inside," said JC, firmly. "Now, we are about to enter a public house, full of civilians. So

I want us all to show a confident and united front, or I may or may not wait until we are alone to dispense savage beatings."

"Bully," said Happy.

''''''''''''''''''''''''

They hurried through the main entrance and found themselves at one end of the main bar; a large open space full of bright lights, wonderfully warm and dry, with a whole crowd of people sitting at tables and standing the length of the long bar-counter. All conversation stopped the moment the three Ghost Finders made their entrance. Everyone turned, or at the very least lowered their drinks, the better to look over the newcomers. It was like facing a solid wall of expectant faces. And then the barman came bustling out from behind the bar-counter to greet them, beaming happily. A big, beefy, older man, with carefully styled grey hair and a hard-used face, wearing traditional country-bartending clothes. He made a point of shaking hands vigorously with all three of them.

"Welcome, welcome! Adrian Brook, proprietor of the King's Arms, at your service! I was beginning to think you wouldn't get here tonight, what with the weather and all; but here you are! Good to see you all! No need to introduce yourselves; the Institute contacted me earlier, gave me all the details . . . Your reputation precedes you! Now, let me introduce you to the regular crowd."

Which was all cheerful enough; but behind Brook's blustering bonhomie, JC could sense a not particularly well-hidden desperation. Like a drowning man clutching at a life-belt.

Some thirty or forty men and women looked eagerly

at JC, Happy, and Melody, as Brook introduced them all by name, as professional ghost hunters. He didn't mention the Carnacki Institute; but then, it was doubtful anyone present would have recognised it anyway. Still, they all seemed pleased enough, and casual enough, with the idea of ghost hunters. Which suggested they took ghosts seriously here. JC looked the crowd over carefully. A fair mix: young and old, prosperous and less prosperous. Pretty much every social group, represented somewhere. They all had wide smiles, and searching eyes. Brook kept up a cheerful stream of chatter as he took the team's coats, hung them up, and handed them each a towel to mop their faces and rub at their wet hair.

The bar itself seemed surprisingly modern, with all the most up-to-date features and fittings. Gleaming metal and polished wood stood out proudly alongside more traditional items like horse brasses and stuffed and mounted wildlife. Large blackboards offered surprisingly ambitious bar food and reasonably expensive wines. The whole place felt cosy and comfortable, easy on the eyes, with a good ambience—everything you'd expect from a standard country inn. Except JC couldn't keep from wondering: why was the building positioned so far outside the town?

Brook started to explain to everyone why he'd called in professional ghost hunters, but JC quickly cut him off. If there was information to be handed out, he wanted to be in charge of it.

"So!" he said brightly to the attentive crowd. "What are you all doing here on such a miserable night?"

"No need to hide the real reason for your visit," said

a red-faced farmer type, nodding and almost winking. "Eli Troughton, dairy farmer. That's me. We all know why you're here. Where are the cameras?"

"What?" said JC.

"I thought they'd send someone famous," said a tall, wispy goth girl, dressed in every shade of black. "I don't recognise any of them."

"What?" said Melody.

"I expect you'll want to hear all the stories, eh?" said an expensively suited man who looked like a local solicitor. "I'm Michael Cootes, local solicitor."

"Famous for its ghosts, is the King's Arms," said a very blonde young lady. "I'm Jasmine. Will there be photographers? I take a very good photo if I say so myself."

"What?" said Happy.

"Famous for its stories, but not quite famous enough, eh Adrian?" said Troughton; and everyone present laughed loudly.

JC felt very much that he'd like to be let in on the joke. He looked at Brook, who was back behind the counter; and the barman quickly declared that the team's first drinks were on the house. So JC had a large brandy, Melody had a gin and tonic, and Happy, rather surprisingly, asked for a glass of Perrier. Presumably because he didn't need anything else. Melody shot him a quick glare that very clearly said *You're not fooling anyone*. Happy looked down his nose at her and sipped his sparkling water with his little finger extended. JC gave Brook a hard look, and the barman nodded quickly.

"I've been telling my patrons all about you," he said defensively. "The three best professional ghost hunters in the game today, come all the way up here from London, to help put things right here. That's why the place is so full tonight."

"Like when the BBC filmed *Songs of Praise* in the local church," said Cootes. "You couldn't move in the pews for new frocks and big hats. Vicar hadn't seen a congregation that big in years. Got stage-fright in the pulpit, and the verger had to take over."

"If you're the Ghostly Busters," said Jasmine, "shouldn't you be wearing those big nuclear packs on your backs?"

"You're thinking of the other guys," Melody said coldly. "We're professionals. They're fictional."

"Even so," said Troughton, "don't you have hawthorn and garlic, crosses and holy water; all that stuff?"

"That's for vampires," said JC. "We don't do vampires. That's another department. We're here to investigate the situation and see what needs doing. If anything does."

"But where are your cameras?" Jasmine said doggedly. "I had my hair done specially for the cameras!"

"What cameras?" said Happy.

"For the television programme!" said Cootes. "For the show! You're here to make a show about the King's Arms and its ghosts, aren't you? Like *Mostly Haunted*?"

JC looked at Brook, who flinched, then shrugged. "I had to explain it to them in terms they would understand, Mr. Chance."

"Which of you is the psychic?" said Troughton. He grinned at Melody. "She looks like she could get inside a man's head."

"Ms. Chambers is our scientific expert," said JC. "Mr. Palmer here is our resident psychic."

Everyone in the main bar immediately turned their gaze on Happy. He wasn't pleased about that but did his best to bear up under the close inspection. The most common reaction in the crowd was disappointment, in that Happy appeared so ordinary and unprepossessing. They'd clearly been hoping for someone a bit more . . . exotic. They couldn't see Happy doing the whole rolling-on-the-floor and speaking-in-tongues bit.

"All right then," said Cootes, leaning forward on his chair to fix Happy with a challenging stare. "Show us something. Go on."

"Oh, this can only go well," murmured Melody.

Happy looked straight back at Cootes, his face surprisingly calm and composed. "I don't do party tricks. Neither am I a performing dog."

"Thought so," Cootes said loudly, looking about him triumphantly. "Fake. They fake it all, for the television."

"We are not part of any television show," said Happy.

"Fake, fake, fake," said Cootes, grinning broadly.

"All right," said Happy.

"Oh dear," said JC, quietly.

Happy looked thoughtfully at Cootes. "You want me to tell everyone here something about you? Something only you would know?"

"Give it your best shot," said Cootes, openly defying him.

"You watch a lot of porn, last thing at night," said Happy.

Cootes stiffened in his chair. "You're guessing. You could say that about anyone."

"But you do it while wearing your mother's dress," said Happy.

Cootes's jaw dropped, and his eyes widened. And in the time it took him to work out a convincing denial, the moment passed. Everyone in the bar erupted with laughter, seeing the truth in his face. Cootes looked like he wanted to get up and leave, but he was trapped in the middle of the crowd. So he buried his face in his glass and ignored everyone. JC took the opportunity to call for a round for everyone. To make up for not being television people and, hopefully, to loosen them up enough to get them talking. Everyone crushed up before the bar, happy at the prospect of a free drink. A little later, while they were all settling down again, JC got Brook to himself, for a moment.

"Why are you working alone tonight?" said JC, bluntly. "You must have known there was going to be a crowd in. Where's the rest of your staff?"

"There's no-one but me," Brook said quietly. "Can't keep staff. Not here. I advertise in all the local papers, offer really good wages, hoping to bring people in from outside who don't know the stories . . . but I can't get anyone to stay for long. Not once things start happening. Even the local trade's dropping off even though the townspeople have been coming here for generations. Point of pride, that they aren't afraid of no ghosts. But there's only a crowd in here tonight because there's safety in numbers. And even the regulars won't stay too late. They don't like to go home in the dark . . ."

He moved quickly away and called for his patrons' attention. They all quietened down, quickly enough. They seemed a good-natured crowd.

"These ghost hunters are here because the King's Arms is justly famous for its many ghost stories," said

Brook. "But recently, I think it's fair to say that things have been getting out of hand. I've been having trouble coping; you all know that . . ."

"What ghost stories?" said JC, cutting in quickly when it became clear Brook was having trouble getting the words out. "Are we talking actual hauntings? Has anyone here actually seen a ghost? Personally?"

It all went very quiet. Everyone looked at everyone else, clearly waiting for someone else to start. In the end, Troughton sat up straight and nodded firmly to JC.

"You sit yourselves down, ghost hunters, and we'll tell you all about it. I'll start."

JC and Happy and Melody pulled three chairs into position facing the crowd and sat down. There were definite signs of anticipation in the regulars' faces now. They all wanted to tell their stories. They needed someone else to take the plunge first. They'd been hoping to do it for the television cameras; but really, any audience would do. Someone new to tell the old, old stories to. Brook shut off the bar's piped background music, and a sudden hush fell across the bar. There was a pause, and Troughton leaned forward.

"I suppose one of the best-known ghost stories features the serving maid from the old Manor House. Must be over two hundred years old, this story, but everyone here knows it. She hanged herself, poor thing. Right here, in this pub, in one of the upstairs rooms. Because the Squire's wicked son, he had his way with her, then wanted nothing to do with her once her belly began to swell. She went to the old Squire, told him what had happened, told him she was in the family way, by his son. He had her whipped for lying and thrown out. She was ashamed to tell her own family after that, so she did away with herself. Upstairs . . . Some say she can still be seen, hanging, in the room where she did it. And even when you can't see her, on some nights you can hear the quiet rasp of the noose creaking as she swings slowly back and forth. Forever . . ."

Men and women were nodding in agreement all through the crowd. They'd all heard the story. And once Troughton had started the ball rolling, there was no stopping them. They all had tales to tell. An old woman in a long, grubby coat was next up.

"I am Mrs. Ida Waverly," she said, in a surprisingly strong and steady voice. "And this story was told to me by my mother, who heard it from her mother. Who was a cleaner at this very inn, back in the day. There is a stain on the old stone path outside. The one that leads right across the car park though the path was there first. It's an old blood-stain, been there for centuries. No-one knows why any more.

"Not even the most modern cleaning fluids can shift it, or make any impression on it. And they've tried everything; down the years. It's not always there, mind; that's how you know it's a ghostly stain. But many have seen it, right enough. When it is there, the stain is always bright red, not dark. Because the blood never dries. And it is said . . . some people, if they touch the old blood-stain, their fingers come away wet and dripping with fresh blood. And then it's a sign . . . that those people are not long for this world."

More general nodding and murmuring in agreement. Names were quietly bandied back and forth in the bar, of people who'd seen the blood-stain and come to bad ends.

Melody turned in her chair to look at the main entrance, clearly considering going outside for a look herself.

"I wouldn't, me dear," said Mrs. Waverly. "You couldn't expect to see it in the dark and in the rain."

Melody settled reluctantly back in her chair, and the stories continued.

"There's this Grandfather Clock," said a tall, thin, young man. His long hair hung down in carefully cultivated dreadlocks, his clothes were shabby but clean, and he looked very solemn. "That clock, that one over there in the corner, that's been here in this pub for many a year. And I heard from my dad, as he heard it from his dad before him, of people who've been right here in this bar when that clock struck thirteen."

Everyone looked at the Grandfather Clock. JC had to turn right around in his chair to get a good look at it. It was an old, perfectly ordinary-looking Grandfather Clock, in a polished wooden case, with a big glass panel in the front to show the heavy brass pendulum as it swung slowly back and forth. In the hush, they could all hear the slow, steady tick of the clock's mechanism. It didn't chime.

"I've never heard the clock chime thirteen myself," said the shabby young man. He sounded a bit disappointed. "But my dad said, if it does, it's a sign that someone present in the bar is about to die . . ."

"And then there's Johnny Lee," said a smart, middle-aged lady in a tweed suit and pearls, with dark, lacquered hair. "My Uncle Jack said he saw him, right here in this very bar, right after the end of the war. Autumn of 1945, it was. No-one here had seen Johnny since he went off to fight, at the beginning of 1940. He walked in here, calm and easy as you please, nodded and smiled to one and all, and ordered a pint of bitter. Of course, everyone was pleased to see him back, especially as there'd been no word to expect him. But he said it was such a shame about his young niece Alice, losing her gold watch that her grandmother had left her. Meant the world to young Alice, did that watch. And Johnny said that if young Alice would look behind the old dresser, in the back bedroom, she'd find the watch, right enough. And then Johnny smiled and walked out, leaving his drink on the bar, untouched. And when the people went outside to look, there was no sign of him anywhere.

"Wasn't till a fortnight later that his family got the telegram. Telling them that Johnny wouldn't be coming home. But Alice found the watch, right where her Uncle Johnny said it would be."

JC smiled and nodded, and the crowd made pleased noises; but JC knew better. He'd heard these stories before, or stories very like them. They were traditional ghost stories, of the kind told in pubs and local gatherings the world over. The names and the details changed, but the stories stayed the same. Which suggested that possibly the King's Arms wasn't actually haunted at all. By anything other than old stories, handed down from generation to generation. He leaned over to talk quietly with Brook.

"Did you see this Johnny Lee yourself, by any chance?"

"Long before my time," said Brook. "And I have to say, if all the people who said they were there were actually there, the bar would have been packed from wall to wall and bursting at the seams."

"I have a story," said Cootes, his voice loud and defiant. "The story goes that this young woman was travelling late at night and had to stop unexpectedly because the weather was so bad. Much like tonight. Luckily, there was an inn nearby, off the beaten track. Even more luckily, they had one room left vacant. The young lady didn't know the inn and thought it a rather rough-and-ready place, but it wasn't like she had a choice. So she allowed the innkeeper to show her to her room. Once inside, she made a point of locking and bolting her door and even jamming a chair up against it. And that was when a voice behind her said, 'Well, no-one's going to disturb us now, are they?' "

There was general laughter. Cootes smiled happily about him. It was clearly as much a shaggy-dog tale as a ghost story, and no-one in the bar took it seriously. But JC saw something in Brook's face, briefly, that made him think there might be something to this particular story, after all. He stood up, to draw everyone's attention back to him.

"Tell me," he said to the crowd. "Have there ever been any great tragedies here? Not in the pub but in the town, or even the general area? Any really bad accidents, or fires, any mass deaths? Anything like that?"

He hadn't even finished his question before everyone started shaking their heads. Brook leaned forward, resting his forearms on the bar-counter.

"Nothing. Nothing at all like that. I did some digging in the local library; and Bishop's Fording has been a quiet and peaceful place for generations."

"Then why are there so many ghost stories associated with this inn?" said Melody.

Again, a great many heads were shaking. Brook shrugged, almost helplessly.

"Have you ever considered having the inn exorcised?" JC said to Brook.

"It's been tried!" said Brook. "Three times in the last forty years, to my certain knowledge. Every time the town gets a new priest, and they hear the stories, they can't wait to take on the infamous King's Arms. Things go quiet for a while, then they start up again. I think . . . it's because what's here, whatever it is that's here, is older than the Church."

The crowd had nothing to say about that. Judging by their faces, it wasn't anything they wanted to talk about.

"Whatever's here," said Cootes, looking challengingly at the three Ghost Finders, "it's best not to upset it."

"Hell with that!" JC said immediately. He glared around the bar and raised a dramatic voice. "To whomever or whatever troubles this place, hear my words! Be advised! This place, and these people, are under my protection and that of the Carnacki Institute! Behave yourself or else."

He looked around him, but there was no response. Everyone in the crowd was very still. They looked tense, braced for . . . something. But nothing happened. They could all hear the wind outside and the rain dashing against the windows; but that was all. JC sat down again and gave the crowd his best reassuring grin.

"You have to stand up for yourself. Ghosts should know their place. You've told me the old traditional stories. Now tell me things you've seen and heard for yourselves. Don't be afraid. I'm here to listen, and to help."

"Sometimes," said Jasmine, quietly, "sometimes, at

night, if you're the last to leave here . . . You look back, and the pub isn't as it should be. There are lights on, in the upper rooms, where nobody goes. And you can see shadows, human shapes, standing before the lit windows, looking out. Or moving slowly back and forth, like people coming and going. Except they're not people."

"I never turn the upstairs lights on," said Brook. "Never anyone staying there . . ."

"I know," said Jasmine, helplessly. She looked at her hands, clasped tightly together in her lap. She looked like she wanted to cry.

"Sometimes," said the old farmer Troughton, "there's a large oak tree standing in the field outside. Only mostly there isn't."

"And sometimes," said Brook, "when I'm in here on my own, I can feel someone following me around. Standing behind me. I never see or hear anything, but I know. Sometimes I hear footsteps upstairs, but when I go up and look, there's never anyone there. And I try not to look in any of the bar's mirrors because sometimes when I look I see someone standing behind me, in the reflection."

The crowd was looking very unhappy now. Shifting in their seats, looking at each other for support and comfort. It was one thing to tell stories out of the past; no-one wanted to contemplate their moving into the present.

"Well, Brook," JC said loudly, "I hope you won't be putting any of us in the room where the servant maid hanged herself."

And it all went very quiet. The crowd looked at each other. Finally, Troughton cleared his throat.

"You're not thinking of actually staying the night

here, in the King's Arms? Are you? No-one ever stays the night here."

"Why not?" said Happy.

"Because the charges here are terrible!" said Cootes.

There was an outburst of laughter at that; but the mood had changed. People were shifting uncomfortably and glancing at their watches, looking around for their coats and belongings. And then Jasmine jumped to her feet and pointed at a window with a quivering hand. Her face was shocked white, her eyes stretched wide. Everyone looked at her.

"What's the matter with you, girl?" said Troughton.

"There was a face!" Jasmine said shrilly. "At the window!"

Everyone was on their feet at once, looking where she pointed; but there was no face to be seen at any of the windows, only the dark of the night, and rain running down the leaded glass. But the damage had been done. There was an awful lot of ostentatiously looking at watches, and saying *Is that the time? I really must be going.* People hurried to pull on their coats and headed for the door. *Got to be going before the storm gets too bad. Or the road gets flooded. Have to make an early start in the morning . . .* JC raised his voice, trying to reach them, to calm them down, but they were already pushing and shoving at each other as they ran for the door, streaming past JC and Happy and Melody as though they weren't even there. The bar emptied in a few moments, the last few actually fighting each other in their need to get through the only exit. And then the main bar was empty, apart from the three Ghost Finders, and Brook, behind his counter.

"And still drinking time left on the clock," said Brook, shrugging resignedly. "You've lost me some profits there. But I have to say, I'm surprised they stayed this long. Given that it's dark out."

JC looked at him steadily. "Why did you call for us, Adrian? What's really going on here?"

"I used to work for the Carnacki Institute before I retired," said Brook. "Though never as a field agent, like you. No, me and my crew, we would turn up long after you were gone, to clean up. Remove the bodies, clear up the mess you left behind, and do whatever was necessary, or practical, to remove the psychic stains from the environment. Not glamorous work, perhaps, but necessary. We all did our best, to prevent nightmares. Anyway, I put in my years, stuck it out as long as I could, then I took early retirement. I'd had enough. I came back here, to my old home-town, and bought this pub. Something to keep me busy, in my twilight years. A chance for a little peace and quiet, at last.

"I should have known better.

"I knew all the old stories, you see. I knew all about the ghosts and the strange happenings. Heard them from my old dad, who heard them from his dad, and so on . . . So many stories, and all with the same point if you took the trouble to listen. That the King's Arms was an unquiet place and always has been. But I thought they were stories, something to give the inn character and pull in the tourists. Tourists love a good ghost story. Money in the bank, as they say. And at first, everything was fine . . .

"But, slowly at first, then more and more, I started to see things. Hear things. Experience things . . . Things I knew from my time in the Institute were well out of the ordinary. And well out of my league. Worse still, my customers started to see them, too."

"What sort of things are we talking about, Adrian?" JC said carefully.

"Not traditional ghosts, like in the stories," said Brook. "Nasty things. Unquiet spirits. Dangerous presences. So I called up my old contacts at the Institute and told them I needed a field team here, to investigate. And a damned good one! I've never seen anything like this, Mr. Chance . . . You've got to Do Something! Put the ghosts to rest or drive them out, or . . . something!"

"So you can get your customers back?" said Melody.

"Because," said Brook, "Something bad is coming. I can feel it."

JC looked at Happy, who nodded slowly. "He might be right, JC. This inn gave me the creeps from out in the car park. Inside, it's like standing in a slaughter-house, listening to the man with the hammer creeping up on you."

He looked slowly around the empty bar. JC could see in Happy's face that he was Seeing something. He moved in close beside the telepath.

"What is it, Happy?" he murmured. "What do you See? The face of the monster?"

"It's not a presence," said Happy, frowning. "Not as such. I'm not picking up any individual ghosts, or poltergeist activity, no real feeling of supernatural manifestations at all . . . but this whole place feels *bad*. Not only the bar, the whole damned building. Steeped and soaked in psychic nastiness, going back . . . centuries. Embedded in the stone and brick and wood. Like Chimera

House, only worse. Much worse. Something spectacularly bad happened here, long and long ago. And I think it's still happening. Calling the dead to it like moths to a flame."

"There was nothing like that in the briefing files," said Melody. "But they were . . . pretty basic. Maybe I should get my kit out of my suitcase. See if I can turn up some solid evidence . . ."

Happy was so disturbed he didn't respond to her open dig at all. He was scowling now, turning his head back and forth in a troubled sort of way.

"Something's here, JC. I mean right here, in the bar, with us. Watching. Listening. Making its plans against us."

"Where?" said JC, looking quickly about him.

"Everywhere," Happy said sadly.

"You're not really going to wait till tomorrow, to make a start, are you?" said Brook, anxiously.

"Not after what our marvellous mutant telepath just said, no," said JC. "But I do think we could all use a break before we get stuck in. A few minutes alone, to get our heads together, get our second psychic wind . . . Do you have rooms prepared for us?"

"Of course, of course," said Brook. "I dusted and aired them out as soon as I knew for sure you were coming. No-one's stayed in them for years, you understand. I never even go up there at night, these days. I have a room, in town . . . But I'll stay here as long as you're here. So let me show you to your rooms, so you can . . . freshen up, and settle in."

"Yes," said JC. "And then we'll come back down, and you can fill us in on all the details you're holding back from us."

Happy turned his head abruptly to look at Brook. "You didn't just happen to come back to your old hometown, to retire. You didn't just happen to buy this pub. Something important to you happened here. You have unfinished business, with the King's Arms . . ."

"Get out of my head!" said Brook.

"I don't need to read your thoughts," said Happy. "Simple deduction. Nice of you to confirm it, though. What did bring you back here, after all these years?"

"Like you said," muttered Brook, looking away. "Something bad happened here. And it's still happening."

He walked over to the back of the main bar and opened a concealed door, uncovering a narrow staircase. "Your rooms are this way."

JC took Happy by the arm and got him moving. They all gathered up their suitcases and followed Brook up a set of thinly carpeted wooden steps. The wallpapered walls were so close on both sides there was only room to go up single file. The lights were all off, upstairs. Brook stopped at the top and switched on the landing lights. He looked quickly about him, as though expecting something to happen; but nothing did. He seemed as much disappointed as relieved. He stepped quickly back, out of the way, to allow the others to join him on the landing. More dully wallpapered walls, distinctly old-fashioned, and more very thin carpeting. And rather more shadows than JC was comfortable with. Brook pointed out their three rooms, close to the top of the stairs. He slapped three large metal keys into JC's hand, then hurried back down the stairs to the relative safety of the main bar.

JC looked at the three keys on his palm. Large, heavy,

old-fashioned things. Melody hauled her heavy suitcase up the last few steps and bent over it, breathing hard. While she was preoccupied, JC looked at Happy.

"Your face is flushed, and you're sweating. Have you taken something?"

"Not everything about me is down to the pills," said Happy. "I don't always need them."

"Why do you need them now?" said JC. "What started you off again?"

"You want the straight answer?" said Happy. "Because I ran out of reasons not to."

JC wanted to say more, but there was a cold finality in Happy's voice that stopped him. So he moved over to join Melody.

"You have to talk to Happy," he said quietly. "He's in a bad way. He'll listen to you, where he won't listen to me."

"He got himself into this situation; he can get himself out," said Melody.

"Harsh, Mel," said JC. "It's not that simple, and you know it."

"Of course I know it!" said Melody. She looked right at him for the first time; and she looked horribly tired and worn-out. "You can't help someone who doesn't want to be helped, JC. He doesn't need you, or me, or the job. He needs his pills. I thought I could change that, give him something else he could depend on. But I couldn't. He's on his own now. Because that's the way he wants it."

"But why does he want that?" said JC.

"I don't know!" said Melody.

She stuck out her hand for the key to her room. JC

gave her the key to Number Seven, and she stomped over to the door, dragging her suitcase along behind, rucking up the thin carpet. She unlocked the door, went inside, and slammed the door shut behind her. JC turned back to Happy, who suddenly threw his arms around JC and held him tight. JC held on to him, not knowing what else to do.

"I'm lost, JC," said Happy, his face pressed into JC's shoulder. "I don't know what to do! It's like I'm drowning, and I'm going down for the third time . . ."

He let go of JC abruptly and stood back. He held out a hand for his key, and JC gave him the key to Number Eight. Next door to Melody. Happy took his suitcase, unlocked the door, and went inside, shutting the door quietly behind him. JC looked at Happy's closed door, then at Melody's. The only thing he knew for sure was that you should never reveal your weaknesses, out in the field. Because the opposition will always take advantage . . . He walked over to his room, Number Nine, then turned abruptly to look back down the length of the landing. All the other doors were closed, everything was perfectly still. Outside, he could hear the wind rising and the rain battering against the single window at the far end.

A bad night to be outside. Or, probably, inside.

FIVE

ENCOUNTERS IN EMPTY ROOMS

JC sat listlessly on the only chair in his room and looked about him, for want of anything else to do. It wasn't much of a room. Dusty, airless, the bed-clothes probably only put on the bed that very day, after Brook was sure they were coming. JC didn't need to be told no-one had used this room in ages. Any sane person would have taken one look around and moved out immediately.

It was a typical country-pub room—barely big enough to hold the bed and some very basic furniture. The bed itself was a single, deliberately undersized to make the room look bigger. JC didn't expect to be spending any time actually sleeping in the bed, which was just as well. He was pretty sure his feet would stick out the end. A battered, old-fashioned wardrobe stood to one side, its unpolished wood covered with scrapes and scratches; and an equally uncared for chest of drawers stood on the other side of the bed. No television, not even a radio. A door at the rear led off to a frankly tiny bathroom. A low ceiling, deeply dull wallpaper; and not even a carpet to cover the bare floor-boards. The pale yellow light from the single bulb seemed flat, lifeless, even oppressive. At least the shadows were staying still. The wind rattled the only window in its frame, while rain spattered against the glass. It sounded cold, and desolate. JC felt like he was a long way from anywhere.

He looked at his suitcase, standing alone and unopened on the bed. The suitcase he always kept packed and ready in his apartment, for those occasions when he had to leave in a hurry, on the Boss's word, for some mission that wouldn't wait. He didn't need to open his suitcase and look inside to know what was in there. The contents never changed. Only the essentials; and a few nasty tricks that the Institute didn't need to know about. Because he wasn't supposed to have them. There was a lot to be said for planning and preparation; but JC had always been a firm believer in cheating. Your opponent can guard against plans and have contingencies in place for what you've prepared; but they're always baffled and helpless in the face of blatant cheating.

JC looked almost fondly at the suitcase, then sat up straight in his chair as the suitcase began to move. It rocked slowly back and forth at first as though making up its mind and gathering its strength, then it edged slowly forward along the bed, humping along in a series of slow, jerky movements, rucking up the counterpane as it went. JC rose out of his chair and glared at his suitcase.

"Stop that! Right now! Or there will be trouble!"

The suitcase stopped moving. It stood very still, halfway along the bed, as though trying to pretend it had never moved at all. Only the crumpled counterpane remained to show the length of its travels. JC stood there for a moment, watching the suitcase carefully, then reached forward and pushed the case hard, with one extended finger. The case rocked back and forth, very slightly, and was still again.

JC opened the suitcase and looked inside, but no-one had sneaked anything in. Everything was as it should be. So he closed the suitcase again, lifted it up, and placed it on the floor by the far wall, where he could keep an eye on it. The suitcase remained where he put it, as though it had got the whole moving thing out of its system.

The door to the oversized wardrobe swung slowly open. The heavy dark slab of wood moved slowly and silently, and the brass hinges didn't so much as creak once. JC waited until the door had stopped moving, then he edged cautiously forward to look inside the wardrobe. Nothing there. Not even any coat hangers. Only shadows and dust. JC shut the door, and looked at it; and it didn't move. Instead, the door to the landing swung slowly open.

JC caught the first movement out of the corner of his eye and spun around quickly to watch the door open all the way, all on its own. Out on the landing, the somewhat brighter lights were still on; and it was clear there was no-one out there who could have opened the door. JC strode forward and stepped through the open doorway and out onto the landing. He looked up and down the long corridor, but no-one was out and about. Happy and Melody's doors remained firmly closed. JC took a firm hold of the door-handle, stepped back inside his room, and pulled his door shut.

He could have locked it. But somehow, he had a feeling that wouldn't make any difference.

On the other side of the room, the door to the tiny bathroom swung open. JC glared at it. There was something eerie and even upsetting, about the refusal of his doors to stay shut. It made JC feel . . . that he wasn't in control of things. And he hated that. He hurried over to the bathroom door and slammed it shut. The wardrobe door swung open. JC slammed that shut as well. And while he was doing that, the door to the landing opened. JC ran across the room and slammed it shut with all his strength; and then stood with his back pressed against it, glaring round the room. Breathing hard, and not only from the exertion of running back and forth. It was all happening so quietly . . . There was no actual threat, or attack, nothing jumping out from behind any of the opening doors. It was as though the room was mocking him and defying him to do anything about it.

"All right!" he said grimly. "Among the many things I'm not supposed to have with me, there is an exorcism grenade in my suitcase. Packed full of holy light; just the thing to dispel unruly spirits. Do you really want to play hard core, this early in the game?"

There was a long pause. JC stood stiffly with his back to the door, glowering around his room, from door to door . . . but nothing moved. JC nodded and allowed himself a small smile. Some phenomena bluff really easily.

Kim walked into his room, passing effortlessly through the outer wall. Which was disconcerting given that they were on the first floor. JC couldn't bring himself to give a damn. He moved away from the door, smiling at Kim. She smiled happily back at him and shot him a sultry look. She'd shifted her ectoplasm again, changing her appearance just for him; and now she was dressed in a traditional tweed suit, complete with strings of pearls. She'd even shortened her gleaming red hair and arranged it in a serious country-set cut. On her, it looked good. JC grinned.

"Someone down in the bar was wearing an outfit exactly like that."

"I know!" said Kim. "I was there, watching unseen, and listening. Honestly, darling, such a bunch of storytellers! Wouldn't know a real ghost if it manifested in their living room, right in front of the television."

"Was that your face at the window?" said JC.

"Of course not," said Kim. "I had a damned good look, and I didn't see a face in any window. I think someone got caught up in the drama of the moment."

The two of them were standing face-to-face now, looking deep into each other's eyes. It was as close as they could come to holding each other. The living and the dead might love each other, but they could never touch. Which was one of many reasons why such relationships were frowned upon, by . . . pretty much everybody. JC and Kim stood so close together, they could have felt their breath on each other's faces if more than one of them had been breathing.

"Why didn't you join us before?" JC said finally. Because it was easier to talk about the job than so many other things. "You could have come with us, on the train. I could have used your company. Happy and Melody were sniping at each other all the way down . . ."

"I travel more quickly on my own," said Kim. "I used the low road, the hidden path of the dead."

"Oh yes?" said JC. "And what was that like?"

"Busy," said Kim.

"I don't really want to know, do I?"

"No, sweetie," said Kim.

"It is good to see you again, my love," said JC.

"And you, my darling," said Kim.

They high-fived each other, their palms not quite touching.

"There are things I can't talk about," said Kim, "And there are things I won't talk about because I'm dead and you're not. One of us has to be the sensible partner in this relationship. So I've been here at the King's Arms for some time, waiting for you to catch up . . . looking around, moving unseen, pushing my nose into things."

"And?" said JC.

"I haven't seen anything supernatural," said the girl ghost, frowning prettily. "But I can say, very definitely; that I don't like the feel of this place. It's hiding things from me."

"So is Brook," said JC. "He knows a lot more than he's telling."

"But he's the one who called you for help," said Kim. "Why would he hold back information that might help you help him?"

"Good question," said JC. "Did you see what was happening just now, here in my room?"

"No," said Kim. She listened carefully as JC explained about the doors that didn't want to stay shut. Kim's eyes gleamed eagerly as she pattered noiselessly round the room, studying everything with great interest.

"I don't See anything, darling. The doors are quite definitely nothing other than doors."

"I never got the sense there was anyone moving them," said JC. "But it wasn't any kind of illusion. And my suitcase really did move, on its own, just like the doors."

"Physical phenomena," said Kim. "Never a good sign. It takes a lot of power, of accumulated energy, for the dead to affect the material world directly. But I don't smell any poltergeist residue . . ." She turned abruptly to grin at JC. "I wish I'd been here to see it!"

"Wish I hadn't been," JC said steadily. "It wasn't very nice, on my own."

Kim was immediately back before him, staring at him sorrowfully. "You have to understand, JC. I'm back; I'm back with you, and the team . . . But I can't always be with you. There will be times when I have to go my own way. Following my own leads, going places you can't . . . and I won't always be able to tell you where I've been or what I've had to do. For your safety as well as mine."

"What aren't you telling me, Kim?" said JC.

"Lots and lots of things, darling," said Kim. "I will tell you what I can, when I can. Except for the times when I can't; and then I'll tell you a comforting lie. Because that's what relationships are all about." She sighed, tiredly. An affectation, of course, because ghosts don't get tired. But JC appreciated the effort. Kim looked at him steadily. "Eventually, this will all be over; and I'll be able to tell you everything. And it'll be such a relief. Secrets are heavy. They weigh you down. But until then, we have to do this one step at a time, for both our sakes. Trust me?"

"Always," said JC.

"I wish I could hold you," said Kim. "Hug you close, feel your heart beating against mine."

"I am working on it," said JC.

"What?" said Kim. "Really?"

"I have a contact in the Nightside," said JC, "who swears he knows someone who can make it possible for people and ghosts to . . . be together. For short periods."

"Not too short, I hope," said Kim. "JC, the Nightside is a bad place. Heaven and Hell and everything in between. I don't like the thought of your going there."

"You can find anything in the Nightside," said JC.

"Or it can find you," said Kim, frowning. She seemed genuinely upset. "You watch yourself, JC. Anything you acquire there will always have a hidden price tag."

"I will be very careful, I promise," said JC. "But you know I'd do anything for you. Pay any price."

"Forever?"

"Forever and ever."

They turned away, ostensibly to study the room again, tacitly agreeing to save the argument for another day.

"I was sad, to see Happy and Melody going off to separate rooms," said JC. "I liked them being together. I've always thought they were . . . stronger, more focused, when they were together."

"Happier?" said Kim.

"Let's not ask for miracles," said JC. "Let's say less grumpy. They've both been a complete pain, all day. Personally, I'm astonished Happy was able to stay off the stuff for as long as he did."

"You can't help an addict if they're determined not to be helped," said Kim.

"The trouble is . . . I'm not sure whether helping Happy is the best thing," said JC. "The pills aren't good for him, not in the long run. They may even be killing him, by inches . . . But there's no denying he's a better team member when he's . . . chemically enhanced. He's braver, smarter, more insightful. I have to wonder, Kim; should I fire Happy from the team, for his own good, to save his life? Or should I encourage him because he's more useful to me and the Institute when he's using? I'd hate to think I was actually that cold-blooded . . ."

"He might fall apart even faster, without you and Melody and me to hold him together," said Kim. "I believe he needs us far more than he needs pills."

"But does Happy believe it?" said JC.

Melody sat on the edge of her hard and unforgiving single bed, in her own small room, with her lap-top set out on the bedspread before her. Typically, she'd hardly given her room a glance before going straight to work. Melody always preferred to concentrate on the job at hand first, and everything else second, if at all. She hadn't expected her room to come with wi-fi, but then, she didn't need it. After all the changes she'd put her lap-top through, she could pick up a signal anywhere. If only by bullying the nearest tower.

She was currently checking out web sites on the most famous haunted pubs in England. Lots of familiar names kept popping up, but, much to Melody's surprise, not only did the King's Arms of Bishop's Fording not make the top ten . . . it didn't even earn a mention in the top hundred. None of the main discussion sites had ever heard of the King's Arms as far she could see. She pursued the inn's history with all her very best search engines, but all she could find were a few old stories from the local newspapers, of people spending the night at the King's Arms and leaving early. The stories were vague and unremarkable and nearly always played for laughs. Silly-season filler pieces. Those foolish tourists, jumping at noises in the night; not like proper country-folk . . . That sort of thing. But when Melody followed the stories through, it quickly became clear that no-one had stayed overnight at the King's Arms since the 1970s.

That had to mean something. Melody pulled her legs up onto the bed, so she could sit cross-legged and glare at the lap-top's screen more efficiently. Why did the phenomenon, whatever it was, start or possibly restart in the seventies? Did something happen then? Had something been disturbed, or awakened? There was nothing in the local press . . .

Melody swung her legs back over the side of the bed, stood up, stretched, and shook her head restlessly. She couldn't concentrate because she was still angry at Happy. And at herself. She shut the lap-top down, slapped the lid closed, then went walking around the room. Not looking for anything, walking around and around. Not going anywhere, roaming around the room in tight little circles, avoiding the furniture because she always thought better when she was on the move. It gave her the illusion that she was doing something.

What made her really mad was that she never saw it coming. She thought everything was going well. She thought she and Happy were . . . well, happy. They talked, they did things together, the sex was great . . . She'd had no idea that Happy had fallen off the edge again and gone back to his bloody pills. And she should have known. She kept a careful eye on Happy, all the time, keeping track of his moods and his needs. It wasn't her fault. She was sure it wasn't her fault. Except . . . if that were true, she wouldn't be feeling so bad. Like there was a great empty hole where her heart should have been.

How did she let him down? What didn't she do? Had she failed him in some way? She did everything for him, went out of her way to make sure she was always there for him. Even though that didn't come naturally for her. No. She didn't let him down; he let himself down. But she still couldn't help feeling that someone else might have noticed something.

There had been times when she was . . . busy. Working on her own, researching The Flesh Undying and the conspiracy inside the Institute. Doing necessary things, to keep them both safe. She couldn't be with him every moment of the day . . . She stopped dead in her tracks, torn between one thought and another, one feeling and another, her hands clenched into fists. She really was in the mood to hit someone.

She caught a glimpse of her face, in the mirror on top of the chest of drawers. She looked at her reflection; and a madwoman looked back at her. Wide-eyed, snarling mouth, face blotchy from a rush of blood, from the passions that raged within her. She didn't want to look like that, didn't want to think she could look like that . . . And then Melody looked more clearly and saw there was a man standing right behind her. A tall figure, all in black. She stood very still, and the man leaned forward to speak directly into her ear, from behind.

"Well," said a cold and nasty voice, "no-one's going to disturb us now, are they?"

Melody smiled. And back-elbowed the man right under his sternum. All the air went out of him in a rush, and he was already bending sharply forward as she spun round to face him, almost as though he was bowing to her. Melody kicked him accurately and extremely violently in the nuts; and a low, whistling scream forced its way out of the man's constricting throat. He dropped to his knees before her, both hands pressed over his crotch. Like that was going to help now.

Melody looked her would-be attacker over. A man dressed in black, with a dark balaclava to cover his face. Melody grabbed him by the arm, hauled him back onto his feet, and threw him around the room. She hung on to his arm with both hands, slamming him violently into the furniture and off the walls, while he made horrible noises of pain and distress.

Melody smiled a really unpleasant smile and eventually let the intruder fall to the floor. She kicked him several times, in very painful places, to make it clear she was still mad at him, then stood over her would-be attacker, breathing hard. She had to admit that she did feel better. She'd needed someone to take her frustrations out on. Melody ripped off the dark balaclava and immediately recognised the pale sweating face underneath.

It was Cootes, the local solicitor.

"How did you get in here?" said Melody.

"Sneaked back in, through the rear door," said Cootes, in a very unsteady voice. "While all the others were hurrying to their cars. No-one noticed I wasn't with them. I came up here before you did and hid inside your wardrobe."

"How did you know which room I'd be in?" demanded Melody.

"I don't know!" said Cootes, miserably. "I just knew . . ."

He seemed honestly confused about that. As though he hadn't even considered the question before. Whatever was working in the inn had messed with his mind . . . Not that this in any way excused what he'd intended to do. Nasty little man . . .

"Please . . ." said Cootes. "I was upset because I wasn't going to be on television. And because of what your friend said . . . Please! Don't hit me! It was a joke, a bit of fun . . ."

"Yeah," said Melody. "I'm really amused . . ."

She grabbed Cootes by the arm and hauled him back up onto his feet. She dragged him over to the door, opened it, and kicked him out onto the landing. He fell sprawling on the floor and scrabbled quickly away on all fours, desperate to put some distance between him and Melody, until he realised she wasn't coming after him. He rose painfully to his feet and glared back at her, tears of shock and pain and shame coursing down his face.

"I'll get you for this!"

Melody raised the machine-pistol in her hand and aimed it at him. "No you won't."

Cootes swallowed hard, the last of the colour dropping out of his face. He nodded slowly. "I think . . . I'll be leaving now. If that's all right with you."

Melody nodded, and he turned and ran for it. She watched Cootes go until he disappeared down the stairs, then she grinned broadly and went back inside her room.

''''''''''''''''''''''''

Happy sat alone, ignoring everything, completely uninterested in his room and its contents. He sat slumped on a stiff-backed chair, before an old-fashioned, black-lacquered writing-desk. He was looking at all the pill bottles and boxes he'd taken out of his suitcase and set out on the desk before him. He honestly hadn't realised how many there were. All of them carefully labelled in his obsessively neat handwriting. A lifetime's collection . . . of chemical excuses. For not being good enough.

He picked them up and put them down, moving them back and forth in patterns and connections that only made sense to him. Setting them out in possible combinations, considering the effects, and the side effects . . . He never used to mix his poisons, but then, he never used to do a lot of things . . .

He'd actually created a lot of these pharmaceutical marvels himself, thanks to his access to the Carnacki Institute's very private laboratories. One of the Institute's most revered research chemists, a certain defrocked Franciscan monk, a genius with access to unstable compounds, was always ready and willing to help Happy out. If only out of curiosity, to see what Happy would do to himself. Apparently the monk saw Happy as his own personal on-going experiment. He kept saying he was going to write a paper, one of these days, on exactly how much damage the human constitution could stand.

One day, Happy hoped to discover what use the Ghost Finders had for private chemical research. No-one else in the labs would even talk to him, let alone discuss what they were doing, or what they were there for. But given that chemicals had no effect on ghosts, Happy did wonder whether the Institute might be trying to develop better field agents, or at least ones who lasted longer, through creative chemistry. If Happy had only known, he would have volunteered.

Officially, Catherine Latimer had no idea what Happy was doing, down in the very private laboratories. But Happy was pretty sure she did know, really. Or they'd never have let him in in the first place.

He picked up a couple of silver pill boxes and rattled the contents thoughtfully. He needed new combinations now, in increased concentrations, because standard pharmaceuticals didn't do the job any more. He'd built up a quite frightening tolerance, down the years. And as a result, he'd had no choice but to start experimenting with stronger and stranger things. He'd tried mandrake root and mongoose blood, green tea and monkey glands, and even diluted doses of Dr. Jekyll's Elixir. That last one, mostly out of curiosity. He'd quite fancied the idea of being someone else for a while. Someone who didn't have his problems, or weaknesses; or at least someone who wouldn't care . . . Someone new who didn't scare so easily. But the diluted dose couldn't even affect his much-altered metabolism; and he was scared to go full Hyde.

In case he couldn't turn back.

His eyes ranged back and forth across the endless handwritten labels, hoping something would jump out and catch his eye. His drug use had never been recreational, never been about getting off his face. It had always been about keeping the world, and especially the hidden world, outside his head. So he could hear himself think and be sure the emotions he was feeling were just his own. All he'd ever wanted was peace of mind; and after all this time and all this effort, he was no nearer attaining it.

Of course, the job, and the weird experiences, and the constant paranoia didn't help. But he couldn't bring himself to quit, not now he knew what the world was really like. Not now his team needed him, more than ever. And besides, where else could he hope to gain access to the kind of chemical help the Institute provided . . .

He sat on his uncomfortable chair and listened to the wind and rain batter against the closed window. It sounded . . . lost, and alone. Sudden gusts of night air forced their way in through cracks in the warped window frame, fluttering the flowered curtains. Happy could feel the storm raging outside, feel its growing, angry presence, like some terrible wild animal prowling around and around the inn, searching for a weak spot, for a way in. Happy felt a sudden impulse to get up and run out of the inn, rip all his clothes off, and run naked through the storm, defying the lightning to hit him. But he didn't have the energy.

He was tired all the time now. Woke up tired, spent the day tired, and went to bed tired. Bone-deep, soul-deep, weary. He wanted to sit there in his room and do nothing . . . feel nothing . . . He wanted to take a pill, any pill, any number of pills, to shock himself out of this . . . At least the pills woke him up, gave him a reason to go on, helped him invest himself in the world. Like it mattered . . .

The pills made him feel alive, but he didn't want to take them any more. Because he didn't like who he was when he took them; because he wanted to be somebody Melody might take back.

Because he had a feeling she might be his last hope. His last life-line.

And because if he did give in to the pills, dived into the great chemical ocean one more time and let it close over his head, he didn't think he'd be coming back.

While Happy was sitting there, quietly thinking about life and death, he heard the sound of a door opening. He looked at the main door, leading out onto the landing; and it was closed. Happy slowly realised the sound must have come from behind him, from the rear of the room. He pushed his chair back from the writing-desk, turned around in his chair, and looked behind him. A door had appeared in the wall at the back of his room, one Happy was sure hadn't been there before. He looked at the door. It seemed ordinary enough, set in an ordinary wall. It was standing a little ajar, no more than a few inches. It wanted Happy to get up and come over to it, he could tell. When he didn't, the door swung wide open, all on its own, revealing a long corridor falling away, lit with a sullen blood-red glow. The walls beyond the door were red, like flesh, or meat . . . something quite definitely organic. And repellent.

It was a really long corridor, falling back and back, stretching off into the distance, much further than the inn could have physically contained. And the more Happy looked down the corridor, the longer it seemed to be. There was a feeling of promise to it, that if Happy would walk through the door and down the long red corridor, something would be waiting there for him.

Happy glared at the door, and the corridor beyond,

and raised his voice. "Do I look like a tourist? How dumb do you think I am? Piss off!"

The door slammed shut, quite silently, and disappeared. Happy was left looking at a perfectly normal, uninterrupted, deadly dull wallpapered wall. He sighed slowly and turned back to the writing-desk. He wasn't surprised to find a young woman sitting beside him, on a chair that hadn't been there a moment before. It wasn't like she'd appeared out of nowhere. More like she'd always been there and he hadn't noticed till now. Except Happy knew she hadn't been there.

The young woman looked real, and solid. She was medium height, with a trim body and long blonde hair falling down around a pretty, heart-shaped face. She had big eyes and a sweet smile. She wore a long white dress—not actually a bridal gown, but that was what Happy thought of when he looked at it. The young woman held her hands neatly folded together in her lap, perfectly calm and peaceful and at ease. She seemed happy to be there with Happy.

He looked at her for a long moment. He didn't even try to raise his Sight, to See what she really was, what was really going on. Not because he was scared to but because he was so worn-out . . . that he couldn't bring himself to give a damn. He wanted someone to talk to, and she would do as well as anyone. And if she turned out not to be real, so much the better. He could be honest with someone who wasn't really there. He smiled at the young blonde woman, and she smiled back at him.

"I'm tired," said Happy. "Really, really tired. It's hard for me to feel anything, to care about anything. Or anyone. Including me. I do try, but . . . it's getting more difficult every day, to force a way through the tiredness, to find a reason to go on. At first, I had the job. I liked helping people, helping the living in their troubles, helping the dead to move on. But the job keeps getting harder, and more complicated, taking more and more out of me, and the pressure never ends . . . When the job wasn't enough any more, I looked for another reason to go on living. Melody tried hard to be that reason, God love her, but . . . She did everything she could to distract me from my problems; but she couldn't solve any of them. She couldn't save me from being me. So I went back to the pills because the pills were always there.

"The effort wears me out . . . the everyday effort of fighting to stay sane. Sometimes I wonder whether it might be better to lie down, and go to sleep, and not have to wake up again. And if God is good, I won't dream . . ."

The young woman shook her head slowly. "Death is worse," she said. "Trust me."

She became suddenly, utterly horrible.

Happy screamed and screamed and screamed. Until Melody kicked his door in and came running into the room, her machine-pistol at the ready in her hand, searching for a target. She was half-expecting another intruder, like the man she'd thrown out of her room, but it only took her a moment to see the room was empty. Apart from Happy, staring at nothing, screaming at the top of his voice. His face was bone-white with shock, his eyes bulging half out of his head.

Melody put her gun away, hurried over to Happy, knelt beside him, and took him in her arms, hugging him to her as tightly as she could. He stopped screaming and buried his face in her shoulder, sobbing like a frightened child. Melody patted his back and murmured comforting words in his ear. She was honestly shocked. She'd seen Happy face down ghosts and gods and everything in between, and never seen his nerve broken this badly. She thought at first he must have taken something, but it only took a glance to see that all the bottles and boxes set out on the writing-table were unopened. And besides, Happy took pills so he wouldn't have to see the things that frightened him. Melody glared around the empty room, desperate for some enemy to lash out at.

JC arrived a moment later. He stopped abruptly in the open doorway as Melody aimed her machine-pistol at him. She quickly recognised him and lowered the gun. JC took a moment to make sure neither she nor Happy were injured, then he prowled quickly round Happy's room, checking the place out. He opened the wardrobe and looked inside, looked out the window, checked the tiny bathroom, and even looked under the bed. When he'd satisfied himself that there was no-one else in the room, he went back to Melody and Happy. They were still holding on to each other. Happy had stopped crying, but he was still shuddering uncontrollably. JC raised an eyebrow at Melody, who shook her head. JC did his best to sound calm and reassuring.

"Happy, this is JC. You're safe now. There's only Melody and me here. Can you tell us what happened?"

Happy slowly raised his head to look at JC, not letting go of Melody. His eyes were puffy, but his gaze was steady. He tried to explain, talking of a door that came and went, and a blonde woman who wasn't real, and said things . . . but most of what he said made no sense. JC understood. Often, it's not what actually happens in a haunting that matters; it's how it makes you feel. Ghosts are very good at finding your weak spots. Your psychic pressure points.

Happy stopped shaking. He took a deep breath and let go of Melody. She immediately let go of him, stood up, and stepped back. Happy mopped at his face with a handkerchief, blew his nose, and rose unsteadily to his feet. He looked at where the door had been in the rear wall, but, of course, there was nothing left to show where it had been because it was never really there. Or at least, never really a door. JC nodded to Melody, and the two of them moved away to stand in the open doorway, so they could talk quietly together.

"This is no ordinary haunted inn, like we were promised!" JC said angrily. "I've never seen Happy like that before . . . There's something really bad here. And much more powerful than we were led to believe."

"I need to set up my equipment," said Melody. "Get some readings. But it's all back in my room, and I don't want to leave him . . ."

"It's all right," said JC. "I'll stay with him. I won't leave him alone for a moment."

Melody nodded quickly and looked back at Happy. "I'm just popping out," she said loudly. "Back in a minute."

Happy barely acknowledged her, his eyes worryingly empty. Melody hurried out the door. JC went back to stand with Happy. He looked at all the pill boxes and bottles set out on the writing-table, and winced. He'd never realised there were so many of them.

"I haven't taken anything," said Happy, finally, not looking at JC or the writing-desk.

"Maybe you should," said JC. "If that's what it takes to get your head back together."

Happy looked at his pills. "You've got to admit, JC, it's an impressive collection. Uppers and downers and sideways . . . Things to shut my mind down, and others to blast it wide open. Pills to make me brave, or smart; but nothing there to make me strong. How do you do it, JC? How do you stay so confident all the time?"

"Because I'm team leader," said JC. "And because I'd rather die than let you and Melody down."

Happy looked at him then and actually managed a small smile. "Word is, you did die, down in the Underground. What was it like?"

"If something like that really did happen," JC said carefully, "which I am not necessarily ready to accept, I don't remember."

"Probably just as well," said Happy. "Why is it, JC . . . that all the people and things we encounter, come back from the dead, are always so very angry?"

"I don't know," said JC. "Perhaps the hereafter disappointed them by not being what they wanted it to be. Or perhaps the hereafter didn't want them because they were unworthy. And spat them out. Mostly, I tend to think of most of the dead things we encounter as escaped prisoners. Jail breakers; bad things, on the run. And it's our job to herd them up and send them back where they belong."

"Except that it's rarely that simple," said Happy.

"No," said JC. "But then, life is complicated. Why

should death be any different? It's important to remember that not all ghosts are bad. Case in point . . . Kim; would you come in here, please?"

Kim appeared immediately, standing demurely in the middle of the room. She'd refined her ectoplasm again and now seemed to be wearing a Salvation Army Girl uniform, complete with tambourine. She smiled sweetly at Happy and dropped him a wink.

"I thought you could use a little cheering up. Hi, Happy!"

He barely smiled. "Thanks for the thought. How long have you been here, at the inn?"

"Ooh, ages and ages. I got here long before you. I've been studying the King's Arms, inside and out. Dreadful place. Not only the inn, mind you, not just the building, but the whole surrounding area. It's all soaked and saturated with retained information. Layer upon layer of memories, ghosts, weird phenomena. Some of it going back centuries . . ."

Happy was already nodding in agreement. "Yes, called here, like moths to a flame." He perked up quickly, the colour seeping back into his face as he became intrigued by the problem. "Something must have happened here, long ago, that made such an impact on this site, and this area, that in a sense it's still happening. A psychic irritant, if you like; like the grain of sand a pearl forms around, inside an oyster. We have to dig down, separate out and identify the original causal agent, and shut it down. Hard. And then everything else should fall apart and disappear. Except, of course . . ."

"Nothing's ever that simple," said JC.

"You read my mind," said Happy. "There are ghosts operating here in the inn. But I think that's just the surface. There are other things here, far more powerful than I am comfortable thinking about. They like being here, like pigs rolling in shit. Something really nasty tried to scare me off. Possibly because it sees me as a threat. I suppose I should feel flattered . . . Kim, can you detect anything out of the ordinary in this room with your more-than-ordinary ghostly senses?"

The ghost girl drifted slowly round the room, taking her time. "I don't See anything," she said, finally. "Which is, frankly, a bit suspicious. I've no doubt something was here, but it's gone to great lengths to cover its tracks." She stopped suddenly. "Someone's coming. A live person."

She turned to look at the door, and the others did, too. The barman Brook peered in through the open doorway and jumped as he found everyone staring at him. He smiled weakly and nodded but decided not to actually enter the room.

"Sorry to intrude," he said. "I thought I heard . . . something. Thought I'd better . . . pop up and check. Is everything all right here?"

He took in Kim properly for the first time, and his eyes widened. She threw him a dazzling smile and rattled her tambourine at him. Brook looked at JC.

"Another one of yours, is she? Working the case on the quiet?"

"You could say that," said JC.

"Will she be requiring a room, too?"

"Almost certainly not."

Melody yelled for Brook to get the hell out of her

way, and when he jumped back, she barged in through the open doorway, with her suitcase. She opened it and pulled out assorted scientific equipment. She quickly set it all up, talking quickly as she did, perhaps so she wouldn't have to acknowledge Happy.

"This is all I have with me. Just the basics. A multi-sensor package, linked in to a very discerning computer. It may look to you like a lap-top plugged into a box, with assorted scanners; but it will do the job."

She piled it all on the bed, then set about firing everything up, still talking to herself. Mostly in terms no-one else there understood. Everyone nodded vaguely, for fear she'd start explaining things. Brook was back peering through the open door again. Still refusing to come in from the landing. Melody studied the readings as they came in and scowled unhappily.

"This inn is old, JC. And I mean really old. We're talking centuries . . . Damn! I'm getting readings that say this building, this basic structure, goes all the way back to the fifth century."

"Druid time," said JC, a bit bitterly. "I should have known . . . I should have known the Boss wouldn't send us off to cover some everyday haunting!"

"You think there's a connection?" said Happy. "Between what happened in London Undertowen and what's going on here?"

"Don't you?" said JC. "Go on, Melody. What else have you got?"

Melody scowled at her glowing lap-top screen. "This is really very limited tech, JC. But . . . I'm picking up serious dimensions. Weak spots, incursions, doorways opening up to God alone knows where . . . There's so much supernatural activity going on here, it's weakened the walls of reality, and all kinds of things are getting in."

She stopped suddenly, to look suspiciously at the rear wall where Happy had seen a door that wasn't a door.

"You had a visitor here, all right, Happy. And it wasn't any ordinary ghost or revenant. I don't think I've ever seen such readings, such raw power . . . Be grateful your training protected you; it would have eaten the soul off anyone else. I'm not picking up any evidence of a cold spot, though, which is unusual. Did you feel one, Happy, at the time?"

"No," said Happy.

"Then where was it drawing its power from?" muttered Melody, her fingers moving quickly across the keyboard. "Ah. Yes. I see . . . Okay, this is seriously not good, people. There's a power source here, maybe inside the building, maybe outside . . . a really old and really unpleasant power source. Been here for ages, maybe all the way back to the fifth century . . . But the really weird thing is, it's not dissipating. In fact, I'd say it's still growing, gaining strength all the time . . . It's what all the other phenomena are tapping into."

"Excuse me," Brook said diffidently from the doorway. "But what is she talking about?"

"Beats me," JC said cheerfully. "I'm usually lucky if I get half of it. Mostly I nod and go along."

"Right," said Happy. "Wouldn't surprise me if she made it all up."

"I do not!" said Melody. "Wait! Wait! Hold on to your underwear, people, I've got something . . . I think, I might be able to bring your blonde woman back!"

"Oh good," said Happy. "Just what I wanted."

"It's all right," JC said quickly. "You're not alone now, Happy. Your team is with you."

"Right!" said Melody. "Anything that wants to get to you has to go through us first!"

"That doesn't sound as comforting as you think it does," said Happy. "This really isn't a good idea, JC . . . I saw . . ."

But he still couldn't put it into words. JC patted him briefly on the shoulder and moved back to stand beside Melody.

"Is this really such a good idea?" he said quietly. "You saw what whatever it was he saw did to Happy. I don't ever want to see him that upset again."

"That bitch even looks at my Happy, I'll rip her ectoplasm off," said Melody. "Look at him; see the state of him. Whatever this thing was, it really did a number on his head. We have to show him that we can kick its arse. Or he'll never be any use to us again."

"Ah well," said JC. "As long as we're doing this for the team, and not just for him . . ."

Melody scowled at JC and punched a new set of instructions into the keyboard. The scanners hummed loudly, the room seemed to lurch briefly under everyone's feet, and the door reappeared in the far wall. Looking as though it had been there all the time, waiting for them to notice it. Happy made a small, frightened noise, but held his ground. All the colour had dropped out of his face again, but his eyes were narrowed, and his mouth was firm. JC walked slowly forward, to fix the door with a steady gaze.

"Don't open it!" Happy said urgently.

But the door was already swinging slowly outwards, of its own accord. There was nothing to be seen beyond it save a flat and empty darkness. And out of that darkness emerged the young woman Happy had seen earlier. She smiled at him, and he flinched; but he still held his ground. Melody left her precious equipment to go stand beside Happy, aiming her machine-pistol directly at the blonde. Who stopped in front of the dark doorway and looked unhurriedly about her.

"Well, well," she said. "Company. How nice."

Kim was suddenly standing there before her, blocking her way. "What do you want here?" she said steadily.

The blonde woman pointed at Happy. "Him. I want him."

"Well, you can't have him," said Melody. "He's spoken for."

"He's protected," said Kim.

"Protected," said the woman, still smiling. "And how are you going to stop me?"

Kim lunged forward suddenly, like an attack dog. She threw herself at the woman and thrust out a single hand. It glowed fiercely, the same golden glow as JC's eyes. The blonde screamed briefly, then exploded into long streamers of light, like so many colourless fireworks. She was gone in a moment, and the door in the wall with her. Kim lowered her no-longer-glowing hand, looked the wall over carefully, and turned back to smile sweetly at her team. A slow, satisfied, and only slightly scary smile.

"No-one messes with my friends," she said easily. "You make one of mine scream, I make you scream. Oh yes!" She grinned at JC and waggled the fingers of her hand at him. "Just a little something that I picked up on my travels."

"Very impressive," JC said carefully. "But what exactly was it that you blew up? A ghost? A presence?"

"No," said Kim.

"Any chance it'll show up again?" said Happy.

"Oh, almost certainly," said Kim. "But I think I can promise you . . . that when we do see it again, it'll be a lot more respectful."

"I think I'll carve some crosses into the tips of my bullets," said Melody.

"Excuse me," said a hesitant voice from the doorway. They all turned to look at Brook, who stood as though he were frozen to the spot. He was staring at Kim. "Who, or what, is that, please?"

"Allow me to present to you the only ghost in the Ghost Finders," JC said grandly. "Her name is Kim, and she's my girl-friend! Be polite to her. If you know what's good for you. Now, I think we've all had as much rest as we can stand, so I think we should go back downstairs and regroup in the bar. So you can tell us all the things you haven't been meaning to tell us, Mr. Adrian Brook."

SIX

DISTURBANCES

Everyone felt much more comfortable, and even comforted, once they were back in the main bar. The lighting seemed brighter, warmer, even friendlier. And the shadows were just shadows. Brook bustled around, chattering cheerfully as he got out what he promised was the good brandy. Everyone else perched on the high bar-stools as Brook set out brandy glasses before them, apart from Kim, who tucked up her feet and hovered cross-legged in mid air beside JC.

Brook poured out generous measures of the good brandy, for medicinal purposes, on the grounds it was good for shock. And if they didn't have shock, it was only because he hadn't presented them with the bill yet. Brook laughed determinedly at his professional joke and started to pour a glass for Kim, until she stopped him with an upraised hand and a sweet smile.

"Spirits don't drink spirits, darling."

Brook blinked at her a few times, and double-taked as he realised she'd rearranged her ectoplasm again. Kim now appeared to be wearing a shimmering white nurse's uniform, complete with a dangling stethoscope and a cute little cap perched on the back of her head. Brook looked at JC.

"She does that," JC said calmly. "I think she spends her spare time reading the ghosts of old fashion magazines. I find it best not to ask questions on the grounds that you're never going to receive any answer you can be comfortable with. Best to smile and nod, and move on."

Brook poured himself a large measure of the good brandy. JC made a point of not looking at Happy and Melody, so he could study them surreptitiously in the big mirror behind the bar. His two living team members were sitting side by side, looking at their drinks. They weren't actually talking, but their body language suggested they were a lot more comfortable around each other. JC was pleased about that. He didn't try to draw them into conversation. He didn't want to push things, yet.

Brook finished his brandy and put the glass down on the bar-counter with more noise and force than was strictly necessary. His face was flushed and blotchy, and his eyes were more than a little wild.

"Whatever you saw up there, or thought you saw, don't let it get to you," he said roughly. "The upstairs floor is its own world, with its own secrets. People have seen all kinds of things up there . . ."

"Such as?" said Melody, challengingly.

"Mostly, things people don't want to talk about," said Brook. "Like your friend, there." He gestured at Happy, who was still staring into his drink.

JC considered Happy for a long moment. "After all the things you've seen, working on the job, everything from ghosts to gods to the ghosts of gods, and this was too much?"

Happy shook his head slowly. "Too personal."

JC turned back to Brook, who met his gaze unflinchingly. JC smiled and pushed his sunglasses down his nose, so he could peer over the top, and fix the barman with his glowing, golden gaze. Brook went pale. He looked like he wanted to look away but couldn't.

"Tell me," said JC, and it wasn't a request. "Tell me what's been going on here, at the King's Arms."

Brook swallowed hard. "So the stories about you are true."

"Stories?" said JC.

"All kinds," said Brook. "About you, and your team. That's why I specifically asked the Institute for you people. Though I never really thought I'd get a famous A team like you."

"Famous?" said Melody. "We're famous?"

"I think he means infamous," said JC.

"Who, exactly, has been telling tales out of school about us?" said Melody. She grabbed the brandy bottle and freshened her glass.

"I still keep in touch," said Brook, almost defiantly. "With some of my old colleagues at the Carnacki Institute. They all had stories to tell, about JC Chance and his team. And there's a hell of a lot more to be found on the Net. Most of it contradictory, of course; but that's conspiracy sites for you. Everyone's fascinated to see what you'll do next."

"You're avoiding the point," said JC. "And I'm afraid

I decline to be distracted. Nice try, though. Now, what's going on here?"

"When I first came back here, to my old home-town," Brook said slowly, "I was looking for something to do, in my retirement. I saw the local pub was looking for a new owner, so I took it on. The regular drinkers immediately took pains to fill me in on all the old ghost stories, but I'd already heard most of them from when I was a kid. With my Institute experience, it didn't take me long to recognise them as just stories. Traditional tales. I thought I knew better. So after I'd been running things here for a while, and I hadn't seen or heard anything unusual or unearthly, I opened up the first-floor rooms for occupation again."

"Even though bad things were supposed to have happened to people who stayed in those rooms?" said JC.

Brook shrugged sullenly. "I thought they were only stories! And running a local pub . . . is harder than you think. I needed the extra money staying guests would bring in. I had all the upper rooms cleaned out and renovated. Including a few tricks I learned cleaning up after Carnacki field teams. To be on the safe side. The local press did a big story about my renting out the rooms again, something that hadn't been done since the seventies. The publicity brought people in from all around. And at first, everything seemed fine. But then the trouble started."

"Ghosts?" Kim said brightly.

"No," said Brook. "Worse than ghosts. Timeslips . . . Open some of the doors, and the room beyond could be from any time in the Past. A different version of the room, from some previous version of the inn. You could look in, quite safely, from the outside, and see places and people long gone. From decades, even centuries, ago. You could travel from one age to another by stepping from the landing into the room."

Melody slammed a fist down on the bar top, and everyone jumped. She was grinning broadly, actually bouncing up and down on her bar-stool in her excitement. "This is fantastic! Actual, practical, Time travel! Oh, I am so going to try this out for myself!"

"No you're not," Brook said immediately.

"Why not?" said Melody. "I'll bet you had a go, didn't you!"

"No," said Brook. "I never dared. The risk is too great."

"Risk?" said Happy. "What risk?"

"The Timeslips come and go without any warning," said Brook. Beads of sweat showed on his slack, grey face. He seemed almost hunched in on himself. "They don't last long, you see. And if you're inside the room, in the Past, when the door slams shut . . . you're trapped in there. Lost in the Past, forever. Because when the door opens, that Past is gone."

Melody looked sternly at JC. "This is far too good to pass up on, JC. Promise me that we will investigate this thoroughly, later."

"If there is a later, yes," said JC.

"Why did I know you were going to say that?" said Happy, not looking up from his drink.

"Maybe you're psychic," said Kim.

"Ghost humour," said Happy. "Ho ho ho."

"This isn't funny!" Brook said loudly. "I lost three customers that way! Until I realised what was happening. I had to report the disappearances to the local police as guests who'd sneaked off, without paying their bills. I didn't like to blacken their names, but what else could I do? Telling the truth wouldn't bring them back. And who'd believe me? The missing guests' families didn't. They made their own inquiries when the police couldn't help them, sent their own private investigators here to talk to me. I didn't tell them anything. I showed them the upstairs rooms, and nothing ever happened because these people only ever showed up during daylight hours. The rooms stayed the same. Looking perfectly ordinary and innocent. As though they were protecting themselves. As soon as the investigators gave up and left, I locked all the upstairs rooms and stopped advertising them."

"But the trouble didn't stop there, did it?" said JC.

"No," said Brook. "I contacted some old friends at the Institute. Told them what had happened. Hoping they'd be intrigued enough to send someone to investigate. Hoping they'd have some idea what to do about the rooms or how to bring the missing guests back. I felt . . . responsible, you see. The Institute said they'd look into it. But they never did. No-one ever came. I kept calling the Institute, trying different people and different departments, calling in every old favour I had, or thought I had . . . Until, finally, they sent you."

Brook stopped there, to look at the team, before looking back at JC. "Would I be right in thinking there's a reason why they finally sent a team, the team I'd been asking for all along? And not necessarily a good one?"

"Could be," said JC. "But these Timeslipped rooms aren't the real reason you need help, are they?"

Brook was trapped by JC's glowing, golden eyes again. He nodded, reluctantly.

"When one of your regulars told the story about a young woman who came to a bad end in one of these rooms, I saw something in your face," said JC. "That story meant something to you, didn't it? Something personal . . ."

Brook licked his dry lips, and nodded quickly, as though bracing himself. "There's another kind of room upstairs. Even more dangerous than the Time-travelling rooms. There's one particular room where, if you go in, you don't come out again. No Timeslips involved; every time I've opened the door and looked in, it's always appeared to be the same room. Perfectly normal, everything as it should be. I've never seen a ghost or anything that shouldn't be there. But I lost four more guests in that awful room before I realised what was happening. Four good men, who went in and closed the door and were never seen again."

"So we now have a grand total of seven people gone missing," said Melody.

"Yes!" said Brook. "Seven! Just . . . gone!"

"Then why keep letting that room to people?" said Happy, looking at Brook for the first time.

"Because the room moves around!" said Brook. "Sometimes it's behind one door, sometimes it's behind another . . . I can't always tell, when I approach the closed door afterwards. Once it's too late to do anything . . . I can feel that the room has changed. It's like there's something lying in wait, inside. Something hungry. And that's when I know I've lost another guest. And I back away, not taking my eyes off the door, in case it should start to open . . . and I run downstairs and hide. Until enough time has passed that I can be sure it's safe to go back upstairs, open the door, and look inside. There's never any trace left of the guest I put in there."

"Hold everything!" said Melody, glaring at Brook. "You noticed something was wrong but not your other guests?"

"Apparently not," said Brook. "Most of my guests had a perfectly good time. Some even congratulated me, on how pleasant it was to stay here. That made it worse, somehow. And you have to understand—I didn't know what was happening, at first. But after a while, the room let me know. I think it wanted to gloat."

"So this hungry room is still up there?" said JC.

"Somewhere," said Brook. "Hiding behind some apparently innocent door."

"We're going to have to look into that," said Kim.

"You never used to be this funny before you went on your travels," said Happy.

"Travel broadens the mind," Kim said brightly.

"I had to explain the new missing guests to the police as more mysterious disappearances," said Brook. "They really weren't happy about that. Missing people are bad for the tourist trade. So the police got a warrant and searched my premises from top to bottom. Never found a thing. Because, of course, they were careful to carry out their search during daylight hours. So they were never going to find anything. They knew that. They were all local men. They knew the old, old stories, like everyone else.

"What a very interesting story," said JC. "Be sure, we will investigate it most thoroughly. Now stop wasting my time and tell me the real reason why you need our help. Or I will get up and lead my people out of here; and you can deal with it on your own."

Brook nodded, slowly. He looked tired, beaten.

"The real reason I came back here, to the town where I was born, and grew up, was a girl. Lydia Woods. I used to walk out with her, back when we were both teenagers. All those years ago. Her father ran this pub, back in the seventies. But, there was a long-standing, really nasty feud going on back then, between Lydia's family and mine. The kind that goes back generations . . . You know what small communities can be like. They clutch their grudges to their bosoms, so they have something to warm their cold hearts in the night.

"Lydia and I, we didn't care. We were young; and we really did believe love conquers all. We even thought, in our naïvety, that we might be the ones to bring our warring families back together. But somehow both our families found out before we were ready to tell them. Bad words were said, on both sides. Scary words. And all kinds of threats; by people we had no doubt were ready to carry them out. Lydia and I were forbidden to see each other, ever again.

"While I was still working out what to do, Lydia hanged herself. Right here in this pub. Upstairs, in her father's room. My father told me and said it was probably for the best. I hit him, for the first time in my life, left this town, and went to London. Ended up working for the Carnacki Institute. And that was my life for so many years. I never came back here, never once talked to anyone from my family. Or hers. They're all gone now, one way or another.

"Finally, when I was getting ready to take early retirement, I got a call from an old friend I hadn't even thought of in years. And he told me there were stories circulating, about Lydia's ghost manifesting in the King's Arms. The poor soul who owned the place then was scared out of his wits because everything had been quiet since the seventies. That's why he was so ready to sell.

"That's why I came back here, to take over the pub. Wasn't like I had a choice. I had to see for myself. And take care of Lydia."

"Is she . . . appearing, here?" said JC, as kindly as he could.

"Yes," said Brook. "Not like the old story, of the wronged servant girl who hanged herself. No hanging body, no creaking of the noose. I look into the room where she . . . did it, and there she is. Looking exactly the way I remember her, from all those years ago. I thought at first it was a Timeslip, but I only had to look at her to know she was dead. I've watched her several times, from the doorway, never finding the courage to go in and talk to her. Because I got old; and she didn't.

"Lydia is why I can't just walk away from this horrible place. No matter how scary or dangerous it gets, I have to be here, for her. I can't let her down again."

"All right," said JC. "I'm sure there's a lot more you haven't told us, but I think we've got the basics now. Tell me . . . exactly what have you seen, and experienced here, yourself? Tell us what you see here after all the regulars have run off home."

Brook nodded reluctantly. "Nothing ever happens during the day. While it's light. But once it starts to get dark . . . the ghosts come out to play. They're everywhere.

First, I hear them upstairs. Footsteps, moving around. Walking up and down the landing and in and out of the rooms. Lots of them, overlapping each other, like there's a whole crowd of people up there. Then I hear voices. Men and women, young and old, but never anyone I recognise. I go to the foot of the stairs, and look up, to the dark at the top of the stairs . . . but I never go up, to see what's happening. Because the one time I did . . ." He stopped abruptly, and looked at Happy. "You know. You understand. They show you things. Unbearable things."

Brook stopped, his eyes far away. JC cleared his throat meaningfully. He wasn't unfeeling; but he couldn't make a start until he knew everything he needed to know. Information is ammunition in the hidden world.

"Sometimes, it gets physical," said Brook. "I've had things thrown at me. Even been picked up and thrown around. Once I heard a child screaming up on the landing. And I wouldn't stand for that. I thought perhaps some local kid had wandered up the stairs; and they'd got her. So I went up. And the moment I stepped out onto the first floor, the screaming stopped. And something laughed at me.

"The landing . . . seemed to stretch away, growing longer and longer, carrying me along with it. I wound up at the far end of the landing, and the top of the stairs seemed impossibly far away. I ran and ran down the landing, and the stairs never seemed to get any closer. I stumbled to a halt, to get my breath back, then forced myself on. I was afraid . . . so afraid I'd never get back. That I was trapped there on the landing, with all the things that haunted it, forever and ever. But suddenly space . . . snapped back, and I was at the top of the stairs.

I ran down them, crying out in shock, and relief; and I could hear hundreds of voices behind me. Laughing."

"All of this happened up on the first floor," said Melody. "Timeslips, and a room that ate people, and ghosts and monsters everywhere . . . *And you gave us rooms up there?*"

Brook's face twitched nervously. He could hear the danger in her voice.

"I had to know . . . whether it was only me. I wanted to see what would happen when the rooms were faced with real professionals. And I needed you to experience . . . what I experienced."

"Yeah," said Happy. "Thanks for that."

"What usually happens next?" said JC. "After the manifestations upstairs?"

"If I stay down here," said Brook, "eventually they come down, looking for me."

"Why do you stay?" said Kim, honestly curious.

"Because if I'm not here, they might leave the inn and come into town, looking for me," said Brook. "It's better to ride it out until it's over; and then I can lock the place up and go into town and get some sleep. It's my pub. I'm responsible. I have to protect the town. And then, there's Lydia . . ."

"What happens when they come downstairs?" said JC.

"They come into the bar," said Brook. "I don't always see things but I can hear them, moving about, talking together . . . You'll see."

Kim left JC's side and went darting off through the bar, sometimes walking on the floor and sometimes tripping happily along several inches above it. Gravity was only ever an occasional thing for her. More an option than an implacable law. She walked right through the tables and chairs, humming cheerfully but tunelessly to herself, while everyone else stayed where they were and watched. Kim rose and fell, looking into every nook and cranny, even drifting all the way up to the ceiling so she could look down on things from above. Finally, she dropped down to hover beside JC again and shook her head firmly.

"Nothing there, now. I couldn't See anything unnatural, sweetie. Not a trace to show anything weird has ever been here. Dull, dull; boring, boring. But, I am getting a feeling . . . that there's something going on outside the inn."

"There's definitely a power source here, somewhere," said Happy. "I can't See it, but I can feel it. Don't ask me what it is. It's . . . elusive. Hard to pin down, even harder to identify. It doesn't feel like anything I've ever encountered before. And like I said before, it's growing. Getting stronger, and stranger. It's attracting Really Bad Things to it, like malevolent moths to an utterly foul flame. Your pub isn't only haunted by ghosts, Brook; I'm picking up traces of everything from elementals to malevolent forces from Outside . . . all of them desperate to Get In."

Kim pouted. "How come you can pick up all this stuff, and I can't?"

"Because I'm alive," said Happy, not unkindly.

Brook looked at Happy, then at JC. "I never heard of half the things he said. What is he talking about?"

"I don't know," said JC. "I think he makes half of it up as he goes along to put the rest of us in the right frame of mind."

"I do not!" said Happy.

"But why are all those things coming here?" said Brook. "What do they want?"

"Us," said Melody.

"Lives, and just as often deaths, are currency to these Things," said Happy. "Eaters of Souls, our ancestors called them. They see us as energy sources. Or snacks, if you like. We're junk food, to Things from Higher Dimensions! And the more they consume, the more powerful they become, and the better chance they have of gaining a foothold in our world."

"By eating real things, they become more real," said Melody. "They want to eat us all up, body and soul."

"Just because they can," said JC.

"I was better off when I thought it was ghosts," said Brook.

"Lots of people say that to us," said Happy.

"The Carnacki Institute has been studying these Things From Outside ever since it was formed," said Melody, "Back in the days of Good Queen Bess. And we're still no nearer understanding what they are. Science keeps advancing, in leaps and bounds, but these Things are still so far beyond us that we're still arguing over what to call them, never mind grasping their essential nature. Aliens, demons, inhabitants of Higher or Lower dimensions . . . I don't think we have the words, or even the concepts, to properly comprehend them. Doesn't matter, though. We can still kick their nasty arses if we keep our wits about us."

"You always make me nervous when you talk like that," said Happy. "You never know Who, or What, might be listening."

"Wimp," said Melody.

Brook shook his head slowly. "I was never big on Theory, when I worked for Carnacki. I cleaned up the mess you guys left behind. We never needed to understand . . . All we cared about was how big a shovel we were going to need. But now I need to know. Why have they come here? What's so important about the King's Arms? Am I right in thinking it's something to do with this strange power source?"

"Seems likely; doesn't it?" said JC.

"How can you be so calm?" Brook said angrily.

"Practice," said JC. "I'm sure this has all been a nightmare for you, but trust me. We have been here before. Now, tell me about the history of the King's Arms."

"Well," said Brook, "after Lydia's father, the inn was run by this gay couple, and the locals named the pub the Queens' Arms. Rustic humour . . ."

"I meant," JC said patiently, "the inn's original history . . ."

"Oh!" said Brook. "Of course . . . Well, if you go back far enough, through the centuries . . . the inn's had hundreds of different names and identities. I did some digging into the inn's past, trying to understand what was happening . . . First on the Net, then down in the town, reading my way through the old church records. None of that's ever going to turn up on the Net, not given the state those records are in . . . There was a local historian some years back who took a special interest in the stories that had accumulated around the King's Arms. A lot of them were contradictory; but then, that's local history for you. Never was a local historian without their own axe to grind. Politics, religion, old scores to pay off . . .

"Anyway, go back far enough, and you find all sorts

of curious chronicles and proceedings. Apparently, there were several occasions when the town council called for the inn to be burned down. Usually after an exorcism had spectacularly failed to work. One priest actually walked all the way up here to curse the inn officially, with bell, book, and candle. Didn't make a blind bit of difference. You would think . . . that with so many bad stories centring on this inn, that the locals would abandon the place and set up another pub, inside the town, and do their drinking there. But somehow, that never happened. Instead, the townspeople seemed to take a perverse pride in doing their drinking in a place outsiders were too scared to visit. And I found a suggestion in the old records that the prosperity and maybe even the safety of the town is linked to the safety and prosperity of the inn. That its continuing presence protects Bishop's Fording.

"It is possible that the very first version of this inn was called The Oak Tree. Because there are old stories, based on even older stories, that the name derives from ancient Druid practices in this area. I have heard it suggested, or at least very strongly implied, that these old-time Druids set something in motion, long ago, that kept on happening. And that's why no-one wants to meddle with the pub. In case its long existence is somehow linked to what the Druids did, and the King's Arms is somehow holding off something even worse . . ."

Brook realised he'd been lecturing JC for some time, got embarrassed, and stopped talking. Happy gave JC a hard look.

"Druids? More bloody Druids? I don't believe in coincidences, JC. Coincidences are the Universe's way of getting you to pay attention."

“The Boss wanted us here,” JC said thoughtfully. “But to do what exactly? And why us?”

“Why is he looking at me?” said Happy, raising his eyes dramatically to the heavens. “Do I look like I have any answers? I am famous for never having any answers! I know nothing! Lots of nothing!”

“Perhaps we’re supposed to die here,” said Melody, quite seriously. “Because of what we found out at the Secret Libraries.”

Happy looked at her approvingly. “I think some of me is rubbing off on you.”

“Moving hastily on,” JC said loudly. “Before someone makes a very inappropriate joke . . . We have to believe Catherine Latimer is on our side or we might as well cut off our own heads. We can’t do this without her. So we’re here because the Boss trusts us to Do Something. About whatever it is that’s really going on here. And that must be important, maybe even significant; or she wouldn’t have sent her very best A team. Would she?”

“Denial ain’t only a river in Egypt,” murmured Happy.

“Shut up, Happy,” said JC.

Melody was looking thoughtfully at Brook. “You said . . . the upstairs phenomena only started up again recently.”

“Yes,” said Brook. “And I have been wondering . . . whether all of this could be my fault. Did I wake things up again by letting out the upstairs rooms? Did I put new bait in an old trap? Throw fresh meat to the waiting Beasts? That’s why I wanted you people here. To find out the truth.”

“I say we nuke the place from orbit,” said Happy. “It’s the only way to be sure.”

"You always say that," said Melody.

"And I'm nearly always right," said Happy.

"Actually," said Kim, "I'm pretty sure I'd pay good money to see that . . ."

"How much?" said Happy.

"But what if the inn is . . . containing the evil?" said Melody. "Destroy the inn, and you might let the Bad Things run loose."

"We don't destroy places," JC said firmly. "We solve problems. And to do that, we need more information. Adrian, what is the oldest part of this inn? I mean, the physically oldest part of the building?"

"This inn's been rebuilt and refurbished so many times, down the centuries," Brook said doubtfully. "It was a tavern before it was an inn before it was a pub . . . God knows what it was, originally, back in those old Druid days . . . The outer stone walls are still original I think. It's definitely local stone, from the quarry over the hill. But I suppose the oldest components . . . would have to be those old oak beams, in the ceiling."

They all looked up, at the long, exposed wooden beams that stretched the length of the ceiling. No-one needed to say *Oak beams . . . The Oak Tree.* It was so obvious. JC took off his sunglasses to better study the ancient oak with his golden eyes; but they looked like nothing other than wood. Kim launched herself up from beside him, so she could hover directly below the ceiling, pushing her face right next to the oak beams . . . and then she drifted back down again, shaking her head.

"I will never get used to that," said Brook.

"You are not alone," said JC.

"You'll believe a ghost can fly," Happy said solemnly.

Melody had a sudden fit of the giggles, to pretty much everyone's surprise. Kim joined in. Happy gave the oak beams his full attention, distancing himself from such frivolity.

"I'm not picking up anything from the ceiling in general or the beams in particular. They're not saying anything to me."

Melody stopped laughing, took a deep breath, and almost immediately dropped into a sulk. "It's not fair! If I had my full equipment here, I could run proper tests. I could shake this whole building by the scruff of the neck and make it tell us everything we need to know. With what I've got here, the best I can hope to do is poke the local phenomena with a stick and hope they feel intimidated."

She hesitated, then before anyone could stop her, jumped down from her bar-stool and ran back up the stairs. In a moment she returned with her suitcase. She opened it and set up her lap-top and scanners on the bar-counter, working quickly and efficiently. No-one offered to help. Melody was very protective of her babies. She was soon scowling into her lap-top screen.

"Of course," she said, to no-one in particular. "It would help if I knew what the hell I was looking for."

"If we knew what we were looking for, we'd already be doing something about it," said Happy.

"At least my equipment provides us with specific information!" said Melody. "Unlike certain psychic people I know who wander around pointing at things, and going *Ooh!*"

"I have never gone *Ooh!*" said Happy. "And I can See things your equipment could only ever dream of."

JC looked fondly on his team-mates as they argued loudly with each other and shared a smile with Kim. He was glad to see Happy and Melody talking to each other again, back to the open bickering of their old relationship. It was how they communicated. Kim leaned in close, to murmur in JC's ear.

"It's all very sweet, but how long do you suppose that's going to last?"

"Beats me," JC said quietly. "I'm glad it's happening at all. I would be the first to admit that I have never known what it is they see in each other. Their relationship would baffle a whole coven of psychiatrists. Hopefully, the shared experiences of this case will bind them together again."

"I have always admired your optimism, darling," said Kim.

"It's the only way to survive, working with those two," said JC. "Or, indeed, with the Carnacki Institute. Melody! Are you getting anything useful?"

"Nothing worth reporting," growled Melody, not taking her eyes off the glowing lap-top screen. "If I didn't know better, I'd swear everything here was hiding from me. Bastards."

"So far, all the supernatural activity we've encountered has been limited to the upper floor," said JC. "Nothing's come down here after us. So, Melody, I think we need to provoke a response. See what you can do. Happy, reach out and make contact with Something. Feel free to be extremely annoying."

Melody grinned broadly, tapping rapidly away at her keyboard. Happy looked thoughtful. Kim leaned in close to JC again.

"Darling, is this wise?"

"Probably not," JC said cheerfully.

Brook shifted uneasily behind the bar-counter. "What, precisely, are you doing?" he said. "What is Ms. Chambers up to with that lap-top?"

"Something very technical that you and I couldn't hope to understand," said JC. "Being the mere mortals that we are. But I have seen Melody work miracles with far less tech, and I have no doubt that she will annoy the hell out of whatever may be lurking in the vicinity. Don't ask me how. Really, don't. Ghost Finder science is very inexact."

"Only because you don't understand it," said Melody. "Don't worry, I'll soon stir these ghostly little shits up and make them squeal like piggies . . ."

"You want to get the ghosts mad at us?" said Brook, incredulously. "Okay; that is it. I am leaving."

"Finally!" said Happy. "A sane man, a kindred spirit, a man after my own heart! Get your coat, Brook, and I'll hold the door open for you."

"Stand your ground, both of you!" JC said sternly. "Happy, concentrate. Melody, anything yet?"

"I am pumping all kinds of psychic chaff into the aether," said Melody, still pounding away at her lap-top. "I am disrupting all the local dimensional frequencies and playing merry hell with all the paranormal patterns I can reach."

JC looked at Brook. "Told you we wouldn't understand. Are you actually achieving anything, Melody?"

"She's giving me one hell of a headache," growled Happy.

"Me, too," said Kim, frowning.

"Good," Melody said briskly. "That means it's working."

All the windows in the main bar suddenly slammed open, and the storm burst in. A bitterly cold wind blasted through the bar, knocking over everything that wasn't nailed down. Overthrown tables and chairs were sent somersaulting the length of the bar, smashing into each other with vicious force. Glasses and drinks abandoned by regulars who'd left in a rush flew through the air, smashing against the walls. The wind roared through the bar, carrying the rain with it, soaking the curtains and the carpets.

Melody crouched protectively over her precious equipment. Happy and JC huddled together. Brook crouched behind the bar-counter, crying out with shock. Kim stood where she was, peering uncertainly around her, as chairs and other things tumbled straight through her insubstantial form. JC yelled to Melody, raising his voice to be heard over the din of the storm.

"You've definitely got Something's attention, Melody! Any idea what?"

"Beats the hell out of me! The readings don't make any sense!" Melody yelled back, fighting to be heard over the storm. "But this is nothing to do with ghosts! It's only weather!"

"Could be poltergeists!" yelled Happy. "Is it poltergeists?"

"Not according to these readings!" said Melody.

Her last few shouted words fell into a sudden silence. The storm had broken off as abruptly as it began, the wind dropping away to nothing. The last of the rain fell away, leaving puddles on the floor. More ran down the walls, and dripped from the bottoms of soaked curtains. The sudden hush was almost brutal, after the rage of the storm. Tables and chairs crashed to a halt and were still, and the windows stopped slamming open and shut. JC and Happy let go of each other and moved quickly around the bar, shutting the windows and fastening them securely. They could still hear the storm howling outside, but now at a safe distance. It wasn't trying to get in, any more. Kim was still looking about her, frowning prettily. Happy went over to Melody, who only had eyes for her lap-top.

"Well?" said JC. "Anything?"

"No," said Melody. "That . . . appears to be it. I prodded the local power source with my science stick, and that was what we got in response. A very basic reaction. Interesting . . ."

"But what does it mean?" said Brook, rising very cautiously from behind the bar-counter.

"I'll have to think about it," said Melody.

She stared at her lap-top screen with such complete concentration she didn't even realise Happy was still standing over her. He nodded, gave up, and went back to JC. Who knew a man who needed distracting when he saw one.

"All right, Happy, you're up."

"What do you want me to do?" said Happy, not unreasonably.

"Reach out!" said JC, waving his arms around in what he hoped was a meaningful way. "Make contact with . . . Something! Slap it around the head in your own special psychic way and get it to talk to you. Say nasty things about its mother . . ."

Happy shrugged briefly and concentrated. Melody finally realised what he was doing and shut down her tech so it wouldn't interfere with his efforts. Brook looked like he wanted to duck behind the bar-counter again, but JC glared at him till he held his ground. Kim stared at Happy, fascinated, and went back to hover beside JC.

"Do you have any idea why the storm invaded the bar?" JC said quietly.

"It wasn't just a storm," said Kim. "I could feel anger in it . . ."

"All right!" Happy said loudly. He was frowning so hard it must have been painful, but he was also grinning in a really unpleasant way. "Everybody please shut the hell up and pay attention! Look around you! We are very definitely not alone here!"

Everyone looked up and down the wrecked and waterlogged main bar, but there was no-one else present that they could see. Everything seemed perfectly still and quiet. And then all the bar taps turned themselves on at once, and a dozen frothing liquids fell to the floor. Beers and ciders and lagers, all spouting out of the opened taps. Brook cried out and ran up and down the bar, closing the taps one after another. But the moment he moved on, the closed taps opened themselves up again. Brook swore loudly, as the floor behind the counter flooded. And then all the bottles on display at the back of the bar exploded, one after another; blasting vicious glass shrapnel through the air. Brook came running out from behind the counter, his arms up to protect his head.

JC grabbed him and pulled him down, away from the

flying glass. Happy was already crouching, both arms wrapped around his head. Melody stayed where she was, peering out from behind her lap-top. And Kim stood still, letting things pass through her with complete indifference. Slowly, things began to quiet down. There were no bottles left to explode, and the taps began to run dry, one after another.

And then, the overturned tables and chairs began to rock back and forth, as though gathering strength and determination. They rolled slowly along the floor towards the besieged people, gathering speed. There was a blind, brutal intent behind their advance, as they headed straight for JC and Happy, Brook and Melody. Kim strode forward to block their way, one hand held out imperiously. The tables and chairs rolled straight through her.

Melody straightened up, her machine-pistol at the ready. She opened fire on the nearest table, and blew it apart with a stream of bullets. Broken wood and jagged splinters flew on the air. But it only took Melody a moment to realise there was far too much furniture, and nowhere near enough bullets. She couldn't hope to stop them all. The rolling tables and chairs kept coming, faster and faster. Dangerously fast, with so much weight behind them.

The overhead lights started to flicker off and on, so that the whole bar went from light to dark, light to dark.

"They're destroying my pub!" screamed Brook. "Do Something!"

"This is us, doing something," said JC.

"Hell with the pub!" said Happy. "I refuse to die by furniture! Do Something, JC!"

The floor-boards suddenly rose and fell, rippling like a slow wave on a wooden sea. Great ragged cracks shot across the walls and ceiling, creaking and groaning loudly, as though the bar was trying to tear itself apart. Tables and chairs rattled and somersaulted across the uneven floor, heading straight for JC and Brook, Melody and Happy, picking up speed all the time. JC stepped forward to meet them, and produced a small round object from his jacket pocket. It shone brightly, the size of a cricket ball. JC held it out before him.

"See this?" he said loudly. "This is an exorcism grenade. Ready to blast holy sanctified light all over the vicinity! So stop this nonsense right now. Or else."

A floor-board lurched suddenly up under his feet, throwing him off-balance for a moment. JC pulled the pin from the grenade and tossed it lightly into the midst of the on-coming furniture. He turned to Kim.

"Get out of here! Right now! It won't be safe for you in here when this thing goes off!"

Kim nodded quickly and dived across the room, running straight through the outer wall, and on into the car park outside. JC turned back to the advancing chairs and tables and stood his ground, arms folded defiantly across his chest. There was a silent blast of overpowering, unbearable light, as the exorcism grenade exploded, filling the bar from one end to the other. And then it was gone. There was a pause, and the electric lights came back on, bright and calm and steady. The tables and chairs rolled to a halt and lay side by side on the quiet floor; rocking slowly back to inactivity again. Everything in the main bar was still and quiet. There was an overwhelming feeling of calm and peace. JC smiled cheerfully about him.

"Let this be a warning to one and all," he said loudly. "I am not always bluffing."

Happy looked at him. "*An exorcism grenade?* I thought those things were banned from field use, pending further testing?"

"I just tested it," said JC.

"One of these days they're going to catch you filling your pockets with whatever you fancy from the Carnacki warehouse," said Melody.

"What the Boss doesn't know about won't give her sleepless nights," said JC.

Kim stuck her head back through the wall and looked about her. "Is that it? Is it safe for me to come back in now?"

"Please don't do that," said Happy. "It's like looking at a serial killer's mounted trophy."

"Get back in here, Kim," said JC.

The ghost girl walked calmly through the wall, ignoring Happy with magnificent disdain, and considered the vanquished furniture, lying scattered the length of the main bar. She nodded, clearly expecting nothing less, and smiled brilliantly at JC. The two of them gave each other their almost but not quite high five.

"Well," Kim said pleasantly, "you wanted to provoke a response, darling. I'd say you succeeded."

"Look what you've done to my bar!" said Brook, almost hysterically.

"Not a bad reaction, as reactions go," said JC, ignoring the barman. "Surprisingly, however; nothing at all to do with ghosts . . . Right then; if the ghost won't come to the bar . . . Adrian! Adrian; where are you . . . Ah, there you are! Stop sulking and pay attention. I think you need to show me the room where your dead girl-friend is still waiting around."

Brook moved forward, reluctantly. "You think Lydia's got something to do with all this?"

"I don't know," said JC. "But she's what brought you back, and it was only after you returned that all this started up again. So I think I need to take a look, maybe have a nice little chat with the young lady. See what she has to say for herself. Happy, Melody, you stay here in the bar. Keep an eye on things. And slap them down hard if they look like they're getting out of hand again. I hereby authorise you to use excessive force because that's the only kind you two understand anyway."

"I'm not cleaning this up!" Melody said immediately, glaring at the mess around her. "I do not do cleaning up!"

"It's true," said Happy. "She doesn't. But since I really don't want to go back upstairs yet, I'm prepared to do a little light tidying, as long as it doesn't involve actual effort."

"I want to go see the ghost," said Melody, sticking out her lower lip. "Why can't I go and see the ghost? I'll be quiet."

"Too many people at once might frighten her," JC said firmly. "Besides, do you really want to leave Happy down here, on his own?"

Melody shot a quick look at Happy and said nothing. JC turned to Kim.

"Be a dear, Kim, and go take a proper look outside. Several quick circuits of the pub, then go flit around the fields. See if you can track down this mysterious local power source. But don't go too far, or get too close to anything unnatural. I'm becoming increasingly convinced that with this much raw power around, there are dangers here for the dead as well as the living."

"Anything for you, sweetie," said Kim. And she strode determinedly back through the wall again. Brook shuddered quickly and headed for the stairs at the back of the bar. JC went with him.

"Lydia's room is at the far end of the landing," Brook said quietly. "Every now and again I unlock the door and take a quick look inside. Make sure she's still there, and that she's . . . all right. But I never go in."

He started up the stairs, but JC stopped him with a sharp gesture. Brook started to say something, and JC gestured savagely for him to be quiet. JC stood very still at the bottom of the stairs, hidden in the shadows, and listened carefully. Because he wanted to know what Happy and Melody might say once they thought he wasn't around. Because he needed to know how things really were with them.

There was a long pause, then . . .

"Just because I'm talking to you again, it doesn't necessarily mean you're forgiven," said Melody.

"I had sort of got that," said Happy. "Even though I'm still not sure why you're so mad at me."

"You have got to be kidding," said Melody. "Really? Why am I so mad at you? You went back on your pills, and you didn't tell me! *Are you crazy?*"

"Sometimes," said Happy. "Goes with the territory. We both do what we have to, to survive what the hidden world throws at us. You lean on your machines, I lean on my medications."

"My machines aren't killing me by inches!" snapped Melody.

"But I can't live without my support mechanisms," said Happy.

"Aren't I enough for you?" said Melody.

"I hoped you would be," said Happy. "God knows I wanted you to be everything I needed. You did try. I know that. But you can't protect me from the pressures of the hidden world the way my pills can. Every day, it gets that little bit harder to keep the bad stuff outside my head. I'm fighting a war, Mel; and I'm losing."

"Oh, Happy . . ." said Melody. And JC winced to hear the helplessness in her voice.

There was another long pause, and then . . .

"Isn't there any special tech you could put together, to help me?" said Happy. He sounded very tired, and desperate. "Some machine that would shut down my ESP and make the world bearable?"

"I have done some research," said Melody. She sounded tired, too. "The only thing I found that might work would just as likely destroy your mind. Lobotomise you. You wouldn't be you any more."

"You say that like it's a bad thing," Happy said gently. "I think . . . I'd find that a relief."

Another long pause.

"Is there nothing else I can do for you?" said Melody.

"Yes," said Happy. "Hold me, while I'm dying."

SEVEN

DARK NIGHT OF THE SOUL

JC followed Brook up the stairs, sticking close behind the barman so he couldn't slow down, or have second thoughts. Brook stepped out onto the landing, looked quickly around him into the gloom, took a deep breath, and turned on the lights. JC moved quickly off the top step and onto the landing beside the barman. After listening to Brook's tales of terror about what the rooms got up to, JC was ready to see the landing with new eyes; but instead he was pleasantly surprised to find it looked like a landing. A long corridor stretching away to both sides, illuminated by reassuringly steady electric lights, with all the doors safely closed. Nothing moved anywhere, and everything seemed entirely still and quiet and peaceful.

JC looked at Brook. The barman was doing his best to look prepared and composed, but already a fresh sheen of sweat was appearing on his grey, haunted face. He looked like a man going to his own execution. He looked like a man . . . who had good reason to be scared. JC patted Brook on the shoulder, and gave the barman his best reassuring smile. Brook did not appear particularly convinced.

After looking up and down the corridor several times, Brook gathered up his nerve and led the way down the left-hand corridor. The only sound on the quiet of the landing was the steady tread of shoes on thinly carpeted floor-boards. JC kept a careful eye on every door they passed, braced for any one of them to suddenly swing open, so Something could jump out and drag them in . . . but the doors were only doors, and didn't so much as stir as JC and Brook passed.

Until they came to the final door, at the very end of the corridor. It looked like all the other doors. Brook stood and looked at it for a long moment, and JC had enough sense not to hurry him. Brook leaned in close, almost but not quite pressing an ear up against the wood, and listened. Then he straightened up, took out his key ring, selected one, and unlocked the door. Another deep breath, and he threw the door open and stepped back, gesturing for JC to go in.

JC looked thoughtfully at Brook; but the barman stood his ground. The expression on the barman's face made it very clear that he had no intention of going into the room. JC could go in if he wished . . . but on his own head be it. Brook would be staying on the landing. JC shrugged quickly, gave Brook another reassuring smile, and strode confidently in. On the grounds that there was nowhere he feared to tread. Because this, after all, was just another haunting; and JC knew what to do with ghosts.

Once inside the end room, JC immediately understood why Brook had first mistaken the haunted room for another Timeslip. The ghost girl hadn't only brought herself back; she'd manifested her old surroundings as well. The room reeked of the 1970s. The decade that taste forgot, or at least gave up on. JC recognised the era immediately, from the terrible earth brown and faded yellow colours, the Laura Ashley wallpaper, and the big, chunky furniture. JC stood in front of the open doorway and looked around, taking his time. He could sense Brook hovering behind him, peering in from a safe distance. Daylight from some past Time poured in through the window, filling the room with a cheerful, midday glow. It all looked very real, very solid, for one dead girl's memory.

Lydia was sitting in a chair by an empty fire-place; and JC knew her immediately for a ghost. She looked real enough, solid enough; but you only had to look at her to know she wasn't alive. Lydia sat at her ease in an overstuffed chair, reading a copy of *Nova* magazine with a photo of a young Germaine Greer on the cover. She seemed completely absorbed in her reading, so JC cleared his throat politely. Lydia raised her head, looked around, then smiled easily at JC. She seemed a little surprised but not in any way disturbed or frightened, at finding a strange man in her room. As though she knew she had nothing to be scared of. She started to get up, and JC gestured quickly for her to remain seated.

Lydia looked to be seventeen, eighteen—a pleasant-looking girl. Average height, perhaps a little heavier than current fashions would allow, with a broad, pretty face and a great mop of curly black hair that tumbled down to her shoulders. She wore jeans and a blue-and-white blouse, and a pale blue bandana across her brow to hold her hair in place. She studied JC openly, reacting to his appearance quite normally, as though both of them were real.

"Hi!" said JC. "Sorry to intrude; I must have the wrong room. I'm JC Chance, visiting Bishop's Fording."

"That's all right," said the ghost girl. "I'm Lydia. My dad runs this place. Are you staying here long?"

"Just passing through," said JC.

"Is my father looking after you all right?" said Lydia. "We don't get many staying guests these days."

"It's been an interesting visit, so far," said JC. "Lots to see and do."

They both smiled and chatted easily together for a while. JC did his best to be kind and gentle with her and not say anything that might challenge her view of reality. She clearly didn't know there was anything unnatural going on. She didn't know she was dead. Didn't remember hanging herself, in this very room. Didn't know the father she talked about so easily had been dead for decades. She still thought she was another teenage girl, with everything to live for. Though JC did notice that she didn't ask him some very obvious questions, like why was he wearing sunglasses indoors.

"I'm waiting for my boyfriend, Adrian," Lydia said cheerfully. "Though . . . it does feel like I've been waiting for him for some time now . . . I hope he'll be here soon."

JC smiled and nodded. He didn't see any point in telling her she'd already been waiting forty years.

Lydia frowned for the first time. "I hope nothing's happened to Adrian . . ."

"I'm sure he's not far off," said JC. "Are you all right, here?"

"I suppose so," said Lydia. "I'm comfortable, I've got everything I need . . . Though every now and again the door opens, and this old man looks in. He isn't any bother, he never says anything; but he always looks so sad . . ."

"Do you recognise him?" JC said carefully.

"Oh no," said Lydia. "He's far too old to be anyone I'd know!" She leaned forward, lowering her voice conspiratorially. "Of course, there is a good chance that he might be a ghost! This pub is famous for them, you know."

"Yes," said JC. "I know."

"Though I can't say I've ever seen one," said Lydia, grinning.

"You're not frightened of ghosts?" said JC.

"No," said Lydia. "I don't know why anyone would be. They're just people, after all."

"I've bothered you long enough," said JC. "I'll leave you alone now. Nice to meet you, Lydia."

"Good-bye, Mr. Chance," said Lydia. "You couldn't do me a favour; could you? Take a look down the corridor and tell me if you see my Adrian coming?"

"Yes," said JC. "I'll take a look."

He left the room and shut the door behind him. His last glimpse of Lydia was of her returning to the magazine she'd been reading for forty years. Out on the landing, Adrian Brook stood with his back to the door, his shoulders shaking as he fought to hold back tears.

''''''''''''''''''''''''''

After a while, they headed back down the landing, to the top of the stairs. It took JC a while to realise that there was something wrong with the light. The electric light bulbs were still burning steadily; but the nature of the light had changed. It had deepened, into an unpleasant orange-red glow, like sunlight that had soured and gone off. The sound of their footsteps had changed, too—softer, muffled, as though the floor-boards underfoot had gone rotten. The air on the landing smelled flat and dusty, like air in a room that's been left shut up for too long. And, one by one, the doors ahead of them began to open, swinging slowly inwards; without making even the slightest sound. They hung back, invitingly, offering access to the rooms beyond, and all that they contained. Brook started to say something, and JC put a steadying hand on his arm.

"Don't look into any of the rooms," JC said quietly. "Look straight ahead and keep walking. There's nothing in any of these rooms that you or I would want to see."

They walked on down the landing. As they passed each door, it slammed loudly shut behind them, in a bad-tempered sort of way. JC kept his hand on Brook's arm, squeezing it reassuringly now and again. He didn't want the barman panicking, so close to the stairs. He had a very strong feeling that this would be a very bad place to show weakness. He remembered Brook's telling how Space itself had become unhinged, here on the landing, stretching away forever . . . JC didn't want to have to cope with that.

They'd almost made it to the top of the stairs when

there was a sudden movement in the last room they passed; and JC shot a quick glance through the open doorway, in spite of himself. He caught a quick glimpse of something like a roomful of vegetation, stirring and rustling; and then he pulled his gaze away. They reached the top of the stairs, and JC allowed himself a small internal sigh of relief as he looked down the stairs and found them perfectly normal and unchanged. This time, he led the way down. Making a deliberately loud clatter on the steps so that Happy and Melody would hear him coming. Melody did still have her machine-pistol, after all, and a frequently stated willingness to shoot first and ask questions at the funeral.

As it turned out, the pair of them barely looked round as JC and Brook re-entered the bar. Happy and Melody were sitting perched on their high stools, at opposite ends of the bar-counter. Melody was bent over her laptop, glaring at the screen and hitting the keyboard so hard the whole machine jumped under her pounding fingertips. Happy was sitting quietly, staring at nothing, or at least nothing any of the others could see. His face was empty, his mouth a flat line; he looked more thoughtful than anything. Brook hurried past JC and went behind the counter to pour himself another large measure of the good brandy. He seemed a little more settled, back in his own territory. But he still had to hold his brandy glass with both hands, to keep it steady. JC moved in beside Melody.

"All quiet upstairs," he said cheerfully. "More or less. Though quite possibly, the quiet that comes before the storm. I met Lydia—charming young lady. Bit sad, of course, but reasonably composed for someone who killed herself forty years ago. Are you even listening to a word I'm saying, Melody? Or are you still sulking because you haven't got all your proper equipment to play with?"

Melody growled under her breath and slapped at the lap-top, to make it clear how annoyed with the machine she was for not doing what it was supposed to do.

"Absolutely nothing useful to report, JC. This piece of shit is acting up like you wouldn't believe. If I had my proper equipment, I could do you a full scan of this pub and the surroundings, and get you some proper answers. As it is, the scanners aren't picking up anything, near or far, and I can't get a single reading on the local power source, wherever or whatever it is."

They both looked around, startled, interrupted by the rising sounds of the storm outside. The wind and the rain were growing steadily louder and more aggressive. The windows jumped and rattled in their frames as the wind slammed against them. The rain was really throwing it down now, pounding against the leaded glass of the windows; while outside the King's Arms, the wind howled and shrieked and prowled around and around the inn, like some great beast trying to find a way in.

And maybe it was, thought JC.

"That storm is not natural," said Happy.

They all looked at him until it became clear he had nothing more to say on the subject.

"I wish Kim would come back," said JC. "I don't like to think of her alone out there, in that storm."

"You sent her outside," said Melody.

"Yes, thank you, Melody," said JC. "I am aware of that."

"Kim is probably the only one of us who isn't in any danger," said Happy, in a calm and only slightly far-away voice. "The only one of us the storm can't touch. I wonder if she could make an umbrella out of her ecto-plasm . . . I think Kim has demonstrated that she is a girl who can look after herself . . ."

"Listen up, people!" Melody said loudly. "Got something . . . I've managed to access the latest weather reports, from the local television news . . . Apparently, this storm we're experiencing is extraordinarily local. As in, it's only raining over this pub and its surroundings. Nowhere else. In fact, outside of a very limited area, it is bone-dry, without even a breath of wind. Meteorologists are baffled."

"Okay," said JC. "That is . . . interesting. It's almost as though Someone or Something has arranged this storm for us."

He peered over Melody's shoulder at the lap-top screen; where the local weather-man was gesturing silently at the animated weather map behind him. Melody worked on the sound, and the weather-man's voice was suddenly there, trying hard to sound knowledgeable and, unfortunately, funny. And then he stopped abruptly, his professional smile falling away as he stared directly at JC and Melody. The weather map behind him disappeared, replaced by the same soured orange-red light JC had seen on the upper floor. The weather-man stepped forward until his face filled the screen. His eyes collapsed and ran away down his cheeks, in dark bloody streams. He grinned and grinned, until his cheeks cracked and split apart, showing the blood-smeared teeth underneath.

"You shouldn't have come here," he said, in a painful, rasping voice. "You're all going to die in this awful place. And after you die, the really bad things will happen to you. Ask your little ghost girl, Kim. Except you can't because she won't be coming back. We have her now, and oh the things we'll do to her . . ."

"Liar," JC said calmly. "If you did have her, you'd show her to me. But you can't because you don't. Because Kim is far more powerful than anything you've got. Now get out of Melody's lap-top, or I'll have her show you what the exorcism function can do."

The bloody-faced weather-man disappeared in a moment, replaced by the head and shoulders of a pretty young blonde woman with cold, dead eyes.

"That's her!" said Happy; and JC and Melody both jumped a little because they hadn't heard him come over to join them. He looked over Melody's shoulder and jabbed a stubby finger at the young woman on the screen. "That is the woman I saw in my room!"

The blonde woman smiled out of the lap-top screen, entirely calm and composed, and when she spoke, her voice was ordinary, and matter of fact.

"You're going to die here. And you won't like it at all. Death isn't what you think it is. Being dead isn't what you think it is. This whole building is soaked in death and suffering and horror. They killed me here. A human sacrifice. The priests nailed my guts to the old oak tree and sang sacred songs to drown out my screams. They told me it was an honour; but I still wouldn't volunteer. They laughed and did it anyway. Because, they said, it was necessary. They should have known better. By sacrificing me in a place of power, they made me powerful. My time has come around at last, and I shall have my revenge on everyone. And taking those won't help you at all, Happy."

JC looked around sharply, to see Happy necking several different colour-coded pills, one after the other. Melody saw it, too, and made a low, soft sound of distress. Happy ignored them both, washing his pills down with several large gulps of the good brandy. He smiled beatifically, then leaned over to stare happily at the face on the screen.

"That's what you think, Blondie. You don't know me at all. These aren't pills to pump me up; they're ammunition. I can See you now, See you for what you really are. You're not real. You're not a person. You're not what you appear to be at all, not a ghost or any kind of surviving personality. You're the door I saw in my room. The blood-red corridor that leads only to death and destruction. You're the last angry, defiant screams of a murdered young woman, given strength and purpose by a place of power. You're the storm. You're what's outside. And if you had any sense, you'd run away and hide, because you . . . should be afraid of us. You've never met anyone like us."

The lap-top shut itself down, and the screen went dead. Melody struggled to get it up and running again, but it didn't want to know. She pushed herself back on her stool and turned her glare on Happy. JC and Brook were staring at him, too. Happy smiled serenely back at them.

"I feel good!" he said. "I'm not scared of anything. Which is, in itself, I'll admit, a bit scary."

"What have you taken?" said Melody. "How much have you taken?"

"Like it would mean anything to you if I explained," said Happy. "Enough to do the job, that's the point. Let us talk about Blondie."

"She said she was killed, sacrificed, by priests," said JC. "And given how old this inn is supposed to be, I think we can safely assume they were Druid priests. According to all the reports, the Druids never met a problem they thought they couldn't put right with a sacrifice. They used everything from sacrificial altars in rings of stones to burning whole communities alive in giant Wicker Men. But what was the point of this particular sacrifice? And why did it go wrong? Why is it still . . . persisting, clinging on, after all these centuries?"

"And why does Blondie want us dead?" said Melody. "I mean, she doesn't even know us!"

"I'm sure she'd like us if she knew us . . ." murmured JC.

"We're not dealing with the ghost of a murdered girl," said Happy, "but her last dying emotions, manifesting in this world as the angry storm outside."

"Is it me?" said Brook. "Or is the storm getting really loud now?"

In fact, the storm was howling so loudly that they'd all had to raise their voices to be heard over it. They turned to look at the rain-lashed windows and jumped pretty much in unison as Kim came running through the wall and back into the bar. She stopped abruptly and looked wildly about her.

"I found something!" she said. "I found something out there; and I think it's followed me home!"

It took them all a moment to realise she wasn't in her white nurse's outfit any more. In times of crisis, Kim always reverted to the long green dress she had been wearing when she was murdered. She moved quickly over to stand before JC, huddling as close as she could get without actually overlapping him. He wanted to hold her and comfort her but knew he couldn't. So he made slow, calming motions to her with his hands and gave her his best encouraging smile.

"What did you see out there, Kim?"

"It's more what I didn't see," said Kim. She was slowly regaining control of herself though her voice was still very small. "The stars have all gone out . . . and the moon is gone. It's all gone dark, JC! Take a look out the window; see for yourself."

JC started towards the windows, then paused when he realised Kim wasn't coming with him. She gestured for him to go on. JC nodded gruffly and went over to stare out the nearest window. Happy and Melody were quickly there with him, staring out the next window. They looked out at the night; but the night wasn't there. Only an endless, impenetrable darkness. Brook listened to their gasps and cries and came reluctantly out from behind the counter to join JC at his window. He leaned in close, almost pressing his face against the glass, and still couldn't see anything but the dark. Brook stumbled backwards, his face slack with fear and disbelief.

"There's nothing out there," he said numbly.

"Nothing but the dark," said JC.

"Kim's right," said Melody, in a shocked, unsteady voice. "No stars, no moon; not even any lights from the town at the end of the road . . . This can't be right."

"And," said Kim, still not budging from the counter, "there's Something out there."

JC looked back at her. "In the dark?"

"I think it *is* the dark," said Kim.

It occurred to JC that Kim was seriously frightened. He hadn't seen her look that scared since both of them were nearly destroyed in the hell train down in the London Underground. He was sure he hadn't seen her look even seriously worried since then. He started to say something; and all the lights in the main bar went out. And stayed out. Everyone made some sort of noise. They couldn't help themselves. Things were bad enough already, without this. The dark seemed so . . . absolute, this time. Like the kind of dark you find at the bottom of the sea, down in the depths where the light has never penetrated.

JC turned his head quickly back and forth but couldn't make out a damned thing anywhere.

"It's all right!" said Brook. "I've got some candles behind the counter, for emergencies! You stay put, and I'll go back and find them! I know this bar like the back of my hand!"

Several loud bangs and crashes and a certain amount of rough language suggested that might not be entirely true, but Brook did make it back to the counter. They could all hear him, scuffling and searching behind the bar. Picking up things that probably felt a lot like candles and putting them down again. JC turned in what he hoped was Melody's direction.

"Melody! Try your lap-top again! The light from the screen should give us something to work with!"

"Way ahead of you, JC," said Melody's voice from

over by the counter. "I've got my lap-top, but it's dead in the water. Nothing's working. I think the faces manifesting through the screen screwed it over, big time."

JC thrust one hand into his jacket pocket. "All right, nobody panic, I've got my lighter here with me."

"Who's panicking?" said Happy. "Who said anything about panicking? I'm concerned, for Melody's sake. And what are you doing with a cigarette lighter? You said you gave up smoking ages ago."

"I did," said JC. "But a lighter is still a very useful thing to have about your person in this business."

Everyone made emphatic and very satisfied sounds as JC's lighter burst into flame. The cheerful yellow glow didn't spread far, but the simple dancing light was enough to warm all their hearts after so long in complete darkness. JC held his lighter up high, but the glow didn't even travel far enough to reach the counter. It was only just bright enough to illuminate his hand and arm.

"Now if this were a movie," said Happy, "that lighter would provide us enough light to do emergency surgery by."

"Hollywood lies to you all the time," said JC. "Get used to it."

"I am not panicking!" said Happy. "In fact, in my current highly medicated state, I don't think I'd panic if an elephant stood on my foot. And then danced Gangnam Style."

Brook set out several assorted candles, in various assorted holders, on top of the bar-counter, and lit them up, one after the other. A flickering pale yellow light illuminated the bar, and everyone hurried forward to stand in the narrow pool of light. JC put out his lighter and tucked it away. Making a careful note of which pocket he put it in, in case he needed it later. Happy moved quickly over to be with Melody, who had given up on her lap-top and pushed it away. Brook was breathing more easily, his eyes fixed on the candlelight. JC had almost reached Kim when she looked suddenly back at the windows and made a loud sound of distress. They all turned to look.

Darkness was seeping through the closed windows, right through the solid glass. It passed swiftly through all the windows and spread out across the far wall, like so much sticky black treacle. It oozed through the windows, without breaking or even affecting the old leaded glass, and covered the entire wall from floor to ceiling in only a few moments. As though the darkness from outside the inn had . . . pressed forward and broken into the main bar. It was inside now and still moving forward. Edging slowly across the floor, eating up the open space, and replacing it with darkness.

There was no sense of physical presence, no sense there was anything in the dark. Just the darkness itself—a huge, impenetrable wall or curtain of utter darkness. A brutal implacable absence of light. Drawing steadily closer to the small, beleaguered group in their pool of yellow light.

"The night's come in here after us," said Kim.

"I really don't like the look of that," said Melody.

"Should we run?" said Happy.

"Where to?" said JC, angrily. "Use your head! There's nowhere to go!"

"We could go upstairs," said Melody.

"Bad idea," Brook said immediately.

"Why isn't my tech working?" said Melody, picking

up her lap-top and shaking it, then slamming it down hard on the bar-counter. "There's no reason why it shouldn't be working!"

"Hold on, Mel," said JC. "Don't let it get to you. Happy, are you picking up anything?"

"I'm getting nothing," said Happy. "And I mean nothing. I can't See or feel anything. There's a total absence of any kind of presence. Which is . . . weird."

"Have you noticed?" Kim said suddenly. "The storm's gone, too. Not a sound anywhere, not even a murmur. It's all gone quiet."

They all stood very still, listening. The entire main bar seemed stuffed full of an eerie, oppressive silence.

"As though . . . the storm isn't there, any more," said Kim. "As though there isn't anything outside this room. Like the darkness has . . . swallowed everything up."

"Nicely put, Kim," said Happy. "Very smart, very succinct, and evocative. Oh yes. If you have any more insights like that, do feel free to keep them to yourself."

"No disagreements in front of the enemy, children!" said JC. "Put on a brave face and a united front and stare the darkness down! I've got an idea."

He grabbed the brandy bottle off the top of the counter and strode forward. He emptied the bottle's remaining contents out over the nearest chair lying on its side on the floor, right in the path of the creeping dark. JC used the last of the liquor to lay a thin trail back to the counter, put the bottle back, knelt, took out his lighter again, and lit the trail of brandy. A puff of blue flames sprang up from the trail, shooting forward to ignite the liquor-soaked chair. It burned brightly with the same blue flame, blazing away in the face of the approaching dark. It made loud crackling and creaking noises as it burned, while everyone watched silently from the counter, waiting to see what would happen. The light from the burning chair helped illuminate more of the bar; but the light stopped dead where it met the approaching dark. Until, finally, the dark wall rolled over the burning chair and engulfed it, stamping out its light in a moment.

And now the darkness covered more than half of the main bar.

"Bugger," said JC, succinctly. "I was hoping for rather more than that . . . Okay, everybody fall back, and get behind the bar with Brook."

By the time he had finished talking and joined them, they were all lined up behind the counter, standing huddled together, shoulder to shoulder. For company and support. Kim stuck as close to them as she could get, staring wide-eyed at the slowly moving dark. The light from the candles on top the counter stopped where it met the creeping darkness; and inch by inch the dark pushed the candlelight back towards the counter.

"JC," said Kim, in a very small voice. "I'm scared."

"Don't be," JC said immediately. "Take it easy. We've faced worse. It's just . . . dark."

"What have you got to be scared of, Kim?" said Happy. "You're a ghost! You're already dead!"

"I don't think the dark cares whether you're alive or dead," said Kim. "It's the end of everything. Can't you feel it?"

"I'd offer you one of my pills," said Happy. "Except I don't think I have anything that would affect ectoplasm."

"Thanks for the thought, though," said Kim.

"Have you got anything incendiary?" said Melody.

"Only metaphorically," said Happy.

The darkness was still moving steadily forward. It had almost reached the counter. Everyone backed up against the back wall, staying inside the candlelight. The flickering, unsteady light only held on behind the counter itself now, as the rest of the room was swallowed up by the dark. The yellow light seemed to shrink back from the approaching dark, as though it were afraid of it. The darkness came right up to the far edge of the bar-counter, so close now any of them could have reached across the counter and touched it. JC picked up an empty brandy glass and threw it out into the dark. They all tensed, straining their ears, waiting for the crash of breaking glass . . . but it never came. No sound at all from inside the dark.

"It's cold," said Happy. "Can you feel that cold? It's sort of like a traditional cold spot—an energy drain. The temperature's plummeting. It's like the darkness is sucking all the heat out of the room. Or the energy. Maybe all the life . . ."

"You can usually Do Something to stop things like that, Happy," said JC. "Are you sure there isn't anything you can do about this?"

"There's nothing here to do anything to!" said Happy. "I keep telling you; there's nothing alive or conscious in that dark, so there's nothing there for me to work with! We're trapped here, and we're helpless. Go on, say something encouraging; I dare you."

The darkness swept over the far edge of the counter, and edged forward, inch by inch. The candles disappeared into it, one at a time, their light snapping off. JC and Brook grabbed a candle each and pulled them right back to the inner edge of the counter, to preserve their light. JC, Brook, Happy, and Melody, and the ghost girl Kim, all huddled together, looking desperately around them; but there was nowhere left for them to go. The dark had already swallowed up both ends of the bar, and they couldn't back away any further. They were already pressed up against the empty shelves that had once been full of bottles. Until they'd exploded.

Brook looked bitterly at JC. "You're supposed to be the great expert; you're supposed to know what to do about things like this! Do Something! There must be something you can do!"

"I'm thinking," said JC. "If anyone else has an idea, feel free to contribute."

"I've still got my machine-pistol," said Melody. "But without something to aim it at . . ."

"Hang on to it," said Happy. "In case we need . . . a final way out."

"Really not helping, Happy," said JC.

He yanked off his sunglasses, took a step forward, and glared at the darkness creeping across the counter like a great black wall. His eyes glowed fierce and golden. And the dark stopped, holding its position on the counter like a dark dividing line. And then it pressed forward again.

"Ah," said JC. "I was hoping for rather more than that."

He broke off as the dark surged forward. It came on in a rush, like a predator pouncing on cornered prey, rolling right over the last of the candlelight. The dark slammed forward and filled all the room. The candlelight disappeared, gone in a moment, and even the golden glow of JC's eyes blinked out. The dark hit the far wall behind the bar; and there was nothing left but darkness everywhere.

''''''''''''''''''''''''''''''''

"Everyone stand still!" JC said sharply. "Nobody move an inch! Now, sound off! Is everyone still here?"

"I'm here, JC," said Kim.

"I'm somewhere here," said Happy. "Can't see a damned thing. Melody, are you here?"

"Of course I'm here!" said Melody. "Right beside you. Here, this is my hand. Grab onto it. That way we can't be separated. I will never let you go, Happy, never leave you. You do know that, right?"

"Yes," said Happy. "But I do like to be reminded occasionally. I can feel your hand in mine, feel your shoulder pressing up against mine. But I can't feel your presence, can't *feel* anything . . ."

"Brook?" said JC. "Adrian? Speak up, man; are you still with us?"

"Yes," said the barman. "Sorry. Couldn't say anything there, for a moment. It's hard to . . . to . . ."

"It's all right," said JC. "Trust me; we're all as shaken as you are."

"Maybe more," said Happy.

"Shut up, Happy," said JC. "All right; everyone stay exactly where you are! This would be a really bad time to go wandering off on your own and get lost. Adrian, you may hold my arm if you like."

"Got you," said Brook.

"I said hold it, not crush the bloody thing!"

"Sorry."

"I wish I could hold you, JC," said Kim. "I feel divorced from the world at the best of times, and this really isn't helping."

"Okay," said JC. "It's important we all to stick together. The light might have gone out of the world, but we haven't gone anywhere. We're still in the bar. I can feel the floor under my feet and the shelves digging into my back. So the dark hasn't transported us anywhere. That's important. We're still in the bar, still in the King's Arms. We just have to figure out how to get the lights back on."

"Very practical," said Melody. "Almost inspiring. Can't say it's helping me feel any better. I've never known anything like this, never encountered a darkness as . . . complete as this. I really can't see my hand in front of my face. I know it's there because I can feel my palm bumping against the tip of my nose; but I can't see anything. Not even those little flashes of light you sometimes get when you turn out the light to go to sleep. And it is so cold, JC! I mean really cold! I am freezing my tits off!"

"It's the dark," said Happy. "No light, no energy, and eventually no life. We can't stay here, JC. The dark is killing us by inches."

"Come on, Happy," said JC, a bit desperately. "Are you sure you can't sense *anything* here in the dark with us? Any motivating force?"

"No," said Happy. "I can't sense anything; as though the dark is suppressing my ESP. I can't See anything; and normally I could See your souls shining at the bottom of a coal mine. Small and insignificant things that they are . . . I can't hear anything except your voices. And all I can feel is the cold. My hands are going numb. Soon I won't be able to feel your hand, Melody."

"Don't say that," said Melody. "I won't be separated from you. I won't."

"What are we going to do?" said Brook, his voice rising hysterically. "I hate this! I hate being here. It's horrible."

"Well, not crushing my arm with your hand would be a good start!" said JC. "Seriously, Adrian, calm down! Or I swear I will find your head in the dark and slap you a good one!"

"Sorry," said Brook.

There was a clicking sound, followed by several more.

"What was that?" Happy said immediately. "You all heard that, right? Somebody tell me what the hell that was!"

"I'm trying to get my lighter to light," said JC. "Ah! Damn!"

"Now what?" said Melody.

"I burned my hand on the lighter's flame," said JC. "And yes, it does hurt quite a lot, thank you all for asking. So the flame is quite definitely burning, but we can't see it. We're being prevented from seeing it, by the dark. Okay, I've turned it off again. Now I have taken off my sunglasses. Can anyone see my eyes shining? Even a little bit?"

"No," said Kim. "Not even a glimmer. And I can usually see them even when you've got your eyes closed, when you're sleeping."

"Far too much information there," said Melody.

"It's like the dark at the end of the world," said Happy.

"When the sun and the stars have all gone out because it's all over."

"It's not over until I say it's over," said JC. "Now everyone hush and let me think."

They stood together in the dark for some time. They had no way of knowing how long. It was hard to get any feel for time passing with nothing to judge it against. Minutes could feel like hours in the dark. Every insomniac knows that. JC glared helplessly about him. He still had his sunglasses in his hand, hoping his altered eyes would let him see something if he gave them enough time to adjust . . . but there was nothing around him except the dark. And the cold. And the silence. JC's thoughts raced frantically back and forth, unable to settle on anything for long, as he raised and discarded one desperate plan after another. There had to be something he could do . . . He'd never felt so small, so helpless and vulnerable . . . It was like being a small child again, abandoned by his parents to the long marches of the night, after the night-light had finally been switched off.

No-one ever really remembers how scared of the dark we are as children because we couldn't bear it.

"I really don't like this," Happy said miserably. "I was very afraid of the dark as a child. Until my psychic abilities kicked in; and then things got really bad. Because then I knew for sure that there really are monsters in the night."

"I was scared of the dark when I was a little girl," said Melody. "I thought there were things in the shadows, in my bedroom, watching me. Bad things. Waiting for me to fall asleep so they could get me. As I grew older, I swore I wouldn't let myself be afraid of anything. And mostly I'm not."

"Only mostly?" said Happy.

"I'm scared of losing you," said Melody.

"Never happen," said Happy. "Though I must say, it is entirely typical of you to wait till we're trapped together in the dark, to guilt-trip me."

They laughed quietly together in the dark.

"I hated the dark when I was young because there could be anything in it," said JC. "Anything at all."

"How the hell did you people ever get to be professional Ghost Finders?" said Brook.

"Therapy," said JC. "And pay-back."

"How's that working out for you?" said Brook.

"I found Kim, in the dark," said JC. "And that makes up for everything."

"Darling," said Kim. "You pick the oddest times to say the nicest things."

"Hold everything!" said JC. "Hush, people; let me think this through. It's just . . . dark. Right? Nothing actually there. No physical threat at all apart from the cold. So we're not in any real danger at all . . ."

"I like the sound of that," said Happy. "Keep talking . . ."

"If we stay in the dark long enough, we'll freeze," said Melody.

"Or maybe even . . . fade away," said Kim. "I think the dark is erosive to our minds and our souls. No living thing can hope to survive for long in conditions like these." She paused, as a thought struck her. "JC, the dark followed me back here. Followed me inside the inn. Maybe, if I was to leave the inn again, the dark would follow me out. I could lead it away; and you'd all be safe in the light again."

"We are not giving anyone up," JC said firmly. "And especially not after I got you back."

"But I'm already dead!" said Kim.

"No!" said JC. "We don't give up anyone on the team to the forces of evil! Not ever! Especially when I've suddenly had this really excellent idea. The dark is stronger than any one of us. But all of us together? Do you remember, Happy, when you joined our minds and souls together to make contact with the ghost of the old god Lud, in the dark of London Undertowen? We all glowed so very brightly, pushing back the dark. We all glowed golden, like my eyes."

"Yes!" said Kim. "I remember! We shone like the sun . . ."

"I can't see your eyes glowing now, JC," said Happy doubtfully.

"But that's only me," said JC. "If you can bind us all together again . . ."

"Happy?" said Melody, when he didn't immediately reply. "Can you do that?"

"I don't see why not," said Happy; and they could hear his smile even if they couldn't see it.

Happy reached out with his mind, forcing it through the resisting dark, jumping from one mind to another, linking them in one formidable thought. He even pulled in Brook's mind, much to the barman's surprise. And then Happy led them all in one great shout of defiance against the dark. They blazed with a great golden light, as though some inner fire had ignited their souls. They burned so brightly in the dark, visible to each other at last, despite all the dark could do to stop them. Like living candles, made of light.

The darkness fell back, unable to face this new light.

It retreated back over the counter, and back across the room; and more and more of the main bar returned, visible again. The dark swept back, in full retreat now, unable to face or block the power of this new, overwhelming light. Until, finally, the dark hit the outer wall, and the windows, and disappeared back through them. And was gone. The main bar was back, looking exactly as it had, every detail sharp and clear in the steady electric light. Happy let out a great sigh, and collapsed, utterly exhausted. His esper link disappeared in a moment, and everybody was alone in their own head again. The golden glow snapped off. Melody was there to catch Happy in her arms as he fell and hold him. JC vaulted over the top of the bar-counter and ran across the room to peer out the window.

He grinned back at the others.

"I can see the moon! And the stars! Everything's back . . . and listen! You can hear the storm again! Everything's back to normal!"

"Well," said Brook, uncertainly, "I don't know about that. As near to normal as it ever gets around here, perhaps." He shook his head, frowning. "Funny; it feels like I've forgotten something, but I can't remember what. A dream of . . . glowing, like a star. But it's already fading."

"Best way," said JC, striding back to the counter. "Let it go."

Kim burst through the bar to meet him, and did her happy dance in the middle of the room, circling JC and stamping her feet and waving her arms. JC even accompanied her for a few steps.

"Since we are now in a winning mood," he announced loudly, "I say we go upstairs and sort out all the bad rooms. Do something positive about the ghost girl Lydia, and the Timeslips, and find out what's in the room that eats people and kick its nasty arse. Because that's what we're here for."

"Cocky," Happy said to Melody, as he got his strength back and his feet under him again. "Definitely cocky. I swear, if I could reduce him to pill form, all my troubles would be over."

EIGHT

CHANGING ROOMS

JC and Brook led the way up the backstairs to the upper floor. JC took the steps two at a time, grinning broadly. Brook stomped along behind him, more or less resignedly. It was hard to say no to JC when he had the bit between his teeth, ready to dash headlong into action and to hell with the consequences. JC glanced back at Brook and flashed him his best encouraging smile. Brook looked stonily back at him. JC shrugged and pressed on. He swaggered out onto the landing and waited for the others to catch up. He could hear Happy and Melody and Kim talking quietly together, further down the stairs.

"It does seem to me," said Happy, "that we are doing this whole joining together thing a little more often than I am comfortable with. Partly because I am, after all, a very private person . . ."

"With so many things it's best to be private about," murmured Melody.

"And also because this whole shining with a very bright light thing strikes me as not always being a good thing," said Happy, doggedly.

"It feels easier every time we do it," said Kim. "As though we're learning some useful, and perhaps necessary, skill."

Happy sniffed loudly. "Is there something you're not telling us, Kim?"

"More than you can possibly imagine," said Kim, smiling brightly.

"We do blaze very brightly when we join together," said Melody. "And everyone knows . . . the candle that burns twice as bright lasts half as long. It worries me, as to exactly what it is we're burning. Our life-force? Our souls?"

Happy sniggered. "Did you just say . . ."

"No I didn't, and you know it," Melody said sternly. "Try and keep up with the adults in this conversation, Happy."

"I have considered the problem," said Happy. "Nothing like being permanently paranoid to give you a healthy interest in all the things that can kill you . . . When we blaze so very brightly, you have to wonder whose attention we might be attracting. Nothing like an unexpected light in the dark to catch Something's eye. All sorts of Somethings . . ."

"Well, we know that the inn, or perhaps more properly the local power source, has been blazing brightly enough to pull in all kinds of Really Bad Things," said Melody. "Like moths to a flame . . ."

"Perhaps we're drawing the attention of whatever it was that first reached down from Outside and put its mark on JC, in the London Underground," said Happy. "After all, the light we project when we're joined does seem very like the light that glows from his eyes . . . Anything you'd like to add, Kim?"

"I'm not disagreeing," Kim said carefully.

"But you're not answering the question," said Happy.

"Some questions have no straightforward answers," said Kim.

"I am changing the subject," announced Melody. "On the grounds that you are making my head ache even more than usual. Hey, JC! Question. Why are we still messing about with the problems of this haunted inn when we know the real trouble comes from the storm raging outside?"

"Because we can do something about haunted inns," said JC, not looking back. "Haunted inns are in the job description. We know what to do. We don't know enough about the storm or the power behind it. Not yet. Happy, talk to me!"

"Any particular subject?" said Happy.

"You said earlier . . . that what was going on here had attracted forces from Beyond, luring them into our reality. So if we can shut down what's happening in the rooms on this floor, then maybe we can break, or at the very least weaken, the link between the inn and the Powers infesting it."

"Good idea," said Happy. "Worth a try. I suppose."

"If only things were that simple," sighed Kim.

They all gathered together at the top of the stairs, looking up and down the long corridor as it stretched away to either side. The landing was presenting its best Perfectly Normal, Nothing To See Here, Move Along face; but none of them were buying it. They could all feel a cold, spiky tension on the still air, a feeling of forces lying in wait, of things waiting to happen. Bad things. The light was steady, and the shadows lay still, and all the doors were safely, sensibly shut.

But the landing still felt like one big trap, waiting to be sprung.

"All right," said Happy. "Where do we start? I'm spoilt for choice, for things to flinch away from."

JC ignored him, giving all his attention to Brook. "Which of these rooms contain Timeslips?"

"You have to be careful," said Brook, looking about him uneasily. "You can't be sure of anything, here. The rooms move around, behind closed doors. Any door you choose might open onto a different Time period."

"And yet you let us stay in rooms up here, without warning us!" said Melody, angrily.

"I said I'm sorry!" said Brook.

"And that's supposed to be enough?" said Melody. "Where's my gun . . ."

"Leave the man alone, Mel," JC said firmly. "He is our native guide in treacherous territory. We need him."

"Yeah," growled Happy. "We can always use someone to throw into a dangerous situation, just to see what happens."

"Don't listen to the nasty telepath, Adrian," said JC. "We would never do that to you. Unless it was necessary. Or funny. Now, tell me how to find a room with a Timeslip. There must be a way . . ."

The barman nodded slowly, reluctantly. "You do

develop a . . . feel for them after a while. That's why I thought you'd be safe in the rooms I chose for you. Be fair; whatever you experienced in those rooms, it wasn't anything to do with Timeslips, was it?"

"Still looking for my gun . . ." said Melody.

"There's a door down here," Brook said quickly. "It's got the right kind of feel to it."

He headed quickly off down the right-hand corridor, looking closely at each door he passed but not stopping until he was half-way down the landing. JC led the others after him, all of them keeping a careful eye out for anything unnatural, or even out of the ordinary. The doors they passed stayed firmly shut, apparently perfectly normal. Brook stood uneasily before his chosen door. It didn't look any different from any of the others. He took out his keys, fumbled through them to find one particular key, then stopped. He looked miserably at JC, who nodded firmly back. Brook unlocked the door, turned the door-handle very carefully, then pushed the door open an inch. He stepped back from the door, retreating quickly until his back slammed up against the wall on the far side of the landing. JC gestured for the others to stay put and moved forward to stand beside Brook.

"What's in this room, Adrian? What lies behind that door? Which particular part of Time Past does it hold?"

"I don't know," said Brook, all his attention focused on the slightly open door. "I never know. The only way to find out is to look inside. But be careful; what's there has a way of sucking you in . . ."

"We ain't frightened of no room," said JC. "Only . . . reasonably cautious."

He moved forward and pushed the door all the way

open with one hard shove. Everyone tensed, trying to be ready for anything; but nothing emerged from the room. JC moved cautiously forward, one step at a time, until he was standing right before the open doorway. As close as he could get without actually entering the room itself. He planted both feet firmly on the threshold and placed both hands against either side of the door-frame, before looking inside the room. The room looked placidly back at him. It seemed like a perfectly ordinary, everyday room. All the usual furnishings. No-one there. JC leaned forward, studying every detail.

"Don't go in!" Brook said loudly from the far side of the corridor. "Crossing the threshold takes you out of this Time and into the Past. And once that door slams shut, you're lost in the Past. Like all my missing guests."

"Are you sure this is a Timeslip?" said JC. "I can't see anything obviously old-fashioned."

"Well, there are two clues," said Brook. "First, none of my rooms have furnishings like that. I had the whole place redecorated when I took over. And second, that's bright sunlight falling through the room's window."

"Ah. Yes," said JC. "Look at that daylight when it's night here. Bit of a giveaway, that. Well spotted, Adrian! So the room appearing so normal was part of the trap, to lure me in. Interesting . . ."

He leaned into the room, took hold of the door's handle, and pulled the door closed again. He stood and looked at his hand for a long moment, half-expecting it to look or feel different from having entered the Past. And then he turned back to Happy and Melody and Kim, all of whom were watching him carefully from a respectable distance.

"Why have Timeslips at all?" said JC. "I mean, ghosts and monsters I can understand, but . . . traps to drag people back in Time? What purpose does that serve?"

"I think it all comes down to the local power source and the unnatural force contained in the storm," said Melody. "With such sheer power involved, it's putting an unbearable strain on local reality. Like Happy said, the rage driving the storm is the rage of the sacrificed victim. I hate to theorise without proper equipment around to back me up, but . . . I think the storm's been building for centuries, becoming so powerful in its own right that it's . . . broken Time. Or at least, local Time. You might say, Time is out of joint, in this vicinity."

"Time . . ." Happy said thoughtfully. "Always tricky . . . I've never felt the same about Time since the Travelling Doctor explained it to me. Anyway, if the storm currently raging round this inn really was born in the days of the Druids, then what we have here is the Past directly affecting the Present. Which is never good. If the storm is powering the Timeslips, that means there's a direct connection between what's inside the inn and what's outside it. So whatever we can do to weaken, disrupt, or even destroy the Timeslips . . . should have a direct effect on the storm."

"I don't know which particular pills you're on right now," said JC. "But I'd stick with them if I were you."

Melody shot JC a hard look but said nothing.

JC looked at Brook. "Have you ever noticed any pattern to the Timeslips? Do they appear in any order? Does any one room seem to prefer a particular Time or period?"

"No," said Brook. "None of this has ever made any sense to me. It's always seemed . . . entirely random. And there's never any warning! The bad doors come and go; and so do the poor people who get trapped inside them."

JC turned to Melody. "Come on, you're the girl science geek expert on this team! Think of something we can try as an experiment. Something to give us more information to work with. And don't tell me all the things you could do if only you had your proper equipment! I need something we can do right now. So think! Improvise!"

"Okay," said Melody, frostily. "What if we sent someone into that room, on the end of a length of rope, tied around his waist? The rope would link him to the Present corridor even when he was in the room's Past; so even if the door did try to close, we could always yank the volunteer back out again."

"She's not looking at me, but she's talking about me," said Happy.

"The rope could snap," said JC. "Or be broken by the forces inside the room."

"And besides," said Kim. "We haven't got a rope."

"Imagine my relief," said Happy.

"All right, one of you think of something!" said Melody.

"Keep the noise down, children," said JC. "Daddy's thinking . . ."

"Oh, I feel so much safer," said Happy.

"The doors open onto Past Time," JC said slowly. "People walk into the room, into the Past, the door shuts, and the visitor is trapped in that Past moment. But! If we could persuade the doors to open onto the exact Time and moment when the doors last closed, and the person was taken, those people should still be there! Time wouldn't have changed or moved on, for them! Which means, if we could persuade those doors to open . . . we could rescue all the lost people! Yes!"

"Love the theory," said Happy. "But how would we do that?"

"Trust you to shoot down a perfectly good theory with a practical question," said JC.

"No! Wait!" Melody said excitedly. "How does each room choose a Time? Each room holds or perhaps generates a different moment of Past Time; so someone or something in the background must be making a decision as to which room holds which Time. And so far, the only thing we've encountered in this inn that even seems like a conscious entity, capable of making such decisions . . . is the blonde woman!"

"I'm not going to like where this is going; am I?" said Happy.

"The blonde woman does seem to like you," said JC.

"It's not mutual!" said Happy.

"She does seem . . . attracted to you, Happy," said Melody.

"I am not volunteering for anything," Happy said firmly. "With or without a rope."

"You first encountered the woman in your room," said JC. "I say we go back there and see if we can summon her. So we can talk to her."

"No!" said Happy. "This is a really bad idea! You don't want to talk to her. You don't know . . . You don't know what she's like, what she's capable of . . ."

"You won't be alone, this time," said Melody.

"We'll be right there with you," said JC. "We won't let anything bad happen to you. I promise."

"What do you plan to do if she does turn up again?" said Happy.

"Improvise!" said JC, grinning broadly. "Suddenly and violently and all over the place! You said it yourself, Happy; she's not a ghost, or any kind of surviving personality. Just a mass of emotions that's somehow hung on for centuries, manifesting as the storm outside, and a blonde woman. If we can't see off a bundle of retained memories, we don't deserve to call ourselves Ghost Finders. Come on, my children, we can do this! We summon her up, then either force or trick her into opening the doors into the Past. And then we rescue all the people trapped inside them!"

"But how are we going to do that?" said Happy.

"Don't spoil another good theory with your voice of reason!" said JC. "I'm working on it!"

"Maybe we should join together again, and glow at her," said Kim, "Like we did in the bar."

Everyone looked at her, and they all thought many things, but no-one actually said anything.

"Just a thought," said Kim.

Brook led the way, back to the room he'd given Happy. The door was still closed, and Brook looked it over carefully before nodding that everything was all right. Kim strode forward and stared firmly at the closed door.

"Don't See anything. Don't hear anything. Can't feel a damned thing."

She walked right through the door, and disappeared.

Everyone jumped a little. There was a short pause, then Kim ghosted back through the door and smiled brilliantly at everyone.

"All clear! No ghosties, no ghoulies, and very definitely no long-leggity anythings. Open her up, Brookie, and let's get this show on the road."

Happy stood at the back of the group as Brook opened the door, pushed it open a few inches, and stepped quickly to one side. JC slammed the door all the way open and strode into the room, turning the lights on with a quick flick of his hand. Kim swept in after him, peering about with great interest. Melody took Happy's hand in hers, held it tightly, and led him into the room. Happy swallowed hard. If Melody hadn't been holding on to his hand so firmly, he would have turned and bolted. Brook came in last, stopping inside the doorway.

"Happy?" Melody said quietly. "What happened to you in here? What did that blonde bitch do to you?"

"It wasn't so much what she did," said Happy. "It was what she said, what she showed me . . ."

"What was that?" said Melody.

"I'm not sure, now," said Happy. "Maybe . . . the true nature of my own mortality."

They all looked around the room, taking their time, and the room looked back at them, seeming entirely normal. Blocky furniture, too-small bed, dull wallpaper, and unwavering electric light.

"Just as I left it," said Happy. "Except that the door I saw in the far wall isn't there any more."

"Where was the door, exactly?" said JC.

Happy pointed out the spot on the far wall, with a surprisingly steady hand, but he couldn't bring himself to go any closer. Melody was still holding on to his hand, giving him what strength and support she could. Kim went right up to the far wall and studied it closely; her nose almost touching the wallpaper. She frowned and turned back to JC.

"There's something here, JC. Something that doesn't belong in this room, or even this reality. This wall, this little bit of our Space and Time, has been overwritten by some force from Outside. It's still there, in principle, waiting to be imposed on our reality again. Like this."

She stepped back and snapped her fingers imperiously. Suddenly, the door was back in place again. Happy cried out involuntarily but held his ground. He looked at the door for a long moment and nodded quickly.

"Yes. That's it. That's the door I saw before."

"You said . . . there was a blood-red corridor on the other side of that door," said JC.

"It wasn't a real corridor," said Happy. "It only looked like one."

"What was it?" said Melody.

"Death," said Happy. "It was death."

"Maybe I should go back out onto the landing," said Brook.

"You stay right where you are, native guide," said JC without looking round. He moved over to stand with Happy. "The blonde woman you saw. Was she part of the corridor?"

"I don't know," said Happy. "I don't think so . . . Connected to it, maybe. One of the faces on what's happening here. The woman, the corridor, the storm . . . they're all the same thing, really. This is a bad idea, JC. You really don't want to summon her. You remember what the dark did to us, down in the bar. She was worse. Crueller."

"Would this woman come to you if you called?" JC said carefully.

"I don't know," said Happy.

JC looked to Kim. "What do we have that we could use to compel her?"

"You're not listening to me!" Happy said desperately. "This is a really bad idea! You have no idea of the kind of Power you're dealing with here!"

"Do you have a better idea?" said JC, quite seriously. "No? Then we go with what we have. Kim?"

"She's not a ghost," Kim said thoughtfully. "She's the human face of the rage in the storm . . . All that's left of the human sacrifice who began all this . . . Happy, can you remember what you were doing, what you were feeling, here in this room, when the door first appeared in the wall?"

"Yes," said Happy. "I was sitting right there, at the writing-desk."

"Okay," said JC. "Go sit there again."

Happy sat down at the desk, and looked at the pill boxes and bottles still set out before him. He didn't touch any of them. Melody crouched down beside him. She put a gentle hand on his arm and patted it a few times. He didn't look at her.

"What were you thinking, Happy?" Melody said quietly.

"I was thinking about dying," said Happy, in a quiet, distant voice. "Thinking about killing myself and what a relief that would be. Not to have to carry the weight of my world on my shoulders any more."

"Oh, Happy," said Melody.

"And then the door showed up, in the far wall," said Happy. "It opened on its own, to show me a corridor that led to death. It was trying to tempt me. When that didn't work, the woman appeared. Except, she didn't try to sucker me in, like the corridor. I suppose you could say, in her own way she talked me out of it. She showed me the true face of death. She saved me. Why would she do that?"

"Perhaps because there's enough left of the original sacrificial victim to appreciate and value life," said Melody. "Okay; I think . . . you need to remember what you were thinking, and feeling. That could draw her back. Do you need your pills?"

"No," said Happy. "Not for that."

He sat still, his head bowed, thinking. About the things that were never far from his thoughts because the tiredness, the bone-deep, soul-deep weariness at the bottom of it all never left him. Melody crouched, close beside him. She'd taken her hand off his arm, so as not to distract him. She could see the pain in him, clear as a wound; and it hurt her almost beyond bearing to know she couldn't help him. Of everyone in that room, she was the only one who could even guess at what this was costing Happy.

The door in the far wall swung slowly open, folding back against the wall to reveal its blood-red corridor. Everyone in the room made some sort of noise as they took in the crimson, almost organic corridor walls, which seemed to fall away forever. To look at it was enough to disturb the thoughts and soil the spirit. It wasn't only death; it was the end of all hope. A road you could walk out of life that promised neither Heaven nor Hell, just the end of everything.

Happy slowly turned around on his chair and looked into the blood-red corridor. He smiled; and it was a brief, savage thing. He considered the corridor's promise, then spat once on the floor, contemptuously. Because when the time did come to end his life, he would be responsible for it. No-one else.

The blonde woman was suddenly there, appearing out of nowhere, strolling calmly down the blood-red corridor. As though she'd always been there, and they hadn't noticed. She seemed to take a long time to reach the opening into Happy's room, as if she was crossing some impossible distance, approaching from some unimaginable direction. She finally reached the doorway and stopped dead, right on the threshold. She looked into the room with cold, dead eyes and a disturbing smile. She looked around at the group gathered before her, dismissed them in a moment, and gave all her attention to Happy.

"Some people never learn. Or else they're suckers for punishment. Haven't you suffered enough, little man?"

Melody was up on her feet in a moment, moving quickly forward to put herself bodily between Happy and the blonde woman.

"Leave my man alone, you bitch!"

The woman cocked her head to one side, like a bird, and considered Melody thoughtfully. "What will you do if I don't? Shoot me with your concealed weapon? I don't think so. I've been dead a long, long time . . ."

"But that's all you've got, isn't it?" said Melody. "You

have death; while Happy and I have life, and love. Show her, Happy."

"What?" said Happy.

"Link with me," said Melody. "Share your thoughts, and your pain, and everything else you have, with me. And then hit her with it, right between the eyes. Show her what she's missing."

Happy grinned suddenly and rose to his feet. He took both of Melody's hands in his and held them firmly. Their eyes met; and everyone in the room felt something move between them. Happy and Melody turned to face the blonde woman in the doorway, and Happy blasted her with everything in their hearts and in their souls, all at once. The woman fell back a step, as though she'd been hit; and then she threw back her head and let out a lost, despairing howl. Some unseen force picked her up and sent her flying backwards down the blood-red corridor, away from something she couldn't face.

And from out on the landing, there came the sound of doors slamming open.

JC raced out of the room and onto the landing, and all the way up and down the corridor, people came spilling out of the open-doored rooms, looking dazed and confused, but clearly very glad to be back in a world and Time they recognised. Brook came out to join JC, saw all his lost guests come home at last, and whooped with joy, jumping up and down on the spot.

"They're back! They're back! Oh you beauty, JC! You did it!"

The returned men and women looked at Brook. There were quite a few more of them than he'd admitted to.

They started forward, filling the landing with questions. JC grabbed Brook by the arm and held him still.

"Get them out of here," he said crisply. "God knows how long those doors will stay open, or how long the blonde woman's control will stay broken. As long as the guests stay here, there's always a chance the rooms will pull them back in . . . So gather them up, don't stop to answer any questions, get them all down the stairs, then send them down the road to Bishop's Fording. They should be safe there. Yes, I know it's raining; yes, I know the road is flooded; and no, I don't care! Do whatever you have to to get them moving. Now go! Go! Go!"

Brook quickly rounded up the bewildered guests, and chased them down the stairs with a mix of publican's authority and really harsh language. Their departing feet made a muffled thunder in the enclosed stairway, and Brook drove them on from behind. He paused, half-way down the stairs, to grin and wink at JC, then he drove his guests on again until they'd all disappeared out of sight. JC allowed himself a brief, satisfied smile, then he went back into Happy's room.

The door in the far wall was gone, with no trace left behind to show it had ever been there. Happy and Melody were standing together, staring into each other's faces, lost in each other's eyes. Kim shook her head and went back to join JC. She shrugged prettily.

"Soppy things," she said kindly. "But it looks good on them. Love is the drug, I suppose. Still, if they hadn't done it, I bet we could have. Right, JC?"

"Love conquers all," JC said solemnly.

Happy finally looked around, to glare at JC. "You used me as bait."

"It worked, didn't it?" said JC. "And you did help to save a whole crowd of lost souls. So be proud! I think the two of you basically overpowered Blondie, with your love and devotion. Either that, or you disgusted her with your lust for life. Or possibly, vice versa. Either way, I am very pleased with you; but if I hear one chorus of 'Love Is All Around,' I will puke. There are limits."

"It was a good plan," Melody said, grudgingly. "But you do realise, all we did was scare her away. She will be back."

"Counting on it," JC said brightly. "I'm not finished with her yet. Now, while we are still in a winning mood, let us go deal with the room that eats people. I am in the mood to kick its arse or whatever it has instead of an arse. You find me something kickable, and I'll kick it. We might not be able to save its victims; but we can at least boot it out of our world. Adrian! Adrian, where are you . . . Oh. Yes. I sent him downstairs, didn't I? Never mind, we can do this on our own. Oh yes we can."

"Have you been at my pills, JC?" said Happy.

"He doesn't need pills," said Kim, proudly. "He was born weird."

"Come along, children," said JC.

He strode out of the room and onto the landing, then paused to glare up and down the long corridor. Rooms stretched away to either side, all of the doors closed again. All very still, like the pregnant pause before the storm. Happy and Melody squeezed through the door to join him, refusing to be separated even for a moment. Kim got fed up waiting for them and ghosted through the wall to stand beside JC. He bounced up and down on his feet, raised his voice, and addressed the empty air in a loud and challenging voice.

"Come on then, you horrible, hungry, little room, you! Where are you? Don't be shy; show yourself! Or don't you have the balls to face a real challenge?"

"Please don't taunt the deadly supernatural threat," murmured Melody. "Not when I haven't got my proper defensive equipment to hand."

Kim looked up and down the long corridor, frowning prettily. "It's hiding. I can't See anything. Happy, can you See anything?"

"More than you can possibly imagine," said Happy indistinctly.

They all looked round in time to see Happy knock back a single fat pill, canary yellow with ice-blue stripes. He dry swallowed the bulky thing with the ease of long practice, then shook his head hard. His eyes bulged, his breathing grew steadily deeper, and he smiled broadly. He started snorting and grunting, and stamped one foot on the ground like an animal getting ready to charge.

"Oh hell," said JC. "What's he taken now?"

"Something he usually only takes with me in mind," said Melody. "I'd stand well back if I were you."

"But what does it do?" said Kim.

"Amplifies some of his more . . . basic instincts," said Melody.

"The two of you never cease to appal me," said JC. "Really. I mean it."

"I can See you!" Happy said loudly, his whole body orientated on the right-hand side of the landing. "Don't think I can't See you!"

And he charged straight down the landing, like a bull who'd spotted a way past the matador's cloak. JC and Melody and Kim hurried after Happy, until he slammed to a sudden halt and stood quivering like a pointing dog, facing one particular room. He grunted and growled at the closed door, his hands clenched into white-knuckled fists. Still grinning his very disturbing grin.

"This is it! I can tell . . . This is the room where if you go in, you don't get to come out again. Except, of course, this isn't a room and never was."

"What are you Seeing, Happy?" said JC, moving cautiously in beside him.

"Oh, I'm Seeing all kinds of things," said Happy, staring at the closed door with wide, unblinking eyes. "JC, you wouldn't believe some of the things I'm Seeing. Hello, can any of you hear that? It sounds like . . . a baby, crying."

JC looked at Melody, then at Kim, and turned reluctantly back to Happy. "I don't hear anything," he said carefully.

"Of course you don't!" said Happy. Sweat was pouring down his face, but his eyes still didn't blink. "You were born with mental blinkers on, like everyone else. Don't worry; it's not actually a baby. It's something that's learned to sound like a baby crying, to lure people in. But I know better. I know a lure when I hear one . . ."

He went suddenly quiet, glaring at the door. JC looked at Happy, at the others, then at the door. It gave every appearance of being completely safe and ordinary, but JC still couldn't bring himself to touch it. All the hairs were standing up on the back of his neck and his arms, in ancient, instinctual warning. It felt like the door was watching him . . .

"Excuse me, everyone," said Kim. "But what are you all looking at? I didn't hear any baby, and I don't see any door. You're all staring at a perfectly unremarkable stretch of wall."

"I told you. It's not a room, it's a trap!" Happy said loudly. "And since it's a trap designed to lure in the living, you can't see it, Kim. Being dead, as you are. The room doesn't want you. Because you ain't got no body, and therefore no chewy bits."

"I think I feel left out," said Kim. "Passed over."

"Ghost humour," said Happy. "Ho ho ho!"

"Calm the hell down, Happy, or I swear I will stick a nozzle up your bottom and rinse your insides out with Ritalin," said Melody. "When this is all over, I am going to have to sit down and work out some serious checks and balances for you."

"Fun time!" said Happy.

JC tore his gaze away from the door, walked back to the top of the stairs, and shouted down them. "Brook! Get back up here! You're needed!"

He waited, but there was no response. JC growled under his breath and tapped one foot impatiently.

"I could ghost through this section of wall," Kim said helpfully. "Or stick my head through and take a quick peek at what's in there . . ."

"Really wouldn't do that," Happy said immediately. "Really bad idea, ghost girl."

"But you said it isn't interested in me," said Kim.

"Not to eat," said Happy. "Doesn't mean it couldn't do something very nasty to your ectoplasm. I suppose there must be something Out There, that eats ecto-plasm . . . There are all kinds of predators, after all. Hate to think what they'd excrete, though . . ."

Melody decided she didn't want to say anything about that and considered the door-handle before her. "Do you suppose it's locked?"

"That door is only locked when it wants to be," Happy said wisely.

JC gave up on the stairs and came back to join them, so he could glare at the closed door, close-up. "Come on, Happy, aren't you picking up anything behind that door?"

"I keep telling you!" said Happy. "There is no room behind this door! A lot of what's happening in this bloody inn is destructive energies and emotions, mixed and fused together, manifesting in physical ways . . . But what we have here is different. This is a predator from Outside that's forced its way through some crack in the walls of the world. There's nothing on the other side of the door, or at least nothing you or I could hope to recognise or understand. It's out of this world. Like Kim said, there is no door there. Just something that's learned to look like a door, for the same reason it learned to sound like a baby crying. To lure the food through and into its belly."

"All right," said JC. "This isn't a haunted room, like yours. Or a receptacle for a piece of broken Time. This isn't another side effect of the sacrificed victim, or the storm, or the local power source. This isn't a room; it's a Beast."

"Finally, someone is listening to me!" said Happy. "Marvellous, wonderful; I may faint. Look! There's

Something in there, a really powerful Something. Possibly one of the Abominations from the Outer Rings. They're always trying to get in at us."

"But if it is some kind of Beast," said Melody, "what's it doing here? What does it want with us?"

"It's hungry," said Happy. "It's always hungry."

"So there's absolutely no chance of getting any of its victims back?" said JC.

"No," said Happy. "They're gone. Not even any bones left . . ."

"Then there's no need to play by the rules any longer," said JC, rubbing his hands together. "No more Mister Nice Guy! Happy; what would happen if I were to open this door?"

"What do you think?" said Happy. "You might as well soak your arm in barbecue sauce and stick it down a lion's throat. But you go right ahead if that's what you want. I shall be right behind you. Way behind you, watching from the other end of the corridor."

"Why not destroy the door?" said Melody. "Remove the Beast's access to our world? I could shoot a whole bunch of really big holes through it."

"Sounds like a plan to me," said JC. "Happy! Stay where you are!"

"My heart is currently brave, but my legs are still chicken," said Happy. "Or, to put it another way—sensible. Bullets won't do it, Mel."

"Why not?" said Melody. "I have cursed and blessed bullets, along with ammo dipped in holy water, sacred blood, deadly nightshade, and fallen angel's urine."

Happy gave her a look. "Only you would have a gun with poisoned bullets. And it still wouldn't work. The door isn't the problem. It's only the mask on the face of the creature."

"If cold iron won't do the job, what about fire?" said JC.

Happy beat a rapid tattoo on the closed door with both fists while he considered the point. "Might work," he said finally. "Fire has . . . cleansing connotations. What did you have in mind?"

JC had already produced something from an inside pocket. He held it out, so they could all get a good look at it. Small and round, easily double the size of a cricket ball, it shone with an almost unbearable light.

"Is that . . . what I think it is?" said Happy.

"Oh yes," said Melody. "I know my supernatural weapons. And for once, I am in complete agreement with you, Happy. Start running, and I'll try to keep up."

"How the hell did you get your hands on the Saint Ignatius Incendiary Grenade, JC?" said Happy.

"You didn't get that from the Carnacki Institute warehouse, or even the armoury," said Melody. "There's only ever been one of those horribly nasty and destructive things; and I only ever saw it in the Boss's office."

"You stole that from Catherine Latimer's very own private office?" said Kim, her eyes wide. "Good for you, JC! I am officially impressed. And a bit frightened."

"The Boss will have a cow," Happy said solemnly.

"Only if she ever finds out," said JC. "And given the clutter in her office, that should take some time. As long as no-one here shouts their mouth off, we should all be perfectly safe. No point in worrying her, after all. She already has enough to worry about . . ."

"Brass," Happy said solemnly. "Solid brass. It's a

wonder to me they don't clang together when you walk down the street, JC."

"Why, thank you, Happy," said JC. "That's got to be the nicest thing you've ever said about me."

"Well, there's a mental image I wasn't expecting to take home with me," said Melody.

"But what does this Saint Ignatius thingy do?" said Kim, leaning in for a closer look at the shimmering thing in JC's hand.

"It goes bang, in a fiery and spiritually cleansing way," said Happy. "And when JC decides to try it out, we should all be somewhere else, a very long way away from here. Or at the very least, hiding behind something heavy."

"You should all be perfectly safe . . ." said JC.

"You see, it's the word *should* that worries me," said Happy.

JC looked at Kim. "Actually, you probably should back off, to the end of the corridor. Or, down the stairs. The Saint Ignatius Incendiary Grenade was designed to wipe out everything of a supernatural nature. As well as burning down the house."

"I'll go with you," Happy said to Kim. "Only to keep you company."

"Me, too," said Melody. "Since I know for a fact that no-one ever worked out the full blast range on one of these things. First rule of engineering; beware prototypes. Along with, avoid anything made by an engineer who doesn't have all his own fingers."

"All right, go," said JC. "You're making me nervous."

Happy and Melody and Kim retreated to the furthest

end of the corridor, while JC sniffed loudly and held his head up, humming a merry tune to show how unconcerned he was. He tossed the grenade gently in one hand and looked firmly at the closed door before him.

"Pay attention, door! This should light you up nicely and leave nothing behind but some consecrated ashes. Or something very like ashes. Maybe I'll make an egg-timer out of you."

He went to pull the pin on the grenade, and the door swung open before him, falling back to reveal something the human mind simply couldn't cope with. JC cried out despite himself, staring into what lay beyond—a man transfixed by the Medusa's gaze. And somehow, he couldn't seem to let go of the grenade. Kim shot down the corridor at inhuman speed and slapped a ghostly hand over JC's eyes, putting her supernatural self between JC's eyes and the unearthly sight that held him.

JC fell back a step, grinned quickly at Kim, and went for the grenade's pin again. A great sucking vortex opened up beyond the door, pulling him in. JC grabbed onto the door-frame with his one free hand, holding himself in place by brute strength. Kim stood her ground, bewildered, her ghostly form unaffected by the physical force. A howling wind shot down the long corridor as all the air was sucked into the room's vortex. Happy and Melody were yanked off their feet and went tumbling down the floor as though it were a cliff-edge.

JC clung doggedly to the door-frame with his one hand, trying desperately to pull his other hand back so he could pull the pin on the grenade; but the pull of the vortex was too great. His feet shot out from under him, and he hung horizontally on the buffeting air. Only his single handhold kept him from being hauled in. Kim tried to help, but her hands went right through him.

Happy and Melody were thrown this way and that as they came sprawling and somersaulting down the landing, trying to hang on to each other while also grabbing at anything within reach to slow them down. Melody managed to grab onto the top of the stairs, while Happy shot straight past her. They cried out to each other as Happy was sucked up into the air, shooting towards the open doorway like an arrow from a bow. He slammed right through Kim's ghostly form, and on into the doorway. He grabbed the other side of the door-frame with both hands and jerked to a sudden halt. He swore harshly at the sudden pain in his hands but hung on, his legs flailing out before him, opposite JC. The two of them flapped like flags in a howling wind.

Melody lost hold of her grip on the top of the stairs and came tumbling down the corridor again. She kept grabbing handholds of the carpeting to slow her down, but the material only tore and came away in her hands. The last stretch of carpet simply disintegrated, and she shot straight through the open doorway. Happy let go of the door-frame with one hand and grabbed onto her. He pulled her to him with all his strength, a few agonising inches at a time, until he could hug her to him with one arm. The impact had almost torn his shoulder out of its socket. Melody clung desperately to him. Happy's one remaining hold was already weakening as the implacable force pulled both of them in. Bit by bit, his fingers were losing their grip. The air blasting past him was growing faster and thinner, and harder to breathe.

"Take her!" Happy yelled to JC.

And with the last of his strength, Happy threw Melody at JC. Immediately, he was ripped away from the door-frame, and fell and fell into the depths of the room that wasn't a room.

JC grabbed hold of Melody with the arm holding the grenade, and pulled her to him. She wrapped her arms around him, even as she craned her neck round to look after Happy.

"JC!" yelled Happy, falling away into an unimaginable distance. "Throw the bloody grenade!"

Melody pulled the pin from the grenade JC was holding, and he threw it after Happy with all his strength. Both objects seemed to drop away in a direction that made no sense, growing smaller and smaller. Melody let out a single cry of despair. JC hugged her to him with his free arm. He'd lost one friend; he was damned if he'd lose another. His fingers locked down on the door-frame with desperate strength, and he hauled himself back, inch by inch. He could hear Kim calling out, encouragingly, but he couldn't spare the strength to turn his head. He caught one last glimpse of Happy, a very small thing, falling away forever, and the grenade rushing ahead of him.

JC forced himself, and Melody, back through the doorway. When she got close enough, she grabbed the door-frame, too, with both hands. Until they were both back out onto the landing, and the door slammed shut behind them. The unbearable suction of the vortex and the roaring wind both cut off in a moment, and JC and Melody fell to the floor. They lay there together, clinging to each other. Both of them crying, harshly, for the good man they'd lost. Kim stood over them, crying her own silent tears.

After a while, JC and Melody sat up, still leaning on each other. Melody cried bitter tears, while JC sat there, exhausted. Kim crouched beside them, wanting to help, trying to comfort them with her presence. Melody turned her face away from both of them, refusing to be comforted.

"After all the things I said to him," she said, "He gave his life for me without a thought, without a single hesitation."

And then the door to the hungry room reopened, and Happy came flying back through it at speed. He shot across the corridor, slammed into the far wall, and crashed to the floor. The door slammed shut behind him; and then they all heard a massive explosion, from somewhere far and far-away. An inhuman scream seemed to issue from everywhere at once, then cut off abruptly. The door was gone, leaving behind nothing but a stretch of unremarkable wall. Happy sat up slowly. He was laughing, shakily. Melody pushed JC away from her and scrambled across the floor to take Happy into her arms. She pushed her face into his shoulder, still sobbing.

"I thought I'd lost you," said Melody.

"I thought I'd lost me," said Happy. "But apparently the many changes I've made to my basic body chemistry made me . . . unacceptable. Bloody thing spat me out! Hah! These Other-dimensional entities think they're so smart; if it had had any sense, it would have kept me and spat out the grenade!"

"Welcome back," said JC. "I really wasn't looking

forward to finding something good to say about you at your eulogy."

Melody stopped crying, sniffing back the last few tears. She pushed herself away from Happy and looked at him directly. "Are you saying it puked you out?"

"Well, yes," said Happy. "Nothing like the supernatural, to make clear your true place in the scheme of things."

''''''''''''''''''''''''''''

It took a while before they all stopped laughing. Finally, they got to their feet again, all of them leaning on each other for support. Kim beamed on them all fondly while they got their breath back and looked around. JC stretched slowly, flexed his aching hands, then looked firmly back down the corridor in a let's-get-back-to-business sort of way.

"One last job, then hopefully we can get the hell out of here," said JC.

"I've always admired your optimism," said Happy.

"I'm going to try to release the ghost girl Lydia," said JC. "I can't help feeling that she's at the back of everything that's happening here. Okay; I want all of you to go back down to the main bar. Too many of us at once would only upset her. Happy, find Brook and bring him back up here, to Lydia's room. He probably won't want to come, so feel free to be very firm."

"I've still got my gun," said Melody. "He'll do what he's told."

Kim planted herself in front of JC and fixed him with her best wide-eyed stare.

"Let me come, JC. I could help. Really I could!"

"Sorry, sweetie," said JC. "But I'm pretty sure you'd scare her. She doesn't know she's a ghost."

Kim nodded, reluctantly, and followed Happy and Melody down the stairs.

JC strolled down the left-hand corridor, all the way to the last door on the left. Lydia's room, for so many years. He knocked politely, opened the door, and went in. The young suicide was still sitting in her chair, still reading the magazine she was always reading. She looked around, and smiled easily at JC.

"Oh, hello! It's Mr. Chance, isn't it? Any sign of Adrian?"

"Not yet," said JC. "But I'm sure he'll be along soon."

"It's all right," said Lydia. "I'll wait for him as long as it takes."

JC heard footsteps outside in the corridor even though Lydia clearly didn't. He stepped back through the door, and there was Happy, leading a visibly reluctant Brook down the landing. JC waited for them to join him, gestured for Brook to go in the room with him, then stopped Happy with a look.

"You stay here," JC said quietly to Happy. "And don't get distracted or go wandering off. I'm going to need you. Adrian, let's go in."

"I can't," Brook said miserably. "I just can't."

"You have to," said JC.

"You don't understand! I can't bear to do anything . . . that might mean losing all I have left of her," said Brook.

"She's only here because of you," said JC. "You're holding on to her."

"Please. Don't say that."

"If you love her, let her go," said JC.

He took Brook firmly by the arm and took him into the end room. Lydia looked round again, her face lighting up as she expected to see her Adrian. Only to recoil a little at the sight of the old man with JC. It was clear she didn't recognise Brook. Didn't know him at all.

"Don't be frightened, Lydia," said JC.

"I've seen that man before," said Lydia. "Is he a ghost? Why does he keep looking in at me?"

"I can't stand this," said Brook.

He tried to leave, but JC held on to him.

"Let me go!" said Brook.

"Happy!" said JC. "Get in here!"

The telepath slouched through the open doorway and smiled at Lydia. She nodded back, uncertainly.

"This is a friend of mine, Lydia," said JC. "Don't worry; he always looks like that. Happy, it's time to do the linking thing again. This time, I need you to forge a mental connection between Lydia and Adrian. Mind to mind, heart to heart, soul to soul, so that they can See each other clearly and know who they are."

"You don't want much, do you?" growled Happy. "I'm still recovering from suddenly not being dead after all. I swear, there aren't enough pills in the world to make working with you worth it."

He frowned hard, concentrating; and Lydia's and Brook's heads snapped round. They looked into each other's eyes . . . and knew each other. After all the years apart, they were finally together again. JC could see it in their faces—a simple, wondering look of recognition. Two lost loves, separated by all the world and Time, brought together again at last. Lydia rose out of her chair and went to Adrian, and they looked at each other.

"I didn't know you!" said Lydia. "You got old, Adrian . . ."

"You didn't," said Brook.

"How long have I been here?" said Lydia. "How long have I been waiting for you, Adrian?"

"Too long," said Brook. "Do you remember . . ."

"What I did?" said Lydia. "Yes. I do now. Such a stupid, selfish thing to do. 'This will show them; this will make them all sorry,' I thought. All those years we could have enjoyed, together . . ."

"You can have all the Time there is, now," said JC. "No more waiting. It's time for you to leave this room, Lydia."

"I won't go anywhere without you, Adrian," said Lydia. "I won't be separated from you any longer."

"Of course not," said Brook. "You're going, and I'm going with you."

"I can't ask that of you!" said Lydia.

"There's nothing left to hold me here," said Brook. "No family, no friends; all I ever really had were my memories of you. If I can't be here with you . . . then I don't want to be here." He looked at JC. "I mean it."

"Yes," said JC. "I think you do."

He nodded to Happy, who nodded slowly.

"The things we do, for love," said Happy.

He reached out, through the link he'd made between a dead girl and a living man, and gave them both a little of his Sight. Brook and Lydia turned their heads, to stare in a direction beyond the sight of the living. And it was over. The Past disappeared and the original room reasserted itself. It looked much the same: old-fashioned, but with dust everywhere. Lydia was gone, and Brook lay dead on the floor. JC knelt beside the body and checked for a pulse. Not because he had any doubts but because that was what you did. He got to his feet and nodded to Happy.

"Good work. This isn't quite the ending I had in mind, but I suppose it will have to do. It's over. And that's all that matters, really."

"It doesn't feel over," said Happy. He rubbed wearily at his eyes. "Dear Lord, I am so tired . . . This has taken a lot out of me, you know."

"Yes," said JC. "I know. It's taken a lot out of all of us."

They left the room, and JC closed the door firmly behind them. They walked back down the landing, past perfectly ordinary doors, all of them closed, and went down the stairs to the main bar.

"How does the upper floor feel to you now, Happy?" said JC.

"Empty," said Happy.

"That's all?"

"Afraid so."

"Damn," said JC. "I was hoping for more than that. Oh. What happened to the people we rescued from the Timeslipped rooms?"

"Brook sent them back to town," said Happy. "The road was flooded by the storm, so he sent them back over the fields. Slogging through thick mud and pouring rain and heavy winds . . . They'll be soaked to the skin by the time they reach Bishop's Fording. But that could be a good thing. Keep them distracted enough that they won't start asking awkward questions till later. And hopefully by then, we'll be out of here." He looked at JC. "Not often we get to save people's lives. It's a good feeling."

"Yes," said JC. "It is."

When they emerged into the main bar, Melody and Kim were waiting for them. JC filled them in on what had happened. The storm outside sounded worse than ever, loud and threatening, battering at the windows, like some furious creature trying to force its way in.

"So," said Melody. "Lydia wasn't responsible for everything that's going on here."

"No," said Happy.

"Then removing Lydia didn't remove the source of the problem," said Kim.

"No," said JC. "But some things . . . just need doing."

NINE

THERE WERE GIANTS IN THOSE DAYS

The main bar of the King's Arms seemed reassuringly calm and normal after the extremes of the upper floor. Only the unrelenting din of the storm raging outside remained to remind them that the game wasn't over yet. JC went behind the bar, found three unbroken glasses, and ceremoniously poured out the last of the good brandy. They all toasted each other solemnly while Kim looked on wistfully. Happy knocked his brandy back in one gulp, ignoring the disparaging looks from the other two, who knew how to treat a good brandy.

"This stuff is feeling more and more medicinal," said Happy, slamming his glass back down on the bar and looking about him distractedly.

"You should know," said Melody.

"Children, children," murmured JC. "Do me a favour and slap each other round the head. I haven't got the energy."

"So what do we do now?" said Melody, deliberately averting her gaze from the bar's windows, as they jumped and rattled in their frames. "I mean, we've dealt with all the obvious trouble, on the upper floor; but it doesn't seem to have changed anything. Listen to that storm!"

"Not a fit night out for man or beast," muttered Happy, looking glumly into his empty glass. "If it rains any harder, it'll be ark-building time."

And then his head came up suddenly, and he looked quickly about him.

"Hold everything and pass the ammunition. Something . . . is heading our way. I can feel it."

JC put down his glass and looked steadily at Happy. "What kind of Something are we talking about here, Happy? Is it the dark, coming back again?"

"No," said Kim. "I can feel it, too. Listen . . ."

JC came out from behind the bar to join the others, and they all stood close together. Listening. The sound of the storm outside seemed to fade away, retreating into the distance, just so they could hear what was coming. Voices . . . voices that seemed to come from every direction at once, drifting in from all around them. A slow susurrus of human voices, whispering. Rising and falling, but slowly growing in volume. Spoken conversations, shouted arguments, raucous laughter, and the sobbing of broken hearts. More and more voices, from everywhere at once, filling the whole bar from end to end. Growing steadily louder and more distinct.

Voices, voices, more and more of them, entire crowds of men and women fighting to be heard. Other sounds arose in the background: what might have been fights, with broken furniture; lovers' quarrels; the raucous singing of disreputable songs. Everything you might expect to hear from every kind of bar.

But it seemed to JC that there was something strange, something decidedly off, about these distant and disembodied voices. Many of them were oddly accented, with the kind of extreme dialects you don't hear any more. Harshly pitched voices, speaking the kind of English that hadn't been spoken for centuries. And as the clamour of voices rose to an uproar, JC was sure he could hear other languages mixed into the general hubbub—Norman, Saxon, Celtic, Latin—all the old lost tongues of England. And some things JC couldn't even recognise. England's linguistic history had always been full of strange bedfellows.

"A whole army of dead voices," said Melody, raising her voice to make herself heard above the din. "It's like everyone who ever patronised this pub has come back, for an after-life reunion."

"All human life is here," said JC. "And all human death, apparently."

Finally, the ghosts appeared. Grim, grey, roughly human shapes, glowing with their own unnatural light as they came walking through the walls from every side at once. Some slipped in through the main door, as naturally as you please, while others came tripping down the backstairs. More and more of them, filling up the bar with their cold, spectral presence. Some rose out of the floor, while others dropped down from the ceiling, following stairways and entrances that had existed once, long ago, in earlier incarnations of the building that eventually became the King's Arms. When it was an inn, a tavern, a meeting-house.

Melody and Happy moved quickly to stand back-to-back.

"Hold your ground," said JC, sternly. "They're only ghosts. We can do ghosts."

And still they came, forcing their way in, an endless flow of the dead, walking right through the tables and chairs, and even each other. Glowing figures overlapped as they tried to occupy the same limited space, dressed in clothing and outfits and even rough armour, from a hundred different periods of Time Past. All of them talking at once, the terrible clamour rising and falling . . . And yet even through the din, JC slowly became aware that he couldn't hear any sounds of movement from the ghosts. No footsteps, no bodies jostling against each other.

And, he couldn't fit a single voice to any particular ghost. As though the voices and the apparitions came from different places.

Melody opened her lap-top on the bar-counter and fired up. She used her scanners to pick out images from the most-recent-looking ghosts, then set them against local records, trying to put some names to the deceased faces. Hoping to work out who they were and why they'd come back. JC could tell from her face that she wasn't having much luck.

"There's one good thing," said Happy.

"Really?" said Melody, without looking up from what she was doing. "Tell me. I'd love to hear it."

"There are two faces I don't see anywhere in this spooky crowd," said Happy. "I don't see Adrian Brook or his Lydia. Their spirits aren't trapped here. They got away."

"You're right," said JC. "That is a good thing. Not a terribly useful piece of information, but . . ."

"I don't do useful," said Happy. "What do you want? Miracles?"

"Yes, please," said JC. "I could use one if you've got one about you. I swear this case is wearing me down. Every time I think I've got it worked out, it changes gear and speeds off in another direction."

"Hello," said Melody. "This is interesting . . ."

"In the absence of a miracle, I'll settle for interesting," said JC. "What have you got, Mel?"

"Look at the ghosts," said Melody. "They're avoiding us. According to my scanners, there's a perfect circle around us that the ghosts aren't entering. They actually change direction at the last moment, to avoid it."

"Yes!" said Kim. "I can feel it. It's you, Melody! Or, at least, you and your lap-top. You've established a circle of scientific reality that the ghosts can't enter. I'm standing right at the edge of the circle, and it is weirding me out big time. As though scientific reality itself is trying to push me away because it doesn't believe in me. It's like a very loud voice telling me I don't exist. If I didn't know better, I think I'd find that very upsetting. These ghosts all around us . . . they're simply memories, trapped in this building. Slowly disintegrating, down the centuries, into little more than sound and fury and increasingly unstable images. Not really proper ghosts at all, to my mind . . ."

She gestured dismissively at the ghosts as they came near, and a grey hand shot out of the crowd and fastened onto her wrist. Kim looked at the hand in shock, unable to believe anything could actually touch her. And then she was dragged sharply out of the scientific circle and hauled away into the crowding ghosts. If she did cry out, she couldn't be heard above the raised voices.

JC immediately went to go after her, but Happy and Melody grabbed him by both arms and dragged him back. He fought them for a moment, then stopped and stood still, breathing hard. Happy and Melody let go of his arms and stepped back, and watched him anxiously.

"You have to stay in the circle, JC," Melody said carefully. "We're only safe from the ghosts as long as we stay inside the circle."

"It's all right; really!" said Happy. "It's not like Kim's in any danger; she's a ghost, right? She can't come to any harm."

"You don't know that," said JC. "They were able to touch her. And ghosts can be hurt. I found that out down in the London Underground."

"That was different!" Melody said firmly. "That was Fenris Tenebrae; these are common or garden everyday ghosts. Kim's been around; she's not just any ghost, now. She can take care of herself. You're the one who might be in danger out there. We don't know what's going on here, JC. We have to be careful."

JC nodded abruptly. He hadn't actually calmed down, but he did his best to seem more in command of himself. He looked at Melody, then at her lap-top.

"Talk to me, Mel. Explain to me what's happening. I am prepared to accept informed guesses."

"It's Time," said Melody, her attention fixed on the information streaming across her lap-top screen. "Time is breaking down in the King's Arms. As in: Time doesn't seem to be as tightly nailed down at the corners as it ought to be. Linear Time is being disrupted, under direct attack from the sheer power of a storm that's been building for centuries."

JC turned to Happy. "All right, you explain it to me."

"It's all concerned with the terrible anger generated by the death of the blonde woman all those years ago," said Happy. "Her sacrifice, in a local place of power, gave birth to Something the Druid priests never anticipated—a great scream of rage given shape and form and power by an unsuspected bad place. So that Something set in motion long ago is still happening. Growing, building in strength, searching for a way to break into our reality. The storm we hear . . . is the smile on the face of the tiger."

"Could you be any more vague?" said JC.

"If you want," said Happy. "Look, the storm started long ago. Back in the Druid days. The rage of the sacrificed victim got mixed up in it and gave it focus. Something's held it off, all these years, but now it's back. And it's mad. Tell me you've got it now, JC. Because all I've got left is mime and finger-painting."

"I get it," said JC. "You're saying that maybe we had it wrong before. The storm wasn't the cry of the blonde woman. Just the opposite. Everything that's happening here, from the rooms to the blonde woman to the ghosts, was really a manifestation of the storm."

He glared about him, into the shifting, overlapping layers of ghosts that filled the main bar from one end to the other. Rank upon rank of shimmering grey figures, some more human or more complete than others. All of them constantly moving and stirring, never still for a moment. There was a general air of . . . restlessness, as though they were all lost, or searching for something they couldn't quite remember. They walked through walls and furniture and even the far ends of the bar-counter.

Still more ghosts came walking in, through the walls and the windows and the closed main door. Some seemed as solid as any real person while others faded in and out, wisps of human-shaped mist. Some had strange lights inside them that came and went, while others seemed oddly out of focus, as though not entirely sure who they were.

"I've never seen this many ghosts in one place at once," said Melody.

"Call Guinness," said Happy. "And yet . . . I have to say, JC; they're not actually frightening, as such. And I am an expert when it comes to being frightened. They don't feel . . . threatening."

And then he broke off and fell back a step. Some of the ghosts were starting to notice that there was one place in the bar they couldn't get into. They'd been banging up against the perimeter of an invisible circle of reason for some time; but now more and more of them were turning their dead gaze on the one place they couldn't go. They turned their heads to look in that direction, with their cold, unblinking eyes, and those on the perimeter crowded up against the invisible barrier. They pressed slowly forward, taking a slow, steady interest in the three living souls inside the circle. And not in a good way.

The ghosts could see them now.

The crash of voices shut off in a moment, replaced by an intent, watchful silence. The ghosts stopped moving. They stood still, staring into the circle. An army of ghosts, with only one thought and one interest in common. To get in.

"Still think they're not dangerous, Happy?" said JC.

"Something's changed," said Happy. "I can feel it."

"Why are they looking at us?" said Melody, one hand resting protectively on her lap-top. "What do they want?"

"What do ghosts usually want?" said JC. "The one thing they can't have. Life. Rooms aren't the only things with unnatural appetites."

"You're not making me feel any better," said Happy. "I really don't like being looked at like this."

"But we're protected!" said Melody, her voice rising. "We had to go through all kinds of training, at the Carnacki Institute, before they'd allow us to go out into the field. Reinforcing our auras against possession, putting in extra layers of psychic protection, so we'd be safe from . . . Things like this!"

"You might want to mention that to these ghosts," said Happy. "Because they don't seem to know that."

"It's the bloody local power source," said JC. "They're drawing on it to sustain their existence . . . Or, more likely, it's using them to get at us. The local power source is the storm! Or it's the rage that drives the storm. Or Something. I swear, this whole case makes my head hurt . . . Either way, the Big Bad has tried every other way to get at us, so now it's using the one thing the King's Arms has more of than anything else—ghosts."

"Yes, but they're still just ghosts," said Melody. "Like you said. We can handle ghosts. They can't reach us inside this circle."

"Maybe," said JC. "Who knows what ghosts can do when you put this many of them together? When it comes to things like scientific reality, I don't think things are as clear-cut here, as everywhere else."

The ghosts were pressing really close now, right up

against the edges of the circle. JC and Happy and Melody huddled close together, looking quickly back and forth to make sure nothing was sneaking up on them. The ghosts were looking right at them, with cold, empty eyes. The sheer presence of so much death in one place was almost unbearably oppressive. JC could feel his heart hammering in his chest. It was getting harder to breathe. Like he had to fight for every breath of air. Some of the ghosts put their hands against the invisible barrier of the circle and pushed. The lap-top burst into flames on the bar-counter, and the scanners exploded. The first ghostly fingertips pushed forward, through the barrier.

Some of the ghosts were smiling.

JC stepped forward, whipped off his sunglasses, and glared right into the faces of the ghosts nearest him. They recoiled, falling back as though thrust away by some unseen force, unable to bear the pressure of JC's golden, glowing eyes. But others immediately pressed forward to take their place, stepping right through the retreating ghosts. None of them could actually meet JC's altered gaze, but it affected some more than others. And he could only look in one direction at a time. The ghosts were surging forward from every side now, and the protective circle seemed to be shrinking. JC looked desperately back and forth; and the ghosts looked back at him.

"So many ghosts . . ." said Happy. "I've never seen so many in one place, even in the oldest parts of London."

"What's calling them here?" said Melody.

JC put his sunglasses back on. "Can't help feeling I'm getting less and less mileage out of my gaze."

"Maybe the world's getting used to it," said Melody.

JC looked at her. "What does that mean?"

"I don't know!" said Melody.

"Whatever's at the heart of what's happening here," JC said heavily, "we must be pretty close to finding it or it wouldn't be trying so hard to stop us."

"I don't think so," said Happy, slowly. "It doesn't feel like that . . . I may be wrong, JC, but it really doesn't feel to me like we're in any danger from these ghosts."

JC looked at him. "They seem desperate enough to get in and get at us. Are you sure about this, Happy?"

"Of course I'm not sure!" said Happy. "There's so much spectral information here, it's swamping my Sight. But look at their faces! That's not hate, or malevolence, or even revenge. That's . . . need, anticipation, maybe even hope. They don't want to kill us; they want something from us. And you know what; I don't see the blonde woman anywhere."

"She isn't a ghost, remember?" said Melody. "Though . . . I suppose she could be orchestrating all this, from a distance."

"Take a good look around, Happy," said JC. "Are you sure you can't See her anywhere?"

Happy snarled and shook his head. "I keep telling you; the aether's so saturated with psychic energies, it's like trying to look through thick fog."

"You make this stuff up as you go along, don't you?" said JC.

Kim suddenly reappeared, right there inside the shrinking circle with them, smiling brightly. Everyone jumped. Melody glared at her.

"How can you be in here, with us—in a circle of scientific reality? Not that I'm not glad to see you, of course, but . . ."

"I can be here because I'm linked to all of you," said Kim. "I belong with you. Your affirmation of my existence overpowers science's need to deny me."

"All right, now you're making stuff up, too," said JC. "Where have you been, Kim?"

"Searching," Kim said cheerfully. "The ghosts didn't want to hurt me; they wanted to point us in the right direction. There's a power behind these ghosts that's trying to distract you. Follow me."

She walked right out of the circle and kept going, and the ghosts fell back on every side, opening a wide corridor for her to walk through. JC and the others moved cautiously after Kim, and the army of ghosts let them. Walking through the ghosts made JC want to shake and shudder. So many ghosts in one place projected a spiritual cold, the absolute opposite of life's warmth and vitality. JC made himself stare straight ahead. Happy and Melody crowded in close behind him. Kim led them through the main bar and all the ranks and rows of watching ghosts, all the way to the main entrance and out the door. The ghosts stood there and watched them go.

Outside in the car park, everything had changed. To start with, the car park wasn't there any more. The concrete base and its surrounding low stone walls had simply disappeared, replaced by a great open area of bare earth punctuated with tufting grass. Like an old clearing in a forest. The sky above was full of stars and a bright full moon. There was no rain, and no wind, but JC could still hear the storm. When he looked up, the storm was circling overhead, like a great whirlpool of disturbed air, hurtling round and round in the sky above the King's Arms. The pub looked as it had, with friendly lights blazing from all the downstairs windows.

It took JC a moment to realise that the sound of the storm had changed. The roaring and the rage was so much clearer now. It sounded . . . like a living thing.

But what drew everyone's attention away from the pub and the clearing and the storm was even more impressive. Standing opposite the King's Arms, on the other side of the clearing, towering high above them, was a giant Wicker Man. A huge, roughly human shape, woven together out of dark green wicker strands, with a great barrel chest set on thick, stumpy legs. Stiff, downward-thrusting arms ended in spiky wooden fingers; and all of it was topped with a blunt, square, featureless head. A massive wicker cage to hold all the people and livestock the Druids would burn alive, in sacrifice. Their gift to their gods, for when they wanted things the gods didn't want to give them, without tribute. Just standing there, its blunt, featureless head rising way up into the night sky, its dark green shape overpowering in the moonlight, the Wicker Man was an ugly, brutal thing.

Its feet stood in a huge pool of recently spilled blood. JC almost choked on the thick copper smell of it. Dark oils dripped from the spike-fingered hands, old-time accelerants to help it burn better. The Wicker Man looked disturbingly real and solid, but it was full of ghosts. All that remained of all the people and animals that had been sacrificed in Wicker Men in the past. They glowed faintly, like ghostly candles, and did not move or speak. They were burned, blackened bodies, faces still stretched in their last, agonised, dying screams. They stared past the wicker bars of their prison with dark, eyeless faces, looking down at the Ghost Finders, begging silently for help. Or revenge. Or—perhaps—their freedom, at last.

Standing before the Wicker Man, smiling calmly and utterly composed, was the blonde woman. She wore a simple white sacrificial shift stained with a great splash of blood across her lower abdomen. Her death wound, still dripping steadily after all the years. She saw JC looking at it and nodded briefly.

"Oh yes," she said. "Nailed my guts to the old oak tree. They really did. Two of them held my arms, while the third rammed an iron spike right through me, pinning me to the trunk of the tree. It took me a long time to die."

"Where are we?" said JC. "Or should that be when are we?"

"We're outside the King's Arms," said the blonde woman. "Outside of Time and Space. For the moment. The inn has been here for centuries, under many names and identities, built to help hold off the awful thing the Druid priests created here, in this clearing. They used the power my sacrifice gave them to perform a great magical working, and it all went horribly wrong. I wasn't killed so they could summon the storm; my death gave them the power to stop it. Except my dying here, in this bad place, gave me power. My dying curse linked me to the storm and this place, which is at least partly why Time and Space are so messed up here."

"You know," said Happy, "I have to say, you speak very good modern English for someone who lived and died fifteen hundred years ago."

"I've been hanging around the inn for ages," said the blonde woman. "Watching, and listening. I paid attention. And it's not like I have human limitations any longer. You've all done remarkably well, dealing with the individual horrors of the King's Arms, breaking the many chains that held me down. So I am free enough now to tell you the truth of what happened in this awful place. Whether you'll be able to do anything about it remains to be seen. But I have hope. At last.

"Before there was ever a building of any kind here, this was a place of worship and sacrifice. The Druid priests practiced their nasty arts here, to help them protect and control their people. And in this place, they performed a great and terrible magic, to put an end to a storm that seemed like it would never end. It rained for months, without pause. Flooding the roads and saturating the fields, washing away the good topsoil. Rivers burst their banks and carried away the bridges. Rising waters washed away the crops, flooded the local habitations, and destroyed settlements for miles around. The livestock drowned, and the people were forced to flee the area.

"The Druid priests couldn't have that. You can't control people when there aren't any people. Those who did remain were turning against the priests, who were clearly not in favour with the gods any more. So the priests raised the power they needed, with one of the oldest forms of magic. Necromancy, the magic of murder. They couldn't stop the storm, or dissipate it, so they did the next best thing and forced it outside our reality. Made a crack in Space and Time and forced the storm through. They sacrificed a lot of people to gain that power. But then, as far as the Druid priests were concerned, that was what people were for. They used Wicker Men, at first. Ranks and ranks of them, stretched out across the land, burning like beacons in the night. And then, when that wasn't enough, they picked out certain significant people and sacrificed them in the local places of power.

"They murdered me here, in a clearing that everyone else had the good sense to stay well clear of. It was a bad place, even then. My sacrifice, in such a place, gave the priests the last piece of power they needed to drive the storm away. And that was that. They thought."

"Hold everything," said Happy. "*Rain, rain, go away; come again another day?* Really? That's what this is all about?"

"They forced the storm outside the world, but they couldn't destroy it," said the blonde woman. "And all this time it's been trying to get back. Growing bigger, and stronger, and more determined. Looking for a weak spot to force its way back in. Because it wasn't just a storm, any more. My dying rage, amplified by the bad place, mixed with the storm. Gave it a purpose. The storm . . . is my dying curse.

"Even after I died, some of me still remained here, linking the storm to this place. So the Druids had a house built, to hold me here, to hold me down. Which, of course, made the bad place even worse. No wonder the King's Arms has always been lousy with ghosts."

"What made you so . . . special?" said JC. "That you could be responsible for all this?"

The blonde woman shrugged. "Perhaps I had magics and abilities of my own, unsuspected. Perhaps the bad place, and my awful death, brought them out of me. Because it is my rage that still drives the storm."

"But all the Druid priests, and the people responsible for your death . . . they're all long gone," said Melody.

The blonde woman shrugged again. "It's a lot easier to start something than it is to stop it. Revenge, like love, is blind. It wants what it wants."

"What's your name?" said JC, as kindly as he could.

"I don't remember," said the blonde woman. "That woman is gone, long gone. It doesn't matter. It's not as if I'm real. I'm only a small part of something much bigger. I've been here so long, held in this place, that I had to give up most of my memories to survive."

"Are you a part of the storm, or is it the other way around?" said Happy. "It sounds like a living thing."

"We're . . . connected," said the blonde woman. "I'm the rage that drives the storm on; but it isn't just a storm any longer. Hasn't been for centuries. It took what it needed from me, to keep it strong. But . . . I have no control over it. I'm only a part of this . . . the part that has watched over this inn, and these people, and this town for so long . . . that I have formed a fondness for them. This small part doesn't want to see them all die. But that's me speaking. Only a very small part of what's happening."

"What do you want with us?" Melody said bluntly.

"I would have thought that was obvious," said the woman. "I want you to stop me. Stop the storm from returning and destroying everything. The storm is so big now, I think it could drown the whole world without getting tired. By removing the layers of ghosts and traps and Things from Outside from the King's Arms, you've managed to remove some of the barriers that kept the storm out."

"How do we stop it?" said JC.

"You don't understand," said the blonde woman. "I'm

only the small rational part that's left. My rage has taken on a power of its own. It drives the storm on. It is the storm. I have no control over it. That's why I need you. I can speak to you, warn you, but that's all. The greater part of me still wants its revenge, denied for centuries. All I can say to you is: remember what Brook told you, about the oldest part of the inn. Remember its significance."

She'd barely finished speaking when a great bolt of lightning slammed down from the circling storm overhead. It grounded itself through the blonde woman, pinning her in place, like an iron spike to a tree-trunk. She faded away, becoming a ghost image of herself. The lightning bolt snapped off, and the faintly glowing human shape rose into the air and was pulled away backwards, faster and faster. The last expression JC could make out on her face was a terrible resignation. The figure flew across the clearing, still rising into the air, until it slammed into the massive curving chest of the Wicker Man and was absorbed.

They could all see her for a moment, looking out through the wicker bars of her cage, a prisoner in the Wicker Man along with all the other dead sacrificial victims. And then she faded slowly away, lost among all the other ghost candles.

The huge Wicker Man creaked loudly as its great blocky head slowly turned to look down on the Ghost Finders. Its whole enormous structure stretched and groaned, as the Wicker Man raised its great green arm, wooden fingers slowly clenching into a jagged fist. The Wicker Man was alive.

"Look on the bright side," said Happy. "At least it isn't on fire."

Two dark yellow flames appeared, burning fiercely in the blank face—fiery eyes for the Wicker Man to see them with.

JC glared at Happy. "You had to say it, didn't you?"

They all scattered, as the giant Wicker Man surged forward, its huge bulk moving with impossible speed. The massive wooden fist came sweeping down and hammered onto the bare ground with such force that the earth split open from one end of the clearing to the other. All of the Ghost Finders were sent sprawling. They heaved themselves back onto their feet again, and JC yelled for everyone to run in different directions, so the Wicker Man would find it harder to target them. But Kim stuck by his side, refusing to leave him, and Happy and Melody wouldn't be separated. They did move quickly away from JC and Kim, as the Wicker Man raised its terrible hand again, glaring down with its flaming eyes. And then it stepped forward on its great stocky legs, making the ground jump and dance as it strode forward to stand between the Ghost Finders and the King's Arms.

Melody produced her machine-pistol and opened fire. Cursed and blessed ammunition stitched long ragged rows of holes across the wide chest, blasting the green threads apart; but the Wicker Man didn't even shudder under the impact. Melody kept on firing anyway, raking the head and chest until she ran out of bullets. She lowered her gun, breathing hard, and looked at Happy.

"I can't reach it!" he said, his hands clenched into desperate fists. "I'm not even sure there's anything in there to be reached! It's not a living thing, it's a construct! A memory of the Past given shape and form and malice by the local power source! JC! Tell me what to do!"

"To start with, keep its attention!" said JC. "I've got an idea."

"Whatever this idea is, I love it!" Happy said immediately. "You have my full and total support! Go ahead and—Oh bloody hell, it's moving again!"

The Wicker Man stooped forward, bending right over, its massive hands opening as they reached out to grab the Ghost Finders. Its huge feet stamped down hard as it moved, so that the bare earth jumped under JC's feet as he ran for his life, Kim hovering at his side. Melody and Happy ran in the opposite direction, trying to distract the Wicker Man. The great jagged hands swept back and forth but couldn't find anything. JC couldn't help noticing that the Wicker Man's movements were becoming more supple, more sure. As though it was leaning how to move, how to be alive. He stopped where he was, took a deep breath, and concentrated. Kim hovered at his side, smiling bravely, trying to be supportive. JC put his head back and addressed the heavens, trying very hard not to look at the storm circling overhead.

"Move, JC!" yelled Melody. "It's coming your way!"

"I am calling for help!" said JC. "You said it was no coincidence that we were sent here; and I think you're right. We're here because of our experiences with old Druid ways, down in London Undertowen, and because we're the only ones who can stop this. Because we have a trump card. Before the old god Lud left this reality, he said he owed us one last favour; and I'm thinking this is the time to call it in. So, Lud! Are you listening? We need your help, right now!"

"No need to shout," said Lud. "I'm dead, not deaf. And I've been waiting for your call."

He stood towering above them, facing off against the giant Wicker Man, who seemed frozen in place. If JC hadn't known better, he'd have said it was shocked. The Wicker Man was huge; but Lud was massive. A great old god from when the land was young, Lud stood a hundred feet tall and more, looming over the Wicker Man; and he didn't look like a fossilised statue any more. His dark, leathery skin gleamed with vitality, and his huge, horned head rose grandly into the night sky. His eyes glowed with the same golden gleam as JC's. Lud looked down and smiled slowly, showing huge, blocky teeth.

"I knew you'd need me here, for this one last unfinished thing from my Time. Go to the inn. Do what needs to be done. And I will buy you some time."

He strode forward and grabbed hold of the Wicker Man with his great clawed hands. The Wicker Man grabbed onto the god, and the two huge figures struggled together, staggering back and forth across the clearing, striking at each other with terrible blows that could have toppled hills. Lud was bigger and stronger, but every time he tore into the Wicker Man, its dark green body stitched itself back together again. They swayed back and forth, their great feet stamping on the bare earth with such force they cracked it apart. The old god Lud struck down the Wicker Man with savage force; but it always rose again, re-formed and remade by the power of the storm circling above it.

JC led his people back to the King's Arms, dodging this way and that to avoid being trodden on; and then they all stopped as a grey army of ghosts came pouring out of the inn, passing through the walls. JC braced himself, but the ghosts swept right past him, their dead gaze set on the two huge fighting figures. They swarmed up and over the Wicker Man, clinging to its arms and legs, struggling to hold it back and slow it down. Because they saw at last a chance to be free from the old power that held them. Lud laughed aloud, and hit the Wicker Man's blunt head so hard his fist buried itself deep inside.

JC gathered up his people and ran back inside the King's Arms.

''''''''''''''''''''''''''

Inside the bar, everything seemed perfectly calm and normal. All the ghosts were gone. But from outside there still came the roar of the storm and the sound of two giant things crashing together. JC looked quickly around the main bar, then up at the ceiling. He pointed a triumphant finger at the long, exposed, oaken beams.

"There! That's it! Brook said those beams were the oldest surviving parts of the pub . . . I'm betting they were taken from the original oak tree the Druid priests used for their sacrifices, the bastards. God knows how much death and blood that wood soaked up in its time."

"So if we destroy the beams, we destroy the one remaining physical link between Past and Present!" said Melody.

"Seems a bit obvious," said Happy. "Are you guys sure about this?"

"Of course I'm not sure!" said JC. "I'm guessing! It's a wild stab in the dark, which is what you'll be getting if you don't stop arguing! Have you got a better idea?"

"Never liked those beams," said Happy.

The storm was growing louder. JC moved quickly over to the nearest window and looked out. The great circling storm was descending out of the night sky, lowering onto the great heads of the Wicker Man and the god Lud as they crashed back and forth in the clearing. JC didn't wait to see what would happen when the storm reached them. He turned away from the window, glared about him, and gestured for Happy and Melody to help him drag one of the tables beneath the oak beams. The three of them pulled it into place, clambered up onto it, and tried to pry the old beams loose. Only to discover the beams had been very firmly fastened in place long ago, with heavy copper nails. They all tugged and pried at the beams but couldn't budge them.

Kim ghosted up through the table and hovered above it, studying the beams at close range. And then she smiled coldly, and wagged an authoritative finger at them.

"Behave yourselves and stop being a pain. Or there will be trouble."

There was a slight pause, and one by one the copper nails rose out of the beams. They squealed loudly as they rocked back and forth, forcing themselves out of the wood. JC looked at Kim.

"Another little trick that you picked up on your travels?"

Kim smiled dazzlingly. "You'd be amazed what I can do when I put my mind to it."

The last of the nails fell away, but the beams remained stubbornly in place. JC and Happy jumped down from the table, grabbed up heavy fire-irons from the open fireplace, then scrambled back up onto the rocking table again. Melody nodded approvingly as Happy handed her a heavy iron poker. The three of them attacked the oak beams with their new tools, forcing them deep into the wooden sides; and one by one they prised the heavy beams loose and sent them crashing to the floor.

By the time the last one fell away, JC and Happy and Melody were soaked with sweat and breathing hard. They had to help each other down from the table and lean on each other for support as they got their breath back.

"I did not sign up for manual labour," said Happy. "If I wanted to work hard for a living, I'd have my head examined."

They all looked round sharply. The storm was upon them. The roar of wind and rain was suddenly deafening, almost drowning out the sounds of battle still going on outside. The glass in the windows shattered as the wind ripped the wooden frames out of the old stone wall. The main entrance door was blown right off its hinges and fell clattering to the floor. Heavy rain blasted into the inn through the ragged openings where windows had been, almost like a storm at sea. For the first time, there were great long rolls of thunder, and jagged bursts of light from heavy forked lightning. The storm had arrived; and it wanted in. That old rage, which would not be denied.

"All right!" said Happy, flinching away from the rain spraying in. "We've got the beams! What now?"

"I say we take a tip from the Wicker Man," said JC. "Burn the bloody things and destroy the physical link forever!"

"In here?" said Melody. "We light this much wood up, and we'll all go up with it!"

"Not if we set a few alight, to get the pile started, then

run like hell," said Happy, judiciously. "I'm really very good at running like hell."

They all looked up suddenly, open-mouthed despite themselves, as the ceiling lights rocked madly back and forth. And then, with a great creaking and groaning, the whole upper floor of the King's Arms was torn away and thrown behind the inn, landing with an impact that shook what was left of the building. And then the whole ceiling was ripped away, revealing the Wicker Man standing over them, holding what was left of the disintegrating ceiling in his great green hands. The fires that were its eyes blazed fiercely. The wind and the rain blasted into the bar, immediately soaking JC and Happy and Melody to the skin. And then two massive hands grabbed the Wicker Man from behind. The Wicker Man dropped the ceiling and staggered backwards, as Lud hauled it away from what was left of the King's Arms.

"Out!" said JC. "Everybody out of here, right now, before this mess collapses on us!"

"Way ahead of you, boss," said Happy.

Back out in the clearing, the storm no longer hung overhead. It had come down to earth, at last, unleashing all the rage it had contained for so long. Gale-force winds blew so hard, JC and Happy and Melody could barely stand up straight and had to cling to each other to keep from being blown away. Rain hammered down with such force, it bounced back from the bare-earth floor of the clearing. Thunder roared, and forked lightning split the sky.

Lud had forced the Wicker Man to its knees and was happily tearing it to pieces. He'd already ripped off one of its arms. It lay twitching on the ground. Lud grabbed the square, featureless head with both hands, digging his clawed fingers in deep. The Wicker Man lurched back and forth but couldn't break free. Lud roared triumphantly and ripped the head right off the green shoulders, crushing it beneath his hands. The two flaring eyes went out. The body stopped struggling and was still. And it seemed to JC that some of the strength went out of the storm.

The ghosts fell away from the motionless body of the Wicker Man, no longer needed. They stood in long ranks, unmoved and unbothered by the wind and rain, glowing fitfully like candles in danger of going out. They looked at the Ghost Finders. Waiting to see what they would do. Lud threw away the crushed wicker head and nodded familiarly to JC.

"So much evil done, in my name," he said. His voice wasn't all that loud, but it rang out easily over the storm. "All because I wanted to be worshipped . . . Nothing like dying to give you an appreciation for life. All life. I am leaving this world now, and it is only right I take some of this old evil with me."

He disappeared, with a great flash of otherworldly light; and when the glare died away, he was gone, and so was the Wicker Man. The wind dropped away, some, and the rain wasn't as bad. JC grinned. He'd suspected that the storm had placed a lot of its power in the Wicker Man.

Happy looked at JC. "What do we do now?"

"Give me a minute," said JC. "I'm thinking . . ."

"I don't think we have a minute!" said Melody. "The oak beams are still back in the inn. Should we drag them out here and burn them?"

"In this rain?" said Happy.

"Oh, I think they'll go up easily enough," said Melody.

"No," said JC.

Melody looked at him. "No? What do you mean, no? It was your idea!"

"I think I've had a better one," said JC. "Fire is the old way. The Druid way. And I have had enough of that old evil."

He looked out across the clearing. Where the Wicker Man had been, the blonde woman stood in her white shift, untouched by the storm. JC walked over to stand before her, smiling reassuringly.

"Go," he said kindly. "Go. There's nothing holding you here any longer. This is still a place of power, the local power source; so use it to do something right, at last. Let your rage go. Let the storm go . . . And be at peace, at last."

The blonde woman considered his words; and then nodded slowly. She rose into the air, light as a moonbeam, until, finally, she hung in the night sky, high above the clearing. Glowing bright as any star. One by one, the ghosts rose after her, taking the rain with them. The raindrops reversed direction, falling upwards. The wind slowed, and calmed, and died out. The storm was gone. After so many years, only the rage had kept it going. One by one, the ghosts winked out, like blown-out candles. Until only the blonde woman remained. She looked around slowly, saying good-bye to the land and people she had looked over for so long, then . . . quietly and without any fuss, she was gone.

''''''''''''''''''''''''''''''''''

JC looked slowly around him. The car park was back, and not a drop of rain or breath of wind anywhere. The King's Arm was still a ruin, though.

"How about that?" said Happy. "After everything we've been through, all it took to put things right was the quiet voice of reason."

"Shame that doesn't work more often," said Melody.

"One big tick in the win column, I think," said JC. "Pity about the King's Arms, but then, it's not like Brook's around to complain about it."

"To save the inn, it was necessary to destroy the inn," Melody said solemnly.

"Cold, Mel," said Happy. "How are we going to explain what's happened to the townspeople?

"Lightning strike," said JC.

"What about the local power source?" said Happy. "Is it still here? And what was it, originally?"

"I don't suppose we'll ever know," said JC. "It's a bad place, that made bad things possible. Hopefully, it will lie quiet now; so long as no-one's stupid enough to disturb it. I'll put a note in my report, for the Institute to keep an eye on things, just in case."

"Let's go home," said Kim. "We're not needed any more."

"Good idea," said JC. "I think we've done as much damage here as we can."

TEN

HOME AGAIN, HOME AGAIN

JC lay on his back, on his bed, back in his own apartment. Legs crossed, eyes half-closed, every muscle so relaxed he felt practically boneless. There's nothing more comfortable than a mattress that knows you and fits the shape of your body like a glove. It was good to be back home, and good to have Kim home with him again. JC lay there and watched happily as Kim fluttered cheerfully back and forth around his new apartment. Clapping her hands, oohing and aahing all over the place, as she checked out absolutely everything. She even stuck her head through closed doors to see what was on the other side. JC couldn't keep from wincing every time she did that.

In the end, Kim stood at the foot of his bed and shook her head firmly. "You've changed the colour scheme!" she said loudly. "I don't like it! And honestly, darling; this room is a mess. Men shouldn't be allowed to live on their own. They don't know how."

"If I'd known you were on your way back, I'd have made an effort and tidied up a bit," said JC. "Sorry it's all a bit of a dump, but . . . I live here."

Kim sat down on the edge of the bed next to him. Or at least, she did her best—hovering as close to the bed as she could manage.

"Have you phoned Catherine Latimer yet, JC?"

"Not yet," said JC. He linked his hands together over his chest. "There's no hurry. We finished the job way ahead of schedule, so she can wait for her official report."

"I thought you wanted to ask her whether she really did send you there on purpose because of the encounter you had with Lud in London Undertowen?"

"Why bother?" said JC. "I think we already know the answer, don't we? She's playing games with us, running us around like rats in a maze, as part of the bigger game she's playing with The Flesh Undying." JC looked thoughtfully at Kim. "Can I ask you a question?"

"Of course you can, sweetie!"

"Did I really die, down there in the London Tube system? Am I only here because some unknown force from Outside took an interest in me, and brought me back to life, for purposes of its own?"

"Of course you're not dead, silly," said Kim. "I mean, I'd know if anyone would, wouldn't I?"

"Yes," said JC. "But would you tell me?"

Kim looked down her nose at him. "You've been spending far too much time listening to Happy, in my absence. Have you been looking after yourself while I was away? Eating properly, and all that?"

"I've been keeping busy," said JC. "Where have you

been, all this time, Kim? What have you been up to? You can talk to me."

"What you don't know can't hurt you," said Kim. "Possibly quite literally. I will tell you everything, JC, when I can. Now hush. You're tired. Go to sleep."

"I've been . . . having trouble sleeping, all the time you were gone," said JC.

"Well, that's all over now," said Kim. "I'm back, so there's nothing to worry about any more. Close your eyes. Don't worry about the dark, or the job, or the Boss, or anything else. You can sleep now. Because I'm here with you, and I will watch over you, all the hours of the night."

JC smiled and closed his eyes, and was almost immediately fast asleep. For the first time in a long time, sleep embraced him easily, and the cares of the day fell away, and were gone. Kim smiled fondly at him, leaned over, and kissed the air very near his forehead.

"Sleep well, my love. You're going to need your strength for what's coming."

Happy and Melody sat side by side, on matching chairs, before the big desk in their study. All the usual electronic clutter had been pushed to one side, so Happy could lay out and sort through all the various pills and potions and special mixtures he'd accumulated. He explained their various uses and side effects to Melody, who wrote it all down in her special note-book. Happy paused, to take a drink of water from the glass before him. He'd been talking for some time, and his mouth was getting dry.

"Do you really need to know all this?" he said mildly.

"Yes," said Melody, firmly. "If I'm going to be a part of . . . this, I need to know everything you're doing. No more secrets. Since it's clear to me now that you can't cope without all this stuff, I need to be able to keep an informed eye on you. How else can I look after you properly?"

"Then don't bother with all the long names," said Happy. "I don't. Go by the numbers. If I've marked something with a low number, that means it's a downer. A high number, an upper. If there's a letter alongside the number on the label, that means it's one of my special mixes."

"I need to know what they all do," said Melody, glaring at the row upon row of bottles and boxes laid out in neat ranks before her.

"It changes," said Happy. "According to my mood, my need, and the circumstances. It's not easy being a drug fiend. What matters is that I know what I need to be able to function."

"How long have you been taking this stuff?" said Melody.

Happy smiled, briefly. "Too long."

"Doesn't your body chemistry . . . adapt to all the changes you keep making in it?"

"Of course," said Happy. "I need larger and larger doses all the time to achieve the same effects."

"But isn't that dangerous?"

"Yes."

"Then . . . what happens when even the largest doses can't help you any more?"

"Then I'm screwed," said Happy. "Hopefully by then, you'll have come up with some kind of tech to help me.

Something to shut me down. Close my eyes and ears to the hidden world. So I can walk along in blinkered ignorance, like everyone else."

"I've already explained the dangers involved in that," said Melody.

"They're not dangers," said Happy. "They're comforts."

"I could burn your brain out!"

"You see?" Happy said gently. "You say that like it's a bad thing. For me, it's something to look forward to. An end to suffering."

Melody started to reach out to him, but Happy sat back in his chair and stretched slowly.

"I'm tired, Mel. Can't we finish this tomorrow? I want to go to bed and get some sleep."

"I need to get the basics down now," said Melody. "I need to know what I'm doing, if I'm going to be able to help you. I have to be methodical; it's how I do things."

"I'm so tired," said Happy. His eyes were closed.

"I could make you something to eat," said Melody.

"I'm too tired to eat."

Melody sniffed. "You've never liked my cooking."

Happy opened his eyes and smiled at her. "Cooking is an art. And you have always been all about the science."

Melody closed her note-book, and sat back in her chair. "All right. That's enough for now. You're going to have to take me down to the Institute and introduce me to these clever chemical friends of yours. See if we can put at least some of this on a firm scientific footing."

She looked at Happy and saw that he was no longer listening. He'd nodded off in his chair, his chin resting on his chest. Melody's heart went out to him. Because she knew that for all her promised support, and all her great intentions, there really wasn't much she could do for him. The only things that made life bearable for him were the same things that were killing him by inches. And both of them knew it. All she could do was keep him company.

And hold him while he lay dying.

Catherine Latimer, great high Boss of the ancient and eminent Carnacki Institute, sat alone in her office at the end of the day. She'd sent everyone else home. She sat in her chair, behind her desk, thinking. She should have gone home long ago, except . . . it wasn't as if there was anyone there, to go home to. There had been loves and lovers, down the years; but either she or the job had always driven them away.

Is this what my life has come to? she thought. *After everything I've done and fought for? To sit alone in an empty room?*

Her head jerked up suddenly, as she pulled herself back from the edge of sleep through an effort of will. How long had she been sitting there, thinking? About all the people and Things that threatened not only the Institute but the whole world? The burden is always so much harder when there's no-one else you can trust, to bear it with you. She smiled briefly. Well, except for the odd person, here and there. She became aware there was indeed another person in the room with her, standing patiently on the other side of the desk, waiting to be noticed. Catherine looked up and smiled.

"Hello, Kim."

From *New York Times* Bestselling Author

SIMON R. GREEN

NOVELS OF THE NIGHTSIDE

Something from the Nightside
Agents of Light and Darkness
Nightingale's Lament
Hex and the City
Paths Not Taken
Sharper Than a Serpent's Tooth
Hell to Pay
The Unnatural Inquirer
Just Another Judgement Day
The Good, the Bad, and the Uncanny
A Hard Day's Knight
The Bride Wore Black Leather

Praise for the Novels of the Nightside

"Simon Green's Nightside is a macabre and thoroughly entertaining world that makes a bizarre and gleefully dangerous backdrop for a quick-moving tale. Fun stuff!" —JIM BUTCHER

"One of fantasy's most memorable constructs."
—*KIRKUS REVIEWS*

simonrgreen.co.uk
facebook.com/ProjectParanormalBooks
penguin.com

M1163AS0812